ASHES TO SCALES

Book 1, The Dragon Age Prophecy

N. A. HYDES

Cover Art By: Neal Hopkins at Elerfine

Original Edits: Vicki Greer at www.vickiedits.com

Developmental and Line Edits: Jennia Herold D'Lima

Proofreading: Roxana Coumans at https://proofreadebooks.com

N.A. Hydes can be reached at https://nahydes.com or on discord at https://discord.gg/pbRmeh6GUn

Created with Vellum

For my Grandmother, Stella

CHAPTER 1
JENNIFER

If Jennifer Wright had known the initial consequences of a kiss, she would have never kissed Matt. Then again, if she'd known how her story would end, nothing would have changed.

Standing in a remote location in a forest in North Carolina, her body pressed against the handsomest man at her college, Matt Davis, she enjoyed their first kiss. The taste of a fresh breath mint covered most of the beer as his tongue danced with hers. And as much as her actions moved her toward intense desire, another need overcame her body as she realized she needed to use the restroom.

Placing her hands on either side of Matt's face, she gently pushed him back, separating their mouths. "Stay here," she slurred. As she backed away, the ground spun from the alcohol she had consumed. Wobbling and giggling, she grabbed the roll of toilet paper resting on a fallen tree limb and headed away from the campfire into the woods.

Jennifer contemplated what had just happened. Matt was one of the few guys who towered over Jennifer during college orientation. At her own 5′9″, most boys met her at eye level. He, however, stood close to 6′4″. With his dark hair and eyes, brilliant white smile, and incredible physique, she initially thought him too much of a jock to be interested in her. Or, for that matter, for her to be interested in him. But, as fate dictated, they were in the same orientation group, spending hours discussing movies, dreams, and goals.

Matt Davis had all the qualities she was looking for in a boyfriend, and she thought he might be the one who would fit into her life plan.

After barely passing seventh and eighth grade due to a virus, she made a simple plan to prove her teachers and classmates wrong—to prove that she wasn't stupid.

One thing led to another, and her parents beamed with pride at their daughter navigating tougher, more challenging courses—all with a seemingly easy A. It wasn't, but only she knew that. Then she won recognition for the state science fair. Granted opportunities to be a Duke Scholar. Colleges contacted her for their S.T.E.M. programs. And now, she had a full ride to South Holt—as long as she kept her grades up.

Being a scholar became her addiction. She pushed herself to be an overachiever, and that became a constant draw on her free time. She'd done it all and accomplished her goals. The only thing lacking in her life, well, was her dating life.

When her schoolmates dated, she stayed home to study. By the time she went to college, her dating experience could be summed up by words from acquaintances, the internet, and movies—her personal experience didn't exist.

She switched up her college goals. Get great grades continued as a theme, but she added find true love. Treating it like she did everything else, she studied excessively, writing her observations in a green spiral notebook.

Other than Matt being soft on the eyes, she picked him because, well, he talked to her about movies and living and doing all the things she couldn't when she sat at home trying to excel.

The first few times she ran into Matt, he jammed his fist

into his pocket and planted his eyes firmly on the ground. She made it a habit of randomly showing up at places and events she knew he would attend—smiling and interjecting into his conversations. After a few of their "accidental" meetings, he finally asked her out—well, invited her to spend time with him and his friends.

By observing and studying romance in entertainment, she concluded that men were more likely to commit to a relationship if they believed they had started the courtship. She assumed this was true because, on some primal level, men needed something to hunt. Following her own set of rules designed to cause Matt to chase her, she kept her phone calls short and sweet and waited for him to make the next move. Rule one was that he had to initiate the relationship, which included taking the first step for all physical contact.

Finally, while they were sitting in the stands at a football game almost a month ago, he reached over and took her hand. By her estimate, it was long past time for the kissing phase to begin.

Camping this weekend seemed like the perfect scenario to "accidentally" bump into his personal space. Perhaps she could trip and use him for balance when she assisted with packing the tent up on Sunday. If she positioned her body correctly and leaned in a certain way, her weekend would follow the plot of romance movies, and he'd kiss her.

At least, that was the plan.

In sudden realization, she stopped walking.

Wait, the breath mint! Who freshened their breath when camping?

The only conclusion she could make was that Matt had planned their kiss! He intentionally kissed her! Two days earlier than her schedule. Which meant she required a new strategy and timeline.

The urge returned, and she did a little pee-dance to force her bladder to hold longer. As she jigged, she caught the faint glow of the campfire. For her to feel free to... partially undress, she needed more distance from their site. Heading in the opposite direction, she thought about the new *make-Matt-her-boyfriend* plan.

On page fifteen of her latest green notebook, she had an idea that might work. She couldn't remember the exact sentence—or even a resemblance of the conceptualization—she scribbled that would apply to this situation, no matter how hard she tried to focus. Distracted, she stubbed her toe on a rock, stumbled forward, and rebalanced.

She recalled two words that Matt said when they arrived, utterly surprised she hadn't noticed the significance earlier. Matt said... one tent! He'd brought only one tent and only one sleeping bag for the two of them.

Worry swept over her as the implications of Matt kissing her this early in the weekend redefined their relationship. Only one tent and *one* sleeping bag for two people indicated even more changes in store before the end of the weekend.

According to all the movies about love she had studied, the current sleeping arrangements meant snuggling and talking under the full moon all night long...or sex!

A daytime vision of Matt leaning over her, his grin mischievous seconds before he removed her panties with his teeth, flashed before her eyes.

Too soon for that, and she cleared her mind of any thought—or at least tried to. Fighting to control her nerves, she fidgeted with the toilet paper in her hands. She didn't need a mirror to confirm her bright red cheeks; heat waves radiating from her face told her what she would see if she looked in one.

They'd never discussed sex or messing around... but did people plan those events? They didn't in movies. So far, Jennifer had never crossed that line with anyone. For sure, she wanted to try everything in books and films, but not tonight. Their relationship required more time to flourish before reaching that step—and she hadn't shaved enough for a close encounter.

A low growl off to her right caused her to stop. While searching the area, she strained to hear a repeat of the sound. Nothing. Though, she did happily realize the campfire was finally out of sight.

With the bright moonlight casting shadows on the path, she bent over to place the toilet paper on the ground, then watched as it bounced and jumped down the hill until it disappeared.

"Great," she said to the air, realizing she had left without a flashlight. If she planned a romantic night with Matt—that might involve missing clothing—she needed that toilet paper!

Another growl echoed much closer, followed by the crack of twigs and crunch of leaves.

Did wolves, panthers, or bears roam these woods? She knew it had deer. The sound probably came from a rabbit, and her mind had made up the snarl.

Even knowing it could be her imagination, her heart raced, and her mind panicked. Could this be a real predator out to kill her? She fought to remain composed, not wanting to draw attention to herself if it was a dangerous animal.

Stay calm.

After pausing and taking deep breaths, she pushed forward, hunting for the missing roll.

Jennifer's gaze zeroed in on a white object, just visible down the steep hill. With a determined stride, she advanced but stumbled abruptly as her foot snagged against an unforgiving root. She careened down the hill and hit the ground with a thud, face first in the dirt. Her drunken haze left her unable to cushion her fall or feel pain... at least no one saw her embarrassing tumble.

The odor of decaying leaves irritated her nose, so she twisted her face to keep from sneezing as she stood. She dusted off the tiny rocks and sticks that stuck to her legs—wearing shorts while camping had not been her best idea.

She could no longer wait.

Standing tall, with her hands on the buttons holding up her shorts, something fuzzy and close blocked out the tree in front of her. As she focused and realized in horror what she saw, two things happened at once: the black bear let out an earth-shattering roar, and something in Jennifer's mind said rather loudly, *"Awaken!"*

The sides of her face grew incredibly hot.

No, not her face—the insides of her ears, as noise erupted through her body, shaking her very bones. An odd expanding pressure caused her chest to swell without a release, like when you held in a sneeze. The uncomfortable warmth spread from her neck to her throat, then her core—all in mere seconds.

In the meantime, the bear's paw pulled back to run its claws through her body, but as the natural weapons slowly approached her face, she grew—like in the video game *Rampage*.

How was that even possible? Did alcohol make you have delusions?

She didn't know bears had facial expressions other than in cartoons, but the creature's eyes changed from tiny anger-filled slits to round, shock-filled circles as its paw slowly extended toward her.

Running wasn't an option with the animal so close. Instead, she shoved to move the beast out of her personal space. With the push, the bear's last expression included eyes now shaped like ovals, and its chin dropped. She recognized this as fear.

An aroma of barbeque saturated the area as Jennifer's fingers met bear flesh that felt a lot like running her hand through water, not as easy as air to manipulate, but not as hard as the ground.

The sweet scent of honey, brown sugar, and pepper caused Jennifer's mouth to water. Before she thought about it, completely on instinct, she bit and pulled out a chunk of bear flesh, chewing and swallowing. The raw meat tasted gamey and tougher than beef, but the blood-rich tissue held a delicious chili flavor. As she chewed, the light of life faded from the bear's eyes.

The thought that she, Jennifer Wright, had killed a bear and then eaten a piece of it was so absurd, so unbelievable, that it left her speechless. Was this real? Was it just a dream? She wondered if she was living in some sort of fantastical world because this sort of thing only happened in fiction and never in real life.

This is real. This has happened, she thought to herself. It didn't stop her hysterical laughter that sounded like some dying animal wheezing.

Naked, she giggled—the giggles coming out in cackles—and released her bladder. Drunk, the thought she no longer had to remove her pants occurred to her as funny, in the way an intoxicated person laughs at anything. As she stared at where her shorts once rested, she observed two ginormous red legs, thick as tree trunks, with red-clawed feet.

Standing in this awkward pose, curiosity got the best of her, and she brought her left hand up to her face. A scaly three-pronged talon obeyed her commands.

While playing with her velociraptor hands, something in her peripheral vision caught her attention. Instead of a nose, a red snout stretched past the point of convergence for her eyes. Jennifer focused on tiny red ruby scales covering it that sparkled in the moonlight. On the very tip were dark nostrils, like on a horse. With her tongue, she felt sharp, jagged, pointed teeth hanging out over her lips that now extended out in an elongated jaw.

Oh! Her imagination held so many layers of depth! She

hoped she hadn't passed out in the field before she went to the bathroom.

Wet pants. That would be so embarrassing!

Moving around, a black flap of skin snapped in front of her, and she thought she recognized a wing. Continuing to jitter, the loose wings flopped around like they were useless. If they were hers, she couldn't control them, but in the few glimpses she saw, they appeared nothing like a butterfly's and closer to broken bird wings. She spun in circles, trying to catch a better view—anything other than red and black flaps of skin.

An oppressive wave of exhaustion swept over her body. She stretched her shimmery, scaly arms to the sky in a yawn. The tiredness dragged on her mind, like an anchor to a sinking ship, begging her to follow it down into a deep, dark abyss. Her limbs felt like heavy stones, and her eyelids grew extra heavy with sleep.

She remembered the anesthetic they used when she had surgery to remove her tonsils at twelve, and how she felt now reminded her of that. No more exploring tonight because she no longer had the strength to keep her lids open.

She mused that the night had a certain magical quality to it, like something from a fairytale. However, this tale was unlike any other. Usually, it was the prince that saved the maiden from a malevolent creature. But for her, a college student, it seemed fate had changed the story—she was the monster.

The ridiculous idea of her being a beast made her want to laugh in hysteria, but she hissed and crackled instead. As she searched for a soft, dry patch of leaves to curl up in and rest, she imagined herself stomping a small city. Finding a passable spot, she laid down in a similar position as a dog.

Just before her eyes drifted shut, she imagined her own fairytale, envisioned herself as the powerful dragon that swooped down to take the fair Prince Matt away to her own secluded cave.

She was determined to keep him forever.

CHAPTER 2

JENNIFER

As Jennifer laid on the bear, she dreamed of a fair lady on her wedding day. However, she wasn't the center of her delusional creation; she became the bride's mother, Lung.

A single window allowed the sun to shine on the gray curved stone walls, giving the room a medieval aura. Her surroundings reminded her of fairytales, especially the ones set in castle turrets. Jennifer guessed it was sometime in the afternoon from the long shadows cast by the daylight outside that hit a faded mirror.

Abruptly, Spring faced her mother, Lung. Silky pale blond strands drifted out of Lung's fingers. The emerald green eyes that stared back were almost identical to Jennifer's, and the face had the same high-arched brows, though less thick.

The rest of her face didn't match Jennifer's at all. Spring was beautiful with a perfect Barbie nose, shapely rose-shaded lips, and a delicate chin—much daintier than Jennifer's fuller face.

Spring spoke with a high-pitched, soft voice and said, "I'm nervous, Mother."

"All will be well, my beautiful and graceful daughter. Your groom is a lucky man," Lung responded with a soft, even voice that reminded Jennifer of an easy-listening radio host. She placed her withered hand on Spring's thin white shoulder strap, noticing the cool, delicate material felt finer than silk Egyptian sheets.

Glancing away from Spring, Lung surveyed her reflection in the old, faded mirror. A thin, frail woman with a mixture of gold and silver shoulder-length straight hair stared back. She wore a white robe with dragons sewn in bright reds, greens, and blues along the shoulders and collar—a representation of their people and city.

Breaking the trance, Spring moved in front of Lung's reflection and patted her outfit. "And the dress, do you think he will like it?"

As Lung watched her daughter, she had conflicting strong emotions of pure happiness and underlying sadness.

The emotions didn't belong to Jennifer, and though Jennifer tried to understand why an event that should be happy was filled with dread, she hadn't a clue why. Something tragic had happened to Spring after the wedding, though what, she didn't know for sure.

"You look beautiful, my love. No man will disagree," Lung answered.

From behind Lung, a creaking door announced someone new had entered. As Lung turned to greet the newcomer, the rest of the room came into view. The gray stone wall, with mortar slapped between each brick, supported long wooden beams and a high ceiling. The ground appeared solid gray, like polished concrete. Near the door, a bear hide rug, complete with its head, rested—more images reminiscent of a castle.

In romance movies, Jennifer had noticed a pattern. The cameras paused on the leading man during his first appearance. Sometimes the wind blew back his hair, and he smiled while the girls drooled.

She found that dramatic pause, well, cheesy. The idea of

love at first sight made her cringe. It wasn't something backed by science or logic — true love required dedication and time. But her understanding of insta-love that came from studying film missed key factors movies could never reveal.

When Lung focused on the man standing in the doorway, something snapped into place. The man was Jennifer's home. His arms were the place she crawled at the end of a long day. The chest she craved to cling to in celebration.

The movies could never explain knowing that the other soul combined with yours made one completed pair.

The tall man with shoulder-length, wavy auburn hair standing in the wooden door frame was Jennifer's other half.

At the part of his hair, he had a white streak down the middle—almost like gray, but with hints of gold. The stubble on his face showed no signs of white, being slightly darker than his locks. Searching his face, she didn't see any wrinkles, so the strange discoloration was either dye or a genetic anomaly. Based on that, she guessed his age to be around twenty.

He had a thin, muscular build that tapered to a lean waist. Dressed from another century, he wore an off-white shirt and dark brown pants that appeared handsewn with thick thread, made of linen and wool. The stitches in his leather shoes were even visible.

Noticing her mind paused her dream so she could obsess over a fantasy man, she realized her subconscious acted just like the movies. If she could huff, she would—and she'd wipe the drool off the corners of her mouth.

She felt a stab of guilt for ogling at the man. She gave in to her desires and let herself appreciate every detail of the fabricated person. He wasn't perfect by any means, but he had a certain something—something she couldn't put into words. His nose was pointy, which wasn't her type, but it somehow made him more appealing. His eyes were an interesting mix of blue and brown surrounded, by a ring of green. He had thin lips that were a reddish-brown shade, resting above a strong chin.

Using her own ability to search Lung's emotions, she hunted for knowledge of this man. A feeling of respect and a name, Petr, was all Jennifer received.

With a mental sigh from Jennifer, the dream continued.

"It's time," Petr said, offering Spring an elbow. Even his deep, throaty voice resonated through Jennifer's soul, melting her heart.

As Spring touched Petr and interlocked her arm with his, a fit of unreasonable jealousy boiled inside Jennifer.

Lung followed the two out of the room and down a spiral staircase with the same gray stone walls on either side. Within a short distance, the way straightened. The left wall disappeared in a few more minutes, revealing a fifty-foot drop and what initially seemed to be the outdoors.

Realizing the enormous cliff-side pathway lacked a guardrail, Jennifer expected to gasp and feel her heart speed up in pure fear. But Lung remained calm, as if she took the risk every day.

Lung stepped down to another set of stairs, and Jennifer realized they weren't outside but inside the largest cavern she'd ever seen. Not even the cave with a full forest and its own ecosystem that explorers had found in Vietnam and then been published worldwide in magazines matched the volume of this chamber.

In the center of the large area, a small village of round buildings was lit by contained bonfires scattered here and there. Candles hung on the outside of the round cob—packed mud and straw—houses. A small fissure above them in the ceiling revealed the clouds passing in front of the sun. The floor or ground seemed to glow with varying shades of orange and red in different locations. A pungent odor of sulfur and smoke permeated the hot and arid air, reminding Jennifer of being in an oven, but Lung ignored it all.

Before the rows of round huts started, an empty circular area, marked by ostrich egg-sized light gray rocks, surrounded a platform. The place reminded Jennifer of a circus or rodeo arena in size and shape.

Maybe two hundred people had gathered around the platform as music and talking echoed off the walls, causing a roar duller than a concert. Jennifer wasn't sure who first noticed Spring and Petr descending, but she thought it was a child who pointed. The ripple of quiet grew as heads turned in their direction.

Someone helped a small, slender, older man onto the red platform—his hair and beard blended into a long, white mass. He reminded Jennifer of either a wizard from a fairytale, a troll doll, or Papa Smurf.

Intense emotions—power, love, strength, comfort—rolled from Lung as she watched the man raise his arms high above his head. The room quieted. He appeared fragile—a deceiving look, for he was deadly. The word mate and the name MiFeng rushed into Jennifer's mind, powerful like a tidal wave.

"Please come to the center of the room," MiFeng said to Petr. With Spring on his elbow, Petr moved forward as the crowd cleared a path to the stage. Lung flowed past Spring and Petr, being helped onto the platform by a man she didn't even glance at, to stand to the right of MiFeng, surveying the crowd—her people, her clan.

The whispers grew to a roar. Once again, MiFeng raised his head and arms, and the crowd hushed. MiFeng's voice boomed, not matching his frail appearance, as he said, "This is our way, an ancient way that has existed since the foundation of our time. Here in our home. Here in our land. We all remember our ways, our birthplace. My daughter has made her choice. A bond that will last forever. A bond that will break two and make one. One that can make or destroy. A bond longer and more dangerous than any mortal can understand."

As the room remained silent, MiFeng locked eyes with Spring. His voice becoming tender, he asked, "Whom do you choose, my daughter?"

"I choose Che-non," Spring answered, almost like she was singing. A man with long, thick, black hair pulled into a ponytail moved in front of the slightly taller Petr.

Jennifer felt overwhelming relief, as she realized Petr was not the groom.

As Jennifer watched Spring's eyes rove over the man with dark brown eyes, thick eyelashes, and sharp eyebrows sitting on an angular face, she recognized the emotions on Spring's face—love, like the kind in movies.

The way Che-non stood, straight, hands tight by his side, reminded her of a warrior on *Kung Fu Theater*, a show she loved to watch as a kid. Though handsome, he did not come close to being as attractive as Petr, who still held Spring's elbow.

"Thank you, my brother," Che-non said, addressing Petr. The differences in their appearances suggested no family relationship existed—maybe different mothers, or a family found?

As Jennifer contemplated the potential meaning behind 'brother,' she noticed the differences how Petr, Lung, and Che-non pronounced words. A strange thought occurred to her. The ceremony was not in English, Jennifer's native tongue. Despite that, she could understand it and tell by how Che-non clicked his last word that Che-non had a strong accent. Whatever language they were speaking, he was not a native speaker.

Breaking up Jennifer's thoughts, Petr gently edged Spring forward, pushing on her elbow. It didn't take much coaxing, since Spring latched onto Che-non's arm with a toothy grin and a twinkle in her eyes. Che-non placed his hand over hers, beaming happiness.

"Many blessings, my brother," Petr said in his fantastic, throaty voice, and he stepped into the crowd, blending in.

To her side, MiFeng focused his attention on Che-non. "The mating of one of our kind is different than you can imagine. We have discussed this, and you are still willing to take this challenge?"

"With all my heart," Che-non answered.

"Then you have my blessing as her father. And you have my blessing as the Head of the Dragon Council."

CHAPTER 3

MATT

A MILLION THOUGHTS RACED THROUGH MATT'S MIND AS HE helplessly searched. Regret weighed heavily on him like a boulder. His throat clenched as he was racked with guilt and anguish.

He had waited too long to find Jennifer! He should have walked with her when she left! Anything could have happened to her by now.

"Jennifer," he cupped his mouth as he yelled, hoping the sound didn't wake the sleeping campers. When no response came, he shined his light over the hill and along the Silly String trail he'd laid out earlier, making sure he could still locate his way back to camp. In the darkness, the fire and tents were no longer visible, freeing him to call out her name without risk of waking a sleeping camper.

"Jennifer!" he bellowed at the top of his lungs. He paused. Nothing.

Taking a few more steps downhill, hoping she went that way, he glanced up at the moon—three hours, maybe four, before dawn.

Why didn't she take the Silly String? Why had she left the flash-

light? They were both beside the toilet paper. He'd explained their purpose. Silly String so you don't get lost and the flashlight so you can see. He demonstrated how to use them when she declared she'd never been camping in the woods. The strange bird had never been drinking either—so not his typical type of girl he'd date.

My gosh, Jennifer was so innocent! Had it not been for Doug, his roommate and best friend, dating a dark, almost emo woman, he'd have never considered wooing a gorgeous nerd. But Doug, the typical jock type, seemed to love Lauren. When he showed Matt the engagement ring he hid in their apartment, Matt decided perhaps he should pursue something other than his usual party, have fun, center of attention kind of girl. Jennifer fit all his needs: athletic, loved movies, and enjoyed relaxing and trying new things.

Some stuff he didn't like. For instance, sometimes she came across as shy, so he worked hard to get her to talk. Then other times, she was too bold and lacking social etiquette, asking personal questions or saying blunt statements he wished she kept to herself.

His other big complaint was her obsessive need to study—aggravating. No one should study that much, ever.

Life is about balance, he thought.

At the sound of leaves crunching and limbs cracking, he stopped. "Jennifer!" he yelled.

Faintly, he thought he heard a woman whisper.

"Jen—"

"Matt," Jennifer said, panic in her voice, but he didn't notice any movement.

"Where are you?" he asked, surveying the area with the flashlight, not seeing anything beyond leaves, sticks, and bushes.

"Over here." Her voice cracked, too high pitched for her normal conversational tone. More like the way she talked when he intentionally scared her to make her jump.

While he bathed the scenery with light, he asked, "Are you hurt? You've been gone for hours."

"No. But I have a problem. I'm behind the oak. The largest one in the area."

Searching the larger trees, something shimmery, glossy, and pale reflected, and he aimed the light at it. He found Jennifer's bare leg. She peered out around the trunk, her long golden blond hair and adorable face cringe-smiled—one of those awkwardly embarrassed grins that meant she was hiding something from him, so he stopped approaching her and waited for the big reveal.

Was this her being bold or shy?

Biting her bottom lip, she glanced up to the sky. "I have a problem."

"I can't help you if you don't tell me what's wrong."

Her hands appeared on either side of the trunk as she gripped the tree, and a long leg came vertically out. He followed the silky length, wondering if this was foreplay.

Matt swallowed and fought to keep the flashlight steady.

Sure, he'd had opportunities for wild nights alone with different girls… he played football, after all. But he chose not to indulge until the right time, the right girl, and the right protection. He'd had plenty of examples from first cousins of what early experience could lead to later in life.

His oldest cousin dropped out of high school to have children with an abusive boyfriend. The middle acquired an incurable disease, whether from drugs or sexual behavior, Matt didn't know. The youngest, about his age, fought tooth and nail to get into Mississippi State University, using Pell Grants to pave his way. Hopefully, he would escape poverty like Matt's dad.

A few friends teased Matt by calling him a virgin, but most respected his decisions. Waiting was his truth and a core value he knew was best for him.

Continuing his study of her mighty fine leg, he made it

down to her foot and discovered the lack of footwear. No sane person went into the woods barefoot, even to tease someone. "Where is your shoe?"

"It's bad, Matt," Jennifer whispered. "What did you put in the beer?"

"Nothing. What happened?" Instinct caused him to glance up and down her body as she clung to the tree. She faced him, the tree between them, but she shifted, and he made out her firm runner's bottom and long legs. This wasn't the time, so he forced his eyes away again.

With his head still turned, he grabbed the edges of his shirt and tugged up on it. "Wait," he said, removing his top. "Please put this on. Jennifer, I'm only human, and I can only take so much." Turning at the hip, he threw the clothing in her direction, and they both watched as it landed on the ground. Hurriedly, Matt faced away from her again and stuffed his hands in his jean's pockets.

Leaves crackled and crunched, then a pause, followed by the rustling of fabric. Thoughts of what her naked body might appear like in the full moon flooded his imagination, so he pinched his eyes.

"Matt, I had hallucinations or something." When he said nothing, she added, "I'm in your shirt. I'm as covered as I'm going to be."

Pieces of leaves stuck in her hair. There were scratches on the sides of her arms. Other than his shirt, she stood naked. He gulped and shifted some to make himself more comfortable.

In the silence, she tugged on the hem of the top, trying to pull it lower. He forced his eyes to her face because he was sure that if she moved too fast or raised her arms, he would see more of her than she wanted. She'd still be covered, but he wanted to respect her wishes.

With her arms crossed over her chest, she stared at the ground. She said, "Thanks." She pointed somewhere behind him, and added, "Back over that way is a dead bear. I dreamed I was a dragon thing and killed it. When I woke up, I was laying on top of it."

The fear in her oval eyes was apparent, so he didn't doubt something spooked the girl, but without a flashlight, how did she know it was an animal?

"I've heard of blackouts, but this…" he answered, turning his head in the general direction she pointed, searching for the animal. He saw nothing and turned back toward her.

Indicating with her chin behind her and grimacing, she said, "I know, right? When I woke up, I had this nasty film all over me, and my clothes were missing. I did search for them, where I might have laid them, but I only found shreds of material. I walked to the stream down the hill, because… I think it was blood, Matt, coated all over me. It took longer to get there than I thought, and I used that nasty water to wash off the sticky substance. Now I'm cold, covered in fishy-water smell, and naked."

He listened for any sounds of a bubbling brook and pointed the flashlight downhill. Not hearing anything, he asked, "You went down to the stream?"

"Not my best decision. But yes. It sounds so close. I guess the sound echoes off the mountains, but it's a lot further than I thought. I just needed to get the gunk off my skin. Can't you hear it?" She glanced up at him.

"No, I can't hear a stream. Listen, we can sort this out later. Let's get you home. Okay?"

"Home sounds good."

Using the flashlight, Matt found the Silly String trail and led her uphill, back to the camp. Periodically, he checked on her progress. A few paces behind him, she moved a strand of her hair behind her ear and bit her lip. Then, her hand returned to the shirt, tugging it downward.

At the campsite, snores greeted them. The fire's last embers still glowed orange but would soon fade.

Gently, Matt touched Jennifer's shoulder. When she glanced at him, he smiled and pointed in the direction of the snoring. She grinned, but her teeth chattered in the cold.

Well, if she froze to death or went into shock, he would be blamed. He grabbed a log from the pile of firewood and added it to the pit, coaxing the flames back to life. As the fire blazed anew, he encouraged Jennifer to move closer to the heat source. She didn't protest and stretched her hands out toward the warmth.

"Stay here," he whispered to her and squeezed her arm before taking a few quick steps to his roommate's tent.

"Doug?" Matt asked while tapping the outside fabric.

With a groggy voice, Lauren, Doug's girlfriend, said, "What is it?"

Seconds later, the zipper lowered, revealing the dark insides and the shadows of resting figures. Doug said in a whisper, "Nothing, Lauren. It's Matt." After sounds of shuffling, Doug's head stuck out of the tent. "Yeah, man, what's up?" Doug asked.

"It's Jennifer. She's sick. In case it's the flu or something, we're heading out. Do you mind taking my things back to the apartment?"

"Sure, but why don't you wait until the sun's up?" Doug asked.

He glanced over at Jennifer again. In those few quick seconds, he glimpsed her skimpy clothing and dazed face while her hands protruded over the flames. "Nah, I'll take her home. Hopefully, this is the worst it will be, but if she gets sicker, I want her to be in bed."

"Okay, man. I hope Jennifer feels better. Be home later," Doug said before disappearing into his tent.

Matt walked to his own tent and retrieved the sleeping bag. He draped it around Jennifer's shoulders, like putting a coat around her. She barely noticed but did place her hands on the zipper, pulling it closed.

"There's nothing I can do about your feet," Matt said. He sighed and pointed down at her bare legs. "They already look cut up." He frowned, thinking about the pain she might experience walking to the vehicle.

Jennifer grabbed her right foot in her left hand and rolled it over. With round eyes and a quizzical face, she inspected the bottom as she removed a small rock. With a shrug of her shoulders, her leg dropped to the ground as she pulled the blanket around her.

Oh boy. Was she in shock from the cold?

Afraid she would fall behind if he didn't lead her, he took her hand. Slowly, they progressed down the mountain and toward his truck. As he unlocked the door, he stared up at the sky. By the time they reached campus, it would be daylight.

On the road to campus, he glanced over at Jennifer, happy to find she had stopped shaking. From habit, he placed his hand on Jennifer's leg. When he felt bare skin, he quickly pulled away.

"Man, Jennifer," Matt said, unable to continue the drive in silence. "You had me scared."

There was a pause before Jennifer whispered, "I had me scared, too." For the first time since she had climbed into the vehicle, she turned away from staring straight out the window and focused on Matt. He smiled and put his hand back on her leg, rubbing her knee.

"What happened?" Matt asked.

"I don't know. I walked into a bear, and before it could hurt me, I changed into a, I don't have a better word for it, dragon. A red, scaley dragon. Matt, I bit the bear and ate a small piece."

"You were drunk, Jennifer. You probably blacked out at some point, sat down, and fell asleep."

"Then why did I wake up naked with my head resting on a dead bear? I searched the area for my clothes, my shoes… I found shreds and pieces of what could only be my clothes. I wasn't drunk then."

Reaching up, he searched for a fever, and she did, indeed, feel warm to him. Shrugging, he said. "I don't know. Maybe you tripped on a bear or a log that looked like a bear, since you left the flashlight, it could have been anything. Dead bears smell horrible. Dead things stink—"

She scrunched up her face, interrupted, and said, "It stank bad after I ate part of it. Flies were all around it when I woke up. I didn't think flies gathered until things had been dead for a long time."

Patting her leg, he said, "That's what I'm saying, Jennifer. You were drunk and tripped on a dead bear. After you fell asleep, you dreamed you turned into a dragon. I can't explain your clothes, but who knows what you could've done with a fever. Why don't I ask Belinda to gather some of your clothes and you can come to my apartment? Or I can drive you to your parents' after you get dressed?"

Jennifer's roommate, Belinda, was part of their friend group. She joined them sometimes for drinking and football games. Nice, but Belinda partied more than Jennifer. Had he not known they met when they started college in August, he would have assumed they were friends in high school. He guessed living with someone, even someone with a different lifestyle, created a bond.

"Your apartment is fine," Jennifer answered, surprising Matt. She closed her eyes and leaned back on the headrest. "Belinda's not at the dorm. After class yesterday, she went home to Michigan to see her parents for Thanksgiving. I'm not so sick I can't grab an outfit or two."

Matt glanced over toward Jennifer and then focused on the road. "I rather like you in my shirt." A wicked grin caressed his lips. But when she didn't smile back and kept her head on the headrest, Matt responded, "Sure, no problem."

Silence filled the vehicle as they drove to Jennifer's dorm.

She periodically tugged on her sleeping bag, covering her body completely. He cranked up the heat in case she was in shock. Beads of sweat formed on his brow, but she stayed tucked away under the blanket.

This date was quite memorable: their first kiss, an unexpected animal encounter, and now an unexpected illness.

CHAPTER 4
JENNIFER

THE NOISE FROM THE BLINKER SNAPPED JENNIFER'S MIND AWAY from the images of the bear falling backward, chased closely by a red talon. She shook her head.

It was just an alcohol-induced hallucination.

As the truck slowed down in front of the dorm, Jennifer searched the area for any students still on campus. At one time, the road in front of her building continued to another part of the school grounds, but the university blocked the street to cars by adding metal pylons. Now, only people-powered devices, such as legs or bikes, traversed that old pathway.

According to the professor for her art class, the university saw the bright yellow pylons as an eyesore. To beautify the campus, they added a circular car turnaround with a baby cherub fountain, green plants that flowered in the spring, ornate benches, and a few lamps with long elegant posts. The area reminded Jennifer of a small park with yellow pylons that didn't seem to fit.

On the head of the fountain's angel, the only living creatures in sight—pigeons—perched, unafraid of Matt's truck.

The vehicle stopped, but she peeked at her dorm window

with her hand on the door before stepping outside. The curtains and the blinds were closed, so she couldn't see into the room. She glanced over her shoulder toward Matt but past him, at the English building. Then, she turned to face the empty path beyond the fountain.

"Don't forget your key," Matt said as she opened the door.

"Yeah, thanks." From the glove compartment, she grabbed her phone and smartwatch. Thankfully, Matt had talked her into not taking them into the woods.

At the thought of the woods, an image of a black bear standing before her popped into her mind. *The bear wasn't real. It was just a hallucination.*

"I'll bring your sleeping bag back to the car," she said.

The first step on the pavement hurt as movement emphasized the small cuts and tears on the soles of her feet.

If the bear wasn't real, why am I naked? Did I leave my clothes thrown about in the forest?

Slamming the truck door closed, she hugged the covering to her chest. Despite the stinging sensation on her feet, she ran to the entrance and, once there, pressed the smartwatch face to the latch. The mechanical parts clicked, and she entered her red brick dorm building.

In the hall to her apartment, she passed the redhead freshman in her art class. Jennifer assumed the other woman must be eating because she whiffed rosemary chicken. Feeling nauseous, it made Jennifer even more queasy. They only talked a few times, so Jennifer nodded, swiftly opening the door to her room and slamming it shut behind her.

When she turned on the light, Belinda's rose perfume filled her senses, almost like her roommate had just left. Scrunching her nose, she flopped on her bed, pulling up her feet. Red welts marked her soles.

The bear wasn't real. It was a hallucination. I'm not a dragon.

Maybe if she said it a few more hundred times, she'd believe it.

She grabbed her favorite Christmas pajamas and loaded jeans, a shirt, and undergarments into a green duffle bag. She sighed; her new running shoes were missing and probably destroyed. At least she still had the old, faded black joggers beside her boots in the corner—the only shoes Jennifer kept at school.

I wonder what happened to the ones I wore in the forest? If the bear wasn't real, I must have taken off my shoes and left them in the woods.

Adding two pairs of socks from the laundry basket, she grabbed a towel and her bathing supplies for a five-minute shower. Once dry, she applied an ointment from her medical kit—her parents insisted she keep one under her bed—to her feet, then dressed in her favorite pajamas, socks, and old shoes.

Done, duffle bag in hand, she confidently made it back to the warm truck with Matt.

As she pulled the seat belt across her lap, Matt glanced at her, focusing on her outfit. "Santa Claus, cute, but I always pictured you in boxer-type shorts and a tight top. I could suggest some," he mumbled under his breath.

She stared at him in shock. It was unlike Matt to make such a lewd statement, but he whispered the words, so perhaps he didn't realize he said it out loud. As a Southerner, she bit her tongue but wanted to ask him how he thought she could walk outside in something like that. Wearing his shirt earlier was embarrassing enough.

He froze, tilting his head to the side. "What's up? What's that look for?" he asked.

"Did you just make a comment about my pajamas?"

"You heard that?" he asked as a warm cherry color grew on his cheeks.

When she nodded, he explained, "Sorry, Jen. Your pajamas are adorable, but you're more sexy than cute. I expected you to dress more like the girls in movies that have pillow fights and giggle, you know?"

She crossed her arms. "You expected me to dress like a porn star?"

Facing forward, he nodded slightly. He pulled out onto the road, flipping a blinker, then merged into traffic. He said, "At least when you sleep. Maybe that's why you took off your clothes in the forest—and then you blacked out? It's a logical assumption. You were tired and wanted to rest and just did the thing you do every night."

I was a dragon, and I killed a bear. It was a hallucination! She saw the image of the bear falling as a red talon sliced it open, and she shuddered. *It seemed so real.*

She forced herself to focus on his logical reasoning. Could she have taken off her clothes in the woods? Maybe to keep them dry while she released her bladder, unsure if she could aim in her drunken state? She could see herself doing that, protecting her clothing. But not to take a nap—Matt was wrong about that. Jennifer didn't sleep naked—even when Belinda was away.

When she said nothing, he said, "Let's forget everything that happened after the kiss until right now. Okay?"

"Agreed."

Once they arrived, Matt found a few empty spots close to his apartment and parked. He searched her face, landing on her lips. "Wait..." he said.

She nodded, and he turned off the engine. She followed him with her eyes as he ran around to the passenger side and opened the door.

"Here." Matt offered her his hand. As she grabbed the green duffle bag, she took Matt's extended arm and climbed out of the truck. Once she was out, he shut the door. "Please hand me that." He reached over and took the bag from her.

Freely releasing the duffel bag, Jennifer watched as Matt

pointed the key fob. The truck's lights blinked as it honked, and Matt claimed her hand.

The sun peeked out from behind Matt's building. As his rough fingers caressed hers, he said, "It's amazing no one saw you at the dorm."

"Yeah, it was. Good thing people went home for Thanksgiving and haven't made it back," she responded. She didn't mention anything about the other dormmate, the red-headed freshman she passed in the hall because it wasn't important. Then she realized, "Ouch, I forgot your sleeping bag at my dorm."

He squeezed, comforting her. "It's okay. You can get it to me later. Are you hungry?"

"Mainly, I'm sleepy," Jennifer answered. An uncontrolled yawn escaped her mouth. "I'm sure you're tired as well."

"Mainly hungry. I'll just grab some pizza when we get inside before I sleep." Letting her hand go, he grinned mischievously, moving out of the way so she could walk into his apartment. "Mi casa, your casa."

As she passed over the threshold, she beamed at his devilish smile right before the overpowering scent of ocean breeze air freshener caused her eyes to water, and she blinked to recover. Compared to the lighter gym socks odor a week ago, it was better, at least. Releasing Matt's hand, Jennifer reached over and turned on the light.

Since her last visit, the simple apartment had been cleaned. Missing were the knickknacks and dirty clothes scattered about. To the left, an outdated entertainment center held precariously stacked books and video games. The area wasn't perfect—for instance, the retro console rested a little crooked on the top shelf, but someone had clearly tried to pick up.

On the end tables beside the white stained couch rested fancy headsets propped on stands. Probably where they gamed on their laptops.

She knew from experience the two outer seats became recliners. Making herself at home, she made her way to the sectional and plopped down. The smell of overripe grape jelly assaulted her nose, so strong she held her breath and jumped back up.

Staring at Matt, she wasn't sure how she could tell him his furniture stank.

No matter how tired I am, I can't sleep with that odor.

Unaware of her inner turmoil, Matt moved to the kitchen, where the brown carpet transitioned to linoleum. He placed the green duffle bag on top of the glass tabletop, gently shoving a vase of flowers out of the way. He leaned on the tall counter that separated the cooking and dining areas and watched her.

Jennifer realized she was biting her bottom lip, and Matt, beyond a doubt, was staring at it. To break the tension, she said, "Wow, you've cleaned your apartment since the last time I was here."

He stood straight at this and dodged the brass chandelier hanging partially above the table. Moving to the kitchen area, he opened the refrigerator. Over his shoulder, he said, "Yes. Would you like a beer? We have two-day-old pizza if you want any."

"No, thank you. The place looks better," Jennifer commented, leaving out the overpowering smells.

Did alcohol poisoning make things smell stronger? She had heard of light and sound sensitivity from movies but had never personally experienced it.

I turned into a dinosaur and killed a bear.

Forcing her mind away from the camping trip, she paid attention as Matt popped open a soda can. After a few swallows, he said, "Lauren said since mid-terms were over, she expected the place cleaned." The corner of his mouth turned up in a smirk. "She was kind of serious about the threat. She said I would find my sheets cut into pieces and all my stuff outside if the apartment wasn't clean." He started laughing. "She's scary when she's angry."

He took another large gulp, and she watched his Adam's apple move. With a loud bang, he placed the soda can on the table. He didn't slam the drink. He just sat it down. Yet Jennifer covered her ears and cowered. "Ouch. Is this part of a hangover?"

"Probably," he answered.

Slowly, she removed her hands, bringing them back to her sides.

"You are so adorable," he said.

She stuck out her tongue. Chuckling at her caused his chest muscles to flex, and her eyes focused on how he appeared chiseled. In his presence, the sculptures of Greek gods would fail in comparison.

"My eyes are up here," he said to her, then laughed again.

"Sorry," she said. Embarrassed, she glanced away. "I forgot your shirt too."

"I'm joking, Jen. You can look and touch if you want." This time, he bit his lip while he grinned.

He moved from behind the counter in front of her in a few short steps. Her fingers trembled as he took her hands and placed them on his chest. Heat rose from his flesh. His oily skin had a strange woodsy aroma that made her want something, but she couldn't put words to it. Closing her eyes, she leaned up and kissed his chin. Tiny hairs pricked her lips in delight.

"I tell you what, Jen. Don't sleep on the couch. I'll rest on the chair after I have some pizza. I changed my sheets and bedcover, so they're clean."

"Thanks, Matt. I'll take you up on that offer." Her fingers dropped. Before she made it to the room, he walked up behind her, spun her around, and bent down for a deep, passionate kiss.

She closed her eyes, waiting for the sparks that accompanied their earlier lip lock. Instead, as his tongue danced with hers, she imagined Petr from her dream.

Petr. Just a fairytale caused by drinking too much alcohol this crazy weekend. Just like the bear wasn't real. *I'm not a winged predator. I'm a simple human kissing the most handsome guy at my college. That's all.*

And with that thought, she threw herself into Matt—running her hands through his hair, biting his bottom lip—before she pulled away and backed into Matt's room.

Matt stood there, a grin splitting his face in two.

"Thank you. I needed that," she said.

He tilted his head like all the cowboys did in the movies when they saved the damsel in distress.

While he stood in that position, she closed the door. Her body collapsed against the frame, and she slid to the carpet. Every time she blinked, the image of Petr appeared, like he was in the room with her.

This is crazy. She controlled her breathing, focusing her mind on blue when she inhaled and pink for exhaling.

Finally, when she closed her eyes, she saw nothing and crawled into Matt's bed. True to his words, the crisp cotton sheets smelled slightly of detergent. The first pillow she grabbed held too much of Matt's manliness, so she sniffed until she found one with less odor.

She tried to rest, but Petr's blue-green irises stared at her when she closed her eyes.

Petr doesn't exist.

There was no way she killed and ate a bear, and all she needed was some rest to make the experience disappear. After sleep, Matt's kisses would curl her toes again.

CHAPTER 5
MATT

MATT'S ARM FELL OFF FROM WHERE IT RESTED AROUND Jennifer's waist, waking him. She stood from the bed, stumbled in the dark, and opened the bedroom door. Seconds later, the bathroom light turned on. He winced at the retching sound. She'd finally thrown up.

Maybe now she'd felt better?

He desperately wanted to rush to her side and hold her hair, to support her, but he held back. If he was in her position, the last thing he would want was for his new girlfriend to see him weak. He gave her that respect and stayed under the sheets, faking sleep.

When she didn't return to the bed and heard her footsteps heading to the living room, he waited, reflecting on what to say.

Voices and laughter from a sitcom played from the room, and he pictured her watching television.

Did he start by apologizing for being beside her in the bed when she woke up? He only meant to close his eyes for a second. Exhausted, he unintentionally nodded off.

And now that she seemed to be on the mend, the other emotion he struggled with—anger—reared its ugly head.

How could she get sick?

Resistance to move increased with each minute that passed. He wanted to avoid an uncomfortable conversation or saying something—such as accusing her of intentionally being sick—he didn't mean because of foolish emotions. He couldn't help the indignation; staying up and checking on someone hour after hour got old. Especially when he had so many fun plans for this weekend.

Your girlfriend is sick. It's normal…all of it…taking care of her, getting bugs, all of it is part of the package, he encouraged himself.

The television turned off, and he sighed—enough stalling.

Deciding not to dress, he stood wearing only boxers, stretched an arm over his head, and leaned on the hall wall facing the couch. This gave her a great view of all the hard work he did in the gym.

Instead of lying in her normal recliner, she sat on the other end, staring toward the patio—her golden blond hair appearing almost brown, tucked behind her ears. Whatever bothered her had created creases on her otherwise perfect forehead.

Even in pajamas with oily hair, she was beautiful. As her eyes locked with his, she sat straight up.

And he smiled. Disarmament would be his first move… His mother taught him a pleasant face hid things one wasn't ready to reveal. In a chipper voice, he said, "Hey, you're up. We were beginning to worry. Jen, it's Sunday." He peeked over at the clock on the wall. It said 2:30 a.m. He corrected his statement and said, "Oops, sorry, Monday. You've been asleep for two days."

The genuine smile on her face caused the resentment and anxiety to seep out of him, leaving his body exhausted.

He could do with a nap.

She said, "Wow! That would explain the hunger."

Time to break the next bit of news. "Your mom and dad

started calling your cell phone Sunday morning. It got a little crazy… ringing again as soon as it stopped."

Her face turned white, and the fear returned.

"Are you okay? Do I need to get you a bag? I think you've had the flu or something."

"No, just concerned about my parents… Mom is a worrier."

Instead of replying, Matt nodded.

"I need to call them," she said, her eyes going wide as they roamed over the apartment's surfaces. He had placed her phone on the nightstand in his room. He'd get it for her in a second.

Tilting his head, his arms dropped. "You can call in a bit." The way she blew out her cheeks like a chipmunk's, round and swollen, he added, "You're not getting sick again, are you?"

Shaking her head, she released the air, and her face returned to normal, yet her eyes hunted the furniture, and she placed her hand on the back of the chair like she was about to stand up. "No… I'm not getting sick. The throwing up was temporary. I'm fine now… If I told you why, you'd understand…"

He crossed his arms and waited.

"Matt, you'd be sick too if you dreamed you were your mom having…" —her cheeks colored in a bright blush — "… getting busy with your dad. That's what I dreamed about, my parents about our age… and… and they had sex. So gross. I feel fine now." She glanced away from him, eyes frantically roaming again. "Help me find my phone. I told them I would call them on Sunday. Have you seen my—"

"Eventually, I answered," he admitted.

Her eyes widened, and her mouth dropped open, but her skin kept the warm blush. He took that as a win.

Now for the tricky part. "Before I gave them a chance to

wonder what stranger answered their daughter's phone, I told them I was your boyfriend."

She inhaled and blinked rapidly. "You told them you were my boyfriend?" she whispered.

"Jen, you've been asleep in my bed for two days. You weren't answering your phone. I thought it would make them feel better, knowing you were safe. You don't mind, do you?"

Claiming his territory, he sat beside her, placed his hand over her fingers on the couch, and brought them to his mouth. He intentionally captured her eyes while he kissed the back of her hand before resting it on her lap. "We can break up if you like. Besides, I got the impression they'd never heard of me."

"I haven't told them about us yet," she admitted and frowned. As she bit her lip, she glanced up at him. "No, Matt, it's fine… I'm your girlfriend." She squeezed his hand and laced their fingers together. "It's just my parents. They love to worry. I told them we would be back Sunday morning."

"Okay, but we were coming back on Saturday."

She sighed. "I know, but they worry, like a lot. If I told them we were coming back on Saturday, they would have called every hour on the hour as soon as the clock turned over to eight a.m."

"Right, sure. Jen—"

"No, Matt, listen. It's so bad before we left, my mom called the doctor to make sure my immunizations were caught up. Seriously, my mom is a massive planner and over-the-top worrier. It's the same reason I didn't tell them about you. I didn't tell them about you because they would want to know everything… where you were born, what high school you went to, your major, your parents… everything. They've probably already done a background check. Did you give them your full name?"

Now that she mentioned it, they had asked him a lot of questions, including where he saw himself in five years. He assumed those were normal things parents wanted to know about their kid's partner.

Playing it off, he answered, "I did, and that explains why they asked for my social." He laughed.

With her free hand, she lightly smacked him. "Not funny, Matt. Were they bad worried?"

"Hm, what is bad worried? I told them you caught a bug when we were camping, and you should be well soon." The grip on his hand tightened, and he saw the fear in her eyes. "Listen, Jen, Lauren works at the hospital as part of her master's program. She checked on you and wasn't worried." His roommate Lauren was finishing her master's in nursing.

For the next part, he needed to watch her expression, so he glanced over at her face and found the windows to her soul. "They invited me to Thanksgiving."

As he expected, fear showed on her face for a mere second, and then her shoulders relaxed.

"What did you say?" she asked.

"Yes, and I would love to, of course. And when I told my parents about you, they obviously wanted to meet you as well. After we eat lunch at your house on Thanksgiving, we're heading to mine."

She removed her hand from his and stood, moving around in the living room, searching once again. "I better call my parents. Where did you put my phone?"

"You don't seem upset about meeting my parents or Thanksgiving," he commented, standing beside her.

"I'm not... not about Thanksgiving or meeting your parents. Once you told them we were dating, it was only a matter of time before they found a way to interrogate you. But I better call them now."

"Relax, Jen. It's kind of early. Would you like to go grab something to eat? You can call them when the sun is up."

On cue, Jennifer's stomach growled. She glanced down at her tummy, and he placed a hand over her belly, rubbing.

"Yeah, something to eat would be wonderful." She moved out of Matt's reach and became stern. "But seriously, I need to call my parents. You told them I had a bug. I can imagine my mom looking in her wilderness books for bugs and fungi that cause symptoms matching mine. Dad is probably trying to find out where you live, and they're planning a surprise visit right now. If we wait until the sun is up, we will be spending the day with them. Thanksgiving is one thing, a whole day with them, probably at your apartment… Do you have beer in your refrigerator?"

He did and wondered why she asked. Did she want a beer? "Why?"

"My parents are teetotalers."

He stared at her blankly. Shaking her head, she picked up the throw pillow on the couch and tucked her hand behind the cushions. Her hand came back with money and a French fry. "Gross, Matt." She placed the fry on the end table near his headset. "Teetotalers, like they never drink, it's against their religious beliefs. Drinking while underage will be like one strike. I'm not ready for that conversation with my parents. Best to avoid it. Where is my phone?" She pushed against the back of the couch, shoving it backward, and found a white sock.

Not sure what to think, he held out his hand before she destroyed the little façade of cleanliness they had created. "Hold on, Jen." Quickly, he located the phone in his room and returned, holding it out for her. As she took it, he said, "The Bee's Knees is around the corner. When you're done, we could grab something to eat. I'm going to get dressed."

She grabbed his arm and had a surprisingly firm grip. "No, sir. The food part sounds great. But you are staying right here. After all, you are my boyfriend." As her fingers flew over the cell's surface, she hyper-focused and hit speaker.

"Jennifer!" Her mother sounded relieved.

"Hi, Momma," she responded. "Sorry to wake you."

"Thank goodness you called. I haven't been sleeping well with worry. Are you okay?" Jennifer's mom asked.

"I'm fine now, just a little hungry." At this, she glanced over at Matt.

In the background, he heard a male voice and recognized it as her father when he said, "Who is it, Pauline?"

Her mom's voice became muffled, but he understood her words. "It's Jennifer, dear."

"Why hasn't she called us earlier? And who is this *boyfriend!*" Jennifer snickered without making a sound.

"Jacob, please. Go back to sleep."

Addressing Jennifer, her mom said, "Do you think you caught something from the woods? You haven't been camping since you were a little girl, and what we did then wasn't really camping."

"I don't know, Momma, but I feel fine now. I'm going to go get some food with Matt."

"Your boyfriend?" It sounded more accusing than anything. Her parents sounded jovial yesterday when he talked with them. Unsure how to react, he locked eyes with Jennifer. She smiled, reassuring.

"Yes, Mother, and you will like him. He's a nice boy."

"I know you have good taste, and I trust you, but I expected to hear that you had a boyfriend from you first."

Jennifer smiled. "I love you, Momma. You can meet him on Thanksgiving."

"Love you too, my sky angel. Please be safe."

"I will."

She ended the call and laid the phone down, then glanced at Matt. "I'd like to grab a shower first."

He rubbed her arm and said, "I can help with that. I have your clothes in my closet, and I have the stuff you'll need in my bathroom, including a toothbrush."

Taking her hand, he led her back to his bedroom and opened the bag he had on the dresser. As she took the items from him, she pulled out a black bra and matching lacy underwear, holding them up. Her head tilted at him like she needed an explanation.

Surprised at Lauren's purchases, he hid it with a shy grin. He only asked Lauren to buy toiletries, not lingerie. He should have checked the bag before he handed it to Jennifer.

Leaning down, he picked up the green duffle bag. "I noticed your gym bag had nothing for you to take a shower. I hope you don't mind; I gave Lauren some money. Enough so she could buy something for herself as well. If they're the wrong size, it's her fault, but please blame me."

She dropped the bra back into the plastic tote and breathed out, but a smile crossed her lips. "Thank you," she said, then glanced up at him.

Instead of a kiss, he touched her on the nose.

"Let me go grab a shower and brush my teeth. Then I'll be ready to go."

As she headed out the door, he said, "Hey Jennifer," louder than he meant to and cringed at the thought that he might wake Doug or Lauren. "I left you two towels and a washcloth. My mom uses two, so I thought you might like two as well."

"Thank you. I'll be right back."

He closed the door to his room after she entered the bathroom. When the water turned on, he exhaled, not sure if that was a victory or a loss.

CHAPTER 6
JENNIFER

SOMETHING WAS WRONG!

Every bump or dent in the road caused Jennifer's head to spin. She'd asked Matt to slow down, and he had, placing his hand on her leg as he decelerated. But the scents were all wrong, too. Naturally, Matt always smelled of body wash, like the kinds in the commercials that made all the girls go crazy, but now the strength of what he wore almost covered everything. And then, every time he stared at her, there was this musk mixed with something floral.

Could she still have a hangover?

The brilliant orange neon light on the overhead sign announcing their arrival at the restaurant did little to soothe her growing stomachache.

Why, at four in the morning, was it as bright as the middle of the day?

"Are you okay?" Matt asked. He seemed unaffected by the surprisingly luminous glare of their surroundings.

The car finally stopped. She swallowed, and the nausea receded. "Yeah, I'm fine. Do hangovers always do this?" she asked as she rubbed her forehead.

He laughed and squeezed her thigh. "No, Jen. I'm pretty

sure you had alcohol poisoning on top of the flu. You should be on the mend now that you're awake." He glanced around the parking lot as he turned off the engine. "Stay here and don't move," he said, then jumped out of the truck.

As he walked around the vehicle, he pulled on his thin jacket and zipped it closed. Once he opened the door, he blew on his hands before bowing and offering to help Jennifer down from the cab. His over-the-top grin—straight white teeth showing just enough gum to look like something out of a magazine—appeared mischievous, with him bent over and his head tilted upward, though she understood that wasn't his personality.

Not a second passed before Matt flung his arm over her shoulder after she planted her feet on the ground. "I could get used to having a girlfriend," he said, then placed a kiss on the top of her head.

Smelling a spicy nutmeg, she picked up her hair and sniffed. And there, on her strands, Matt's body spray lingered along with the floral perfume of the shampoo.

What's wrong with me? Why are my senses on overdrive? she asked herself as Matt held open the door to the diner. Seconds later, all thoughts left except the need to eat as the overpowering odor of grilled steak caused her tongue to swim in saliva and her stomach to growl.

To focus on something other than her overwhelming hunger, she inspected her surroundings—orange booths along the wall, fake plants here and there, and tables in the center; other than the wood-paneled walls, nothing special compared to any other restaurant.

When a server approached them, her hair up in a beehive, Jennifer had a flashback to her dream last night. Her mother watched a TV show about a waitress with similar hair—raised on top of her head, curls going in every direction, even the same reddish blond. The similarities were striking, and Jennifer just stared.

In my dream, what year was that? She couldn't remember. Intentionally, she blocked out most of what transpired. Seeing your parents kiss was one thing; actually being your mother while it happened, absolutely disgusting!

Well, that helped with feeling less hungry.

"Ready to be seated?" the woman asked.

"Yes, please," Matt responded, pushing on the small of Jennifer's back to encourage her to follow the waitress.

The hostess showed them a booth. Jennifer scooted next to the window and removed the jacket Matt loaned her.

As the hostess positioned the menus on the table, a curl fell in front of her face, and the waitress tucked it behind her ear. Something in that simple movement seemed so familiar; she had to know her from somewhere. Jennifer asked, "Is your name Flo, by chance?"

Flo was the name of the main character in the comedy she dreamed her mother watched years before Jennifer's birth. Maybe Jennifer had met the waitress before, and that inspired that small part of the dream?

The woman stopped with her hand on the menu as she placed it at Matt's spot. "Usually, only older couples ask me that. Is that show offered with a streaming service now?"

Shocked and confused, Jennifer hoped that the image of watching a series through her mother's eyes was nothing more than her imagination. "No," Jennifer said, not glancing at the woman. Instead, she hyper-focused on the list of food options in front of her.

That part of her dream was real?

"Oh, I thought you asked me that because," the woman said, and she touched her nametag. "My name is Tiffany. The owner is from Texas, and he likes things big. He asked all of us to style our hair in beehives, like a way of showing solidarity. Most of us just pull our hair off our necks. Since I'm the night manager, I thought I would lead by example, you might say. I used that old TV show to model my hair after, and not one of the influencer's updos." Dropping her hands to her sides, she added, "Your waitress will be with you shortly. I hope you enjoy your meal."

Glancing at the woman, Jennifer nodded as she said, "Thank you." But Matt said the same thing, drowning out her words.

Once the hostess left the area, Matt tapped her hand. He asked, "Do you feel rested up?"

"No. All my senses are still in overdrive. Even this lighting hurts. I think if I had more sleep, I'd feel better."

Off to her right, steak charred in the kitchen, and she inhaled deeply. Handing the menu to Matt, she said, "I think I'm going to get a meat lover's omelet. How about you?"

"Scrambled all the way." He smiled.

About that time, their waitress walked up. She appeared years younger than the first woman, and true to the hostess's words, she only pulled her auburn hair back in a bun. Pulling a pen from behind her ear and holding it in front of a notepad, she asked, "What can I get y'all to drink?" The strong Southern accent came out clipped.

Leaning against Jennifer, Matt whispered, "You first, Jen."

Taking the cue, she said, "I'll have water."

Matt turned to the waitress. "I'll take a Coke." Once the waitress had their orders, she left the table.

Carefully, Jennifer unhooked the paper wrapper from around her silverware and napkin at the seams.

"So, do you want to go see a movie?" Matt asked.

Without glancing at him, she began folding the paper. "Maybe. I was thinking of going for a jog this afternoon. At some point, I need to ask my parents when they can pick me up. Then there's a report I need to finish, or at least work on before next week. I thought about writing a good rough draft on that today."

To avoid making eye contact, she focused on reshaping the wrapper in her hands. "Thanks for getting all that stuff to take a shower. It was very thoughtful, Matt. I was getting pretty nasty." She felt a warm glow from a blush creep into her face despite her attempt to seem meek.

"Nah," Matt said, unhooking his silverware and playing with his fork. "Okay, maybe."

Jennifer laughed and lightly smacked him on his wrist.

"Hey! Only a little nasty." Dropping the utensil, he turned toward her, placing his fingers under her chin, forcing her to stare at him. Leaning in, his lips caressed hers.

When he moved away, he still touched her face. "You had a beer smell to you." An ear-to-ear grin stretched his face as he released her, turning his attention back to the fork. "You smell better now, almost good."

"Thanks," she responded sarcastically.

"I can take you home, if you like. That way you don't have to bother your parents—if you don't mind staying around for a few days. We can catch a few movies, go on a few jogs," he said. Bumping against her shoulder, he added, "We can even do a little homework, but not so much that it hurts my brain. This is, after all, called Thanksgiving break for a reason." He emphasized the word "break."

Grinning, she made the napkin into a duck. "What about gaming? I heard your friends talking about that new pirate game. Do you think you could show it to me?"

Reaching over, he grabbed her hand, and she dropped the paper bird. "I didn't think you liked games."

"I don't know. I've never really tried, but I'm willing."

"Let's play Phasmaphobia instead of the pirate game. You go as a team into a haunted house and use clues to find and remove the ghost—fun, and you can use your brain." He tapped his head.

"Does it have scary noises like a horror movie?"

"Huh, I never noticed—don't remember. It's been a while since I played, but we can find out later."

Instead of glancing at her, he stared at their intertwined

fingers. "Listen, I can't tell you what to do, but I don't think you should drink again—first, the blackout, running a temperature, and then sleeping for two days. I'm sure you were just sick, but still—in case your body doesn't do well with alcohol... At least consider never doing it again, and if you do, don't do it without me. I want to make sure you're safe."

She saw the way he hyper-focused, not making eye contact. "Matt Davis, I will consider both your proposal to watch me drink and to never have a drink again," she said, squeezing.

A familiar odor, a musk similar to cashmere and sandalwood with a taint of wrongness—pungent and moldy, but nothing she could accurately describe—wafted in her area. She knew that person's scent in her heart, and her pulse quickened as her head snapped around the room. The recognition happened so quickly that she felt her face drain of color. Across from them, she watched a man with shaggy auburn hair, a small patch of blond at the center, and a full beard, take off his coat.

It's the man from my dream, Petr! Will he recognize me? This can't be real! He doesn't exist!

As fast as her neck could turn, she faced the window and tried to hide. She controlled her breathing to slow her frantically racing heart.

Why am I hiding? There is no way he could recognize me! In my dream, I was someone else... and hello, it was a dream!

Matt released her hand, yet all her senses honed in on the scent that belonged to Petr, the man from her dream.

"Dr. Smith," Matt said, standing. It felt like time stopped. She refused to look. Instead, she watched the shadowed reflection as her boyfriend greeted a man who shouldn't exist.

CHAPTER 7

PETR

THE BEE'S KNEES STAYED OPEN TWENTY-FOUR HOURS AND offered comfort food. As a single man with no strong attachments in the area, Petr regularly ate at the restaurant.

With a smile, Connie, the waitress who usually worked his table, held open the door for him. "Isn't it surprising how fast it turns cold around here? Your normal table, Dr. Smith?"

It took a second to remember he went by Doctor Nicholas Smith, but he doubted she noticed the pause in the conversation while he recalled his name for this century. "Amazing. Warm just two days ago. I would love my normal table if it's not too much trouble, and if no one is already sitting there, please," he answered.

As he came around the corner, he recognized Matt sitting beside a blond. Making sure he placed the note he found slipped under his office door into the zipped pouch, he hung his jacket over the chair.

Turning to greet Matt, he watched as the tall boy with dark hair and brown eyes stood. Matt's appearance was nothing like Petr's long-dead twin sister's, but Petr was sure —Matt was her descendent.

The only reason Petr took the job at South Holt University as an anthropology teacher was to watch Matt. Petr's twin gave him a task and the means to do it. While she died birthing a dragon's son, Petr promised to guard and wait until the blood ran true and her descendant shifted into a dragon.

"Dr. Smith," Matt acknowledged him first.

As they shook hands, he said, "Hello, Matt. It's awful late or early to be at The Bee's Knees. How is your Thanksgiving break going?"

Petr glanced around Matt toward the girl. She faced the window, her long golden hair down her back, two eyes peering at him from the reflection on the glass pane. He heard her heart race, and he wondered why. Did he interrupt a moment between Matt and the girl?

Unbeknownst to Petr, his sister hid dragon parts in his food, giving him two dragon abilities—a long life and dragon hearing, or he might not have caught the uptick in her blood-pumping muscle.

"Good. No complaints. All we've done so far is camping in the mountains near Canton. Good time. Let me introduce you to my girlfriend. Jennifer, this is Dr. Smith. Dr. Smith, this is my girlfriend, Jennifer." Matt stepped out of the way.

At hearing her name, she swallowed, but she turned to face him.

That's when he knew his breath caught. She was beautiful, but when she fully faced him, he recognized those eyes—emerald green so pure, they were like two cut stones reflecting light. He'd never seen that color on a human, and he'd only met two dragons, in human form, with that color. Staring at her reminded him of his long-dead friend, Spring.

Hoping no one observed his shock, he forced himself to portray a calm expression. Instead of touching her in acknowledgment, he nodded.

Grab ahold of yourself. Spring died without an heir. The only person she could inherit those eyes from, Lung, hasn't had a child since River, and River never mated.

"Nice to meet you, Jennifer," he said. Only centuries of practice kept the nerves out of his voice.

Petr believed in fate. Two days ago, he heard a human awaken into a dragon shifter. He estimated the distance to be a two-hour drive by car west of Charlotte, North Carolina—about the same distance of Canton, where Matt said they camped.

When he heard the awakening, he called others like him, those sworn to protect dragon shifters. At least one Nose, someone who could smell dragons, planned to head to the U.S. as soon as possible.

Then, yesterday, when he opened the door to his office, he found a note in a dialect he didn't recognize. The language reminded him of an old tongue, making Petr believe that the group that hunted dragons to kill them had gotten a good whiff of him recently.

Petr sniffed the air. Though Petr couldn't detect any strange odor, dragons told him he stank of something wrong and old. His friend River compared the aroma to brewing alcohol—yeasty, moldy, and off.

Fate brought Matt to the same restaurant as me. Right after the awakening. Are the Immortals on campus hunting the new dragon shifter? Could the new dragon shifter be a student on campus?

Is Matt the dragon shifter?

Forcing his attention back to Matt, he asked, "Do you mind if I join the two of you for a while?"

"No problem," Matt answered, and motioned for him to sit across from them. Petr slid into the seat, his pants audibly sticking on the plastic.

There were ways to detect dragon shifters other than scent, even if he couldn't detect odors. A dragon shifter experienced dreams of their ancestors that seemed realistic, causing them to act crazy, and often spoke in languages they shouldn't be able to understand.

Sitting across from the couple, Petr searched Matt's countenance for a sign of insanity, but other than his hair appearing disheveled, he looked normal. Perhaps while they talked, Matt would mention something from his mother's past. Plus, Petr knew Matt's grandfather. If Matt had made it to his grandfather's dreams, then maybe Matt would recognize him and call him by the pseudonym Matt's grandfather knew him by.

As Matt sat back down, he placed his arm around Jennifer.

It was subtle, but her shoulders hardened for a second, and she glanced up at Petr. Almost like she asked him for permission to allow Matt to snuggle with her. Maybe he read too much into the intense way her eyes pleaded with him. It could have been simply that she and Matt had argued, and she didn't want to be touched. That could explain her racing heart as well.

"So, what brings you out here this late?" Matt asked, disturbing his inner dialogue.

With a force of effort, Petr ignored the prickling sensation of being watched. The scar above his beard burned as if someone poked it, and he knew that Jennifer's eyes bore a hole into it.

"I couldn't sleep." Petr smiled and moved his left hand through his hair to calm his nerves.

Could Matt be the dragon shifter?

Could Jennifer be the dragon shifter?

The group bent on protecting dragon shifters found a link between descendants from dragons. Offspring from dragon and human couplings were naturally attracted to each other.

"Jennifer, Dr. Smith is my anthropology teacher," Matt explained.

Acknowledging the statement, he nodded at her, glad for the opportunity to discover what she focused on so intently.

Her bright green eyes locked onto his, and if he didn't know better, he would say he glanced again into Spring's. Not that the rest of her face matched his friend's. Jennifer's coloring was warm, whereas Spring's had been cool. And Jennifer's hair appeared like sunshine. Spring's more the pale white of the moon. Also, their noses were different: Jennifer's more of a sharp point compared to Spring's button nose. They could pass as sisters if Spring had been alive, despite the differences.

Not intending to dwell on her so long, heat grew in his cheeks, but he couldn't look away.

Could Jennifer be the dragon shifter? How could she be related to people who passed away? Could she be Yangdi's daughter? Yangdi, Lung's only living descendent?

Jennifer asked, "So, how long have you taught at South Holt University?"

Finally, the spell she wove with her emerald eyes broke and snapped him back to the now. He glanced down at the table.

What did she ask me? Oh, yeah.

He said, "It's been recent. I'm not tenured. I'm actually a biologist who has enough credentials to teach anthropology." When he finished talking, he searched Jennifer's face, again tangled in the familiarities.

Connie returned to the table, carrying three glasses. While she placed two cups in front of Matt and Jennifer, she asked him, "Can I get you the usual?"

Maybe it was just him, but Connie always seemed to flash her cleavage. Like now, as she bent over to place their drinks and talk to him, her top button open and her chest in his face. Politely, he glanced away.

Jennifer said, "Thank you." However, Connie ignored her and batted her eyelashes at him.

"Yes, I would like my usual, please. Could you put my

drink at my regular table?" he answered, trying to be both courteous and indifferent.

"No, eat with us," Matt insisted. Almost as an afterthought, he added, "That is, Jennifer, if you don't mind?"

In response, her heart rate accelerated, and she focused intensely on him, which seemed like she was pleading with him to stay. If he didn't know better, he'd think Jennifer was attracted to him, not Matt. He ran his left hand through his hair again.

Placing her hands on the table, she said, "Yes, I insist. Besides, I might want to take one of your classes next semester. It's always good to have a head start on such things as grades, and finding out more about the class could help me decide if it would make a good general education course. I need at least three more."

He smiled at Jennifer. To Connie, he said, "Please leave my drink here and bring my food to this table."

After Connie placed his tea in front of him, she asked for Jennifer's and Matt's meal orders. He stood to retrieve his jacket from his regular table, but while he was away, his thoughts lingered on Jennifer.

How was it even possible for this person to have Spring's eyes? He'd never seen the rich color so pure and vivid they shimmered on any human in the many years of his life. The color belonged solely to Spring and Lung—both dragons. River, Spring's brother and Lung's son, had blue eyes. Lung's oldest son, Yangdi, her only rumored living child, might pass the emerald eyes to his young. But Yangdi, mated? If that were true, where was the evidence? After Yangdi left the dragon prophecy, he disappeared.

Connie departed the table as he brought the coat back to the booth, throwing it in the seat before sliding over beside it.

As he made himself comfortable, Jennifer asked him, "What other classes do you teach? Anthropology and? Or is that it?"

She didn't give him time to get settled before she started throwing questions at him. He admired her desire to learn but felt like this much younger girl was interrogating him. He answered, "I teach all the 101 classes they can assign me. I have Anthropology of Native Americas next semester, which will be the first time I teach this subject. I'll be teaching the first semester of biology, the first semester of paleontology, and another anthropology course. Basically, all the lectures they can give me." He laughed.

Scrunching up her eyes, she tilted her head. She said, "You look too young to have been teaching long."

Did she say that to pry for my age? Is she hitting on me?

Assuming innocence, he said, "Thank you. I'm older than I look."

"I can hear a slight accent. Where are you from?" Jennifer asked.

Such a direct question. Wait, weren't Southern girls known for being timid?

Stopping himself from running his hand through his hair again, he said, "Most people don't even notice my accent—I've been in the States for so long. The last place I lived before the States was in South Africa. And you?" he asked, taking a sip from his drink before he stared at Jennifer. Now it was his turn to interrogate her.

She smiled. "My accent isn't giving me away? I'm from North Carolina, not too far from here."

"And what are you studying?" he asked.

"Like Matt, I've not decided."

"What are you leaning toward, might I ask?" Petr tilted his head but maintained eye contact. Spring asked a lot of questions, too, he remembered.

She shook her head, breaking her penetrating stare, and laughed, the sound warm and inviting. "I'm sorry, Dr. Smith. Have I met you before? You look very familiar." Placing her elbows on the table, she leaned forward.

Given the opportunity to really study her, he did so. Not overly pronounced soft lips, just plump enough to kiss for hours, sitting in a beautifully sculpted face. Her lobes were close to her head, her fingernails not manicured but not bitten either. Overall, she was probably the prettiest girl he'd ever seen. One that he would consider breaking his rule of not dating mortals for, if she had a matching personality, but she belonged to Matt.

Guiltily, he stared over at Matt. Currently, he had his straw in his hand, drinking from his glass of soda. Wherever Matt's thoughts roamed, it wasn't on his conversation with Jennifer.

"I don't think so," Petr responded. He took a sip of his drink and continued to watch Jennifer. When their eyes met again, a prickling sensation in his stomach he associated with the start of desire rose, and he had to find something else to distract him. Connie stood near the doorway, and he glanced at her as she wiped the glass door with a rag.

When he turned back toward Jennifer, he found her staring out the window.

A while back, the other people protecting potential dragon shifters found a pattern. People who descended from dragons were more attracted to other people who descended from dragons. He knew Matt's heritage, but he didn't know Jennifer's. Did she have the potential to be a dragon shifter—if she wasn't already one? If they were playing get to know the professor, he could find out some of the answers now. He asked, "So, where are your parents from?"

As she snapped back around, he heard her breath catch. Then her breathing became erratic. Her skin flushed.

The bubbles of desire in his stomach rumbled even louder, and he questioned his motives.

She recovered quickly and replied, "My parents are both from North Carolina. Where did you get your doctorate?"

The thought of an interview in this much detail with

someone he just met reminded him of speed dating, so he started laughing.

When he remembered Matt sitting beside her, he calmed down and took a sip of his tea. Matt, Jennifer's boyfriend. Matt, his sister's descendent.

The most recent doctorate came from the University of Colorado, but she didn't need to know that. He answered, "I think I got it everywhere. So, Matt, what are you leaning toward?"

Jumping back into the conversation, Matt said, "I'm leaning toward mechanical engineering. I've almost completely decided on it. Jennifer's been thinking about architecture."

So Matt had listened to their conversation.

He leaned back in his seat, watching Matt. For whatever reason, Matt didn't think he was a potential suitor for Jennifer. And, for that matter, the assumption was correct. More than anything, Petr needed to identify the dragon shifter and help that person. His plans at South Holt didn't include finding a female partner for a few years before she passed away. Only needing a few more details, he could then cross Jennifer off his list of candidates who were potentially the dragon shifter, and then he could forget he ever met her.

CHAPTER 8
JENNIFER

Nervous sweat beaded Jennifer's forehead. While Dr. Smith focused on Matt, she cleared the droplets with her hand and breathed.

She studied the man from her dreams. Brown to blue to green irises framed his pupils, and she found she wanted to stare into them for hours. As odd of a thought as it was, he didn't have a beard that went up above his cheeks. Instead, it rode low, close to his chin. Around his eyes, small, but there, crow's feet cracked outward from the corners. Yet his skin seemed healthy. She estimated his age to be around twenty-six or seven.

Dang, she thought, *I find Dr. Smith hotter than the man in my dream, Petr, despite the professor's outfit.* Even his voice sent chills up her spine, deep and throaty, like the bad guy in *Highlander*.

"Interesting." Dr. Smith rubbed his beard with his left hand, as if tasting Matt's words. "So, Matt, where are your parents from?" he asked.

"Both my parents are from North Carolina. Well, Mom was born in India, but she spent most of her life here. My grandfather is from China, but his parents were from Germany," Matt answered.

"Ahh. Matt, do you have any siblings?"

"No siblings. Only child." Finished talking, Matt took a sip of his drink.

"And you, Jennifer, do you have any siblings?" Dr. Smith asked, his eyes darting over to her. Her gaze roved his face again. In the dream, he didn't have a scar above his lip parting the hairs of his auburn mustache. Her subconscious got that wrong.

To calm her breathing, she brought her glass to her mouth and swallowed. "Yes," she said and placed the drink on the table. "I have a younger brother. Are you married with children, Dr. Smith?"

Her question caused him to pause and lean against the back of the seat, as if tasting her words. His shoulders relaxed, and she didn't like the meaning that she somehow understood. He'd finished his search and found her lacking.

But she wasn't done with this confrontation. Risky words dripped out her mouth like a leaky faucet despite her everyday docile discourse. He toyed with her, like the sport of cat and mouse. An odd image of him sitting across from her while they played a board game with stones flashed in front of her mind. In this vision, he reacted the same way, like she lost the match. Something she said caused him to think her not a contender in whatever contest they were competing in, yet he still searched for a specific clue. She wasn't sure how, but she knew this man. How he thought and how he acted.

Elbows on the table, she leaned her head in her hands as she waited for her answer. *Did he have a wife or a significant other?* His response was imperative to her heart.

"No." Dr. Smith hesitated. "No, on both accounts."

The weight of a thousand mountains fell off her shoulders, and she recognized that she would hate any woman who touched this man.

Before she realized she was talking, words poured from her trap as she said, "And your sister's children, do you talk with them?"

He sat up straight and stared at her with a new intensity.

Before he answers me, he will run his hand through his hair, she thought, seconds before his fingers combed his loose curls.

"Yes, I talk with them," he answered.

The waitress returned carrying trays of hot food. She placed the dishes at each of their spots. Jennifer's stomach growled, but she ignored her hunger. The game she battled with Dr. Smith was in full swing, and she feared if she gambled by glancing away, it would admit defeat or, even worse, end the round.

Unaware of their battle, Matt moved his hand from behind her to grab his fork. Until that second, she'd forgotten about him. Earlier, he told her he wanted scrambled eggs. She leered as the traitor took a large bite of his pancakes.

Taking a nibble of her omelet, she enjoyed how it seemed to melt in her mouth. The flavor was so wonderful, she lost focus on the game and ate half before returning her attention to Dr. Smith. So far, he politely answered all of her questions despite how prying and inappropriate her inquisition had been. Especially given that there was no way this was the same man from her dreams. He must think her crazy. The more satiated she became, the more ridiculous all her assumptions about this professor she never met seemed.

Maybe the universe was telling her this was the man for her? Or perhaps she'd seen him across campus and dreamed of him because of how handsome she found him.

The latter was the most probable explanation.

Matt broke the silence. He asked, "So, what do you do when you're not in class? I mean, do you like sports? Do you play video games? I've always wondered what professors do in their free time." Instead of glancing at the professor, Matt grabbed the nearby syrup dispenser and applied a second helping to what remained of the hot cakes.

Dr. Smith also had a steak omelet meal, except he placed a healthy dose of salsa on top of his. Laying his fork back on his plate, he chewed before answering. Her eyes fell onto the white streak in the center of his hair. It was such an odd detail for her mind to include in her dream.

He grabbed the glass of what she assumed was tea. He replied, "I enjoy reading and playing video games, but usually, I'm doing research."

"What do you research?" Jennifer asked, surprised that she had said anything.

"Just migration of different species, nothing special, nothing to win me a Nobel Prize. But I do spend copious amounts of time on it," Dr. Smith said.

"Neat," Jennifer responded, putting more food in her mouth to keep from talking.

Matt had finished most of his plate of pancakes and pushed them to the side. He drank all the liquid in his glass and slushed the ice around. "Dr. Smith, why did you become a college professor?"

He will bite his bottom lip.

His teeth chewed on the corner of his mouth.

Next, he will take a bite of food, contemplating how to respond.

Instead of answering Matt, he grabbed his fork and put another piece of omelet in his mouth.

Finally, once he swallows, he will answer Matt with something non-descript but still an answer.

"When I was in college, I knew I wanted to help people. This seemed like the best way. Plus, it affords me time to do my research," he said.

Chills ran up Jennifer's spine. *How did I know how he would respond? Could we be soul mates?*

Almost as though Matt could hear her thoughts, Matt pulled Jennifer closer, wrapping his arm around her shoulder.

On instinct, she glanced at Dr. Smith and caught the slight downturn of his lower lip. He disapproved of something. Was it because Matt snuggled her close to him? *Can he feel a strange attraction to me, like I do to him?*

Before she could decide, the waitress laid the bills on the table and winked at Dr. Smith.

Snatching both checks before Matt could grab one, he handed the waitress a credit card and the tickets. "Here. This meal is on me."

"Are you sure?" Matt asked. "I don't mind paying."

"My treat." Dr. Smith stood up, laid some tip money on the table, and grabbed his coat. "It was nice meeting you, Jennifer. Hopefully, I'll see you in my class in January. You two have a wonderful day."

Before he made it to the door, he backtracked. "Jennifer, what is your last name, if you don't mind me asking? That way, I will know if you sign up for my class in the spring."

"Wright," she answered.

"If you don't mind my further boldness, where in North Carolina were you born?"

The guy from her dreams, undoubtedly not Petr, but Dr. Smith, wanted to know more about her. Before answering, she peeked at Matt. He seemed oblivious to the awkward question. She gawked as she realized Matt didn't seem to be threatened by the professor.

The ridiculousness of the whole thing suddenly occurred to her. A guy from a dream, who obviously was someone so different from the man she created, stood in front of her. In comparison, she sat beside her boyfriend, one of the most gorgeous guys on the planet. She placed her hand on top of Matt's leg. Answering Dr. Smith, she said, "I'm from Cherryville, North Carolina. My dad is Jacob, and my mom Pauline, though I'm not sure that shows up on class rolls."

Color crept into Dr. Smith's cheeks. *Has he been hitting on me? Why is he embarrassed?*

"Thank you, Ms. Wright. I will see you in class on Monday, Mr. Davis. Hope you both have a great day, and thank you for letting me sit with you." He bowed slightly and left.

On his way out, he stopped by the waitress and talked to her as she handed his credit card back to him.

The woman batted her eyes at him. An unrealistic desire to separate the woman from Dr. Smith caused her fist to ball at her side, but she forced it to get under control.

Still, as she scooted out of the seat and stood, Jennifer asked, "Do you think he's asking her on a date?"

As Matt shrugged and wrapped her in his coat, he whispered, "Yeah, possibly. She flirted with him enough during the meal to think there was a strong interest on her part. For an older guy, he is good-looking, if you're into fossils. But who cares? If he wants to date the waitress, good for him, but it's none of our business."

He grabbed his jacket from the chair, swung it around his shoulders, and zipped it up. "Ready to go get cold?" he asked.

Glancing toward the door, she watched as Dr. Smith exited the building.

"Sure," she said but continued to focus on the entrance.

"Tell you what, when the sun's out, we'll go for a run, and then we'll go see a movie. What do you say?"

Kissing the side of his face, she said, "Sounds like a plan." But as they left the restaurant, she wondered where Dr. Smith lived and what his plans were for today.

CHAPTER 9

PETR

THE SLATE-BLUE MODERN CRAFTSMAN-STYLE HOUSE HAD LARGE white columns framing a generous front porch. Petr bought the home before the builder finished the interior, allowing him to hand-pick some of the design's finer elements. Just past the porch swing, he opened the wood door with its frosted oval window.

Inside and on the left, he had an Amish-made washstand. He purchased it because the mirror's shape matched the front door and had hooks on either side of the glass. Hanging his keys on one of them, he admired the skill apparent in this piece. As someone who spent more than one lifetime as a carpenter, Petr recognized the talent it took to build the furniture.

He hung his coat on the rack to his right, taking the note from the zippered pocket. Opening it, he read what he thought it said again—something about knowing he ate a dragon heart, something else, and then death or kill. He wasn't sure—only that it sounded more like a threat than anything good.

The entranceway and the kitchen existed as one room in what the real estate agent called an open-concept design. In front of him, the lime green cabinets and cooking area lined the wall. He had purchased a tall table with lime green chairs that sat across from the sink. The only thing on the white quartz countertop was a coffee pot with a hot water reservoir for quick brewing. He hit the on switch and watched as water dripped into a pitcher. Preferring his drink black, in a few minutes, he poured a cup and headed for his study.

No decorations lined his walls. No photos of family or friends, and he didn't have any living children or descendants himself, so he didn't see the point. Once, he thought about hiring a decorator but decided he wasn't sure how long he would stay in Charlotte, so why bother? He was only here to watch Matt earn an undergraduate degree. Then he would change his name and attend college to start a new life, again.

His office also served as a guest bedroom. He had few visitors and, so far, no overnight stays. The life of someone who searched and protected dragon shifters really embodied the phrase *hurry-up-and-wait*.

Taking a sip of coffee, he thought, *Guardians would be a good name for my merry group of friends that protect dragon shifters.* Perhaps he'd suggest it.

Before Friday, the last human to turn into a dragon, a process the dragon community called an awakening, occurred thirty years ago. The guardians never found that poor creature. Without guidance, he doubted the dragon shifter still lived.

The one before that was in Africa, almost eighty years earlier, when several churches sent missionary families to the continent. And that didn't end well—the townspeople killed the young dragon after they witnessed him transform. The folder with his lessons learned from that dragon in Africa sat on his desk in front of him.

When Petr wasn't at the university, he spent hours at the standing desk that faced the window. Right now, he had the motor set at seventy-two, which meant sitting. He placed the black coffee on the surface and scooted his ten-hour-rated chair under to have more room to maneuver on the ground.

With the note in hand, Petr dropped to the hardwood floor and searched under the single twin bed for a shoebox in which he kept all the facts he had gathered through the years. Inside, he'd find a key to help decipher the mysterious language on the note.

Periodically, he summarized and destroyed the larger stack of evidence. This kept the information from seeping over the edges when a box became full. Soon, he'd purchase a new container—maybe he'd switch to a plastic box—and merge his documents again.

As he moved things out from under the frame, his head hit the wooden leg. On that post, he made out the image of a carved bear facing a small, brave boy who held a spear in his hands.

After making the dark cherry furniture, he chiseled out scenes from his childhood. On that day so long ago, he earned his manhood. He sighed. The animal was what his tribe called "brown death," because they were afraid to give the creature a name for fear it might come to steal their souls.

Moving to comfort his head, he saw the box. Pulling it out, he opened the top and retrieved a small book with letters shaped as both items and people, handwritten on the front.

After years of honing his translation skills, he identified rough meanings. He wrote the possible words for the scribblings on a notepad he had on his desk.

> Place you/I obtained/found a (dragon or power) heart/life or when group of people pinpoint/marked block/stop. Stronger plural family/business, death.

In English, he interpreted the words to say, "*We aren't sure where you obtained the dragon heart or when, but family (or business) will kill you if you interfere with our plans.*"

The family or business part confused him unless that was the word the other group called themselves—the group that killed dragons and harvested their body parts. Petr's side, who protected dragons, called that mob of evil-doers the Immortals.

Rolling his eyes, he threw the cryptic note into the trash and turned on the computer. This person wasn't the first to threaten him. He doubted it would be the last.

Sun blasted his eyes, and he squinted to make out the computer screen. Reaching up, he twisted the lever on the blinds, darkening the room.

Throughout the eighties, when computers first became popular, he avoided purchasing one. Now, though, he needed to step into the modern world. The university recently scheduled him to teach a remote class next fall. He had a year to prepare for the cyberworld, and in preparation, a tech company wired his house for the internet less than two months ago.

His first search of the day was to gather information on Jennifer Wright.

The name of Matt's girlfriend, Jennifer Wright, burned into his mind as a permanent record. Even now, hours after leaving the restaurant, her perfume lingered as a clean lavender scent around him. He typed in his password as images of her emerald eyes stared back at him.

I know those eyes!

When he paid the waitress, he'd glanced at her as Matt placed the jacket around her shoulders. Being a leg guy, he first noticed that Jennifer matched his height. He swallowed and wasted another ten minutes thinking about her hair cascading down her back, the simple jeans she wore, and those flipping long legs!

Could Jennifer Wright be the dragon?

Not all humans could one day spontaneously shift into a dragon. First, the human had to descend from a dragon. Why someone who might have had an ancestor thousands of years ago that was a dragon suddenly exploded into the creature, he didn't know.

Petr estimated one percent or less of the modern population had the ability to become one of the legendary monsters.

There were many reasons for his conclusion. First, dragons seldom mated, let alone with a human. Conception could occur once every fifty years. Low fertility carried to any offspring, no matter how many generations passed. It was very rare for a dragon descendant to have multiple children.

Thus, with a sibling, Jennifer Wright had several strikes against her being the dragon shifter.

The odds of someone being descended from a dragon were close to the odds of being struck by lightning. Being descended from a dragon and having a sibling were closer to the odds of being hit by a meteorite. Could it happen? Yes. Was it likely? No.

Jennifer is beautiful, though.

"Matt's girlfriend. Matt, your great-great-nephew. Lucky Matt," Petr said, dropping off several greats from Matt's relationship to him.

Thinking back to this morning, he misled Matt into believing he played video games. When the tech guy installed his ethernet through his home, he bragged about his diamond ranking in some war game, Underwatch, or something. That was when Petr realized most individuals used the World Wide Web to negotiate the vast Esports arena.

Petr fought the urge to open chess and solitaire, the only two recreational programs he liked on computers. *Those count as games, right?*

At breakfast, the banter between him and Jennifer almost reminded him of a different game—flirting.

"Matt's girlfriend," he said again.

Sure, lots of girls flirted with him, yet he enjoyed how off-guard Jennifer made him. She surprised him by asking direct questions and seemed to anticipate his answers. After years of the same tedious attempts made by other girls pretending to be coy or making overly sexual suggestions, she attempted to understand him from day one while maintaining a shy and presumptuous approach. He found the diversity of conflicting words and actions intriguing.

Then again, feasibly, it was her long legs.

Shifting focus to his task at hand, he stared at the screen. Pop-ups littered the backdrop, and he clicked each one away. How could over one hundred unopened emails accumulate since the last time he turned on this machine?

Giving up, he shut his email and opened a browser.

He paid a yearly fee to run background checks on people, but he could never remember the process to access or use the program. Biting his lower lip, he moved to the bookcase and pulled out the green camel-back notebook.

Before scooting back to his desk, a reflection on the book-case caught his attention. He examined a long dark mark in the wood. He made that piece himself from an old oak tree. One night, a hundred years or so ago, while he worked outside, nearby lightning struck and split that tree. The dark groove, made by wild electricity, reminded him that he, too, could be divided in two by a force of nature.

After he placed the notebook on his desk, he ran his hand along that marking, closed his eyes, and remembered to stay humble, work hard, and enjoy every second. Then, he returned to his task.

Finding the right page, he moved to his computer and finger-pecked, following the instructions.

Next lifetime, I'm majoring in keyboarding and programming! he promised himself.

Creating what his tech guy called an incognito sandbox, he pulled up the Cherryville High School yearbooks.

Researching last year's graduating class revealed a not-so-different Jennifer. She'd been on the debate and robotics teams. And then, filling an entire page, he found a color picture of Jennifer in a pale blue formal ballgown. Her soft hair pulled to the front appeared full, her features perfect, her shoulders bare in a strapless dress. She smiled, showing beautiful white teeth and a healthy glow to her skin. This image he printed out for his folder on the bed.

Next, he searched the yearbooks for her sibling. Eventually, he found a Randy Wright so similar they had to be related. Locating him in the current list of students for ninth grade, her brother was four years younger, with blond hair and blue eyes. He appeared to be on the tall side as well. They were too much alike not to be genetic brother and sister.

Based on the pictures, Jennifer had a blood-related brother. Her chances of being the dragon shifter or descending from a dragon decreased. Not that it was impossible. It was just extremely, infinitesimally small.

Retrieving the photo of Jennifer from the printer in his closet, he traced the outline of her face and wondered about that day. Did she have a date? Did she go out with her friends afterward?

The phone rang, and Petr jumped. No one saw him lusting after Jennifer, but guilt consumed him.

He found the portable home phone on the bookshelf and retrieved it. "Hello," he answered.

"My friend," said Che-non. In his mind's eye, he pictured him with his dark hair cut short, intense eyes, and angular features. Che-non lived because of a fruit found in the ancient City of Giants. Spring, his wife, died on their wedding day many years ago. She died before they consummated their marriage, or Che-non, too, would be dead.

Dragons mated for life—which meant if one died, the other died. A true mating only occurred after *the deed*. Personally, Petr believed it was a chemical reaction. Still, he'd never researched why sex bonded dragon couples to life and death, only that it did.

"My friend. Any news? Is the Nose on the way? I received a note under my door since the last time we talked. Based on the language and the message, the Immortals are here on campus," Petr said.

"Kamar, a dragon, and I are both on our way to visit you. Even if the dragon shifter is not on campus, we can start our search there. Any chance that it's your dragon ancestor?"

"I ate breakfast with him and his girlfriend this morning. Right now, neither are showing any signs of an awakening."

"Okay. Keep watching them. Kamar is on his way, and I will leave when I can."

"What do you mean, you will leave when you can?" Petr asked as he leaned against his chair.

"I mean, I haven't left the mountains in so long that I don't exist. There is no record of me in any governmental database, and if there were, it would show me as over two hundred years old. I have a friend here, Fritz, who is helping me get the necessary paperwork to fly over to see you, but it will take some time. Hold tight until I get there."

"And Kamar, then? If I had a dragon's nose, my search would be faster. This time, I'm close. I had a threatening note from an Immortal."

"Hm, there is an issue there," Che-non said.

"An issue?"

"Without going into the details, Kamar is swimming across the Pacific to the Atlantic, then up the coast until he hits the island chain outside your city," Che-non said.

"The islands...Oh, the Outer Banks. Why can't he just fly? We have a large airport in Charlotte." Petr ran his hand through his hair.

"He is afraid to fly. Something about water dragons not meant to be in the air; I'm not arguing with him. Besides, he has already left. Onto something more important—have you checked your sister's descendant for the traits I sent you?"

"Hold on," he said, stood, and walked over to the bed,

where he laid several papers. Sorting through the documents, he found the list of traits with strange symbols.

Picking it up and holding it in his hand while the phone rested by his ear, he said, "Yes. I've got it right here."

"Good. Go ahead and mark up his picture. And do you know his friends? You mentioned his girlfriend."

"Che-non, please, my friend, stop questioning my skills. I have the checklist and the list of symbols. All of Matt's friends' pictures are marked up. Only one person to go—Matt's girlfriend, Jennifer."

"You need to mark up her picture as well. Since we have found evidence that dragon descendants are attracted to other descendants, almost like nature intended to fill the earth with dragons again, do you see any evidence that Jennifer could be the dragon shifter?"

Studying the picture of Jennifer, despite the flat two-dimensional image, her green eyes appeared like gems. Should Che-non ever see the girl, he would notice the undeniable similarities with Spring.

"Petr?" Che-non asked, interrupting his thoughts.

"Yes."

"Is it possible for Jennifer to be the dragon shifter?" Che-non asked.

Sighing, he thought about how to answer that. "Jennifer has something familiar about her. Her eyes, really."

"Oh," Che-non answered, but didn't elaborate.

"What?" Petr asked.

"It's that voice you get when you are attracted to a girl."

Feeling the need to defend himself, he raised his eyebrow in defiance and said, "She reminds me of Spring."

"Oh," Che-non said, and Petr thought he detected sadness. Che-non never married after Spring's death.

"I doubt she is a dragon or descended from a dragon. She has a brother," Petr said to change the subject.

"It does sound doubtful, but wyverns and ludwigs were

known to birth multiple children. We shouldn't rule her out yet. Have you observed better than normal senses?"

"I haven't talked with her long enough to detect anything out of the ordinary."

"Does she act strange, like the missionary's son?"

"No. A little bold, but she acted like a normal human."

After a pause, Che-non continued. "Does Matt act differently?"

"No. So far, no one is acting strangely."

"Okay, well then, what are you doing while I'm working on finding my way to the United States?" Che-non asked.

"Tomorrow, I will head to Jennifer's hometown. I hope to find the census, birth, and death records. I can check how long Jennifer's ancestors lived and if they had siblings. That should give me more of an idea. But I doubt it, Che-non. If she didn't have a younger brother, maybe."

The line was silent, then Che-non said, "Sounds like you have a lot to do and prepare yourself. Remember, this person will dress funny, act funny, and prefer to be alone. The real telltale sign is if they suddenly started speaking and understanding a language they didn't previously know. I wish we knew what happened after the dreams. It could help us find the dragon child sooner. All right, my friend. Fritz is giving me dirty looks. I better go. I will be at your house soon."

"All right then. Talk to you later, Che-non," he said.

With that, the phone went dead. The best method for him to investigate her family would be to search for her mom and dad's history. If he could find her family's history, he would go back in her lineage as far as he could. If her parents and grandparents were only children with no siblings, and her grandparents died at a ripe old age, she could conceivably be the dragon. But if she had multiple aunts and uncles, she was definitely just another human.

With any luck, tomorrow would paint a clearer picture.

CHAPTER 10

JENNIFER

...I TURNED OVER TO FACE MY HUSBAND, RICHARD, AND KISSED him one last time before dozing off to sleep. He'd worked me into a stupor with our lovemaking. How he could stay awake after all the energy we expended together was beyond me. He leaned over to the nightstand and picked up his latest automotive magazine.

He said he kept the lamp on because he enjoyed watching me shatter with each delve into my hot core. But in truth, it allowed him to read when we finished.

I sighed as he flipped the pages and snuggled close to his chest.

For his new job, he kept his strawberry blond hair cut short. I liked how it felt, so I touched his baby's fine hair at the nape of his neck.

"Love you, Josephine," he whispered in response. "I'm going to read for a bit. You get your sleep." He placed a hand on my back, holding the magazine with the other.

Cuddled close, I allowed the heaviness of happiness to bring me to the prince of dreams...

The weight of the arm that dangled over Jennifer's waist seemed heavier than usual, and she glanced down at the thick fingers. For a second, her heart raced. Richard's familiar skin never tanned to that warm olive, and the chunky girth of the digits on this hand didn't match her husband's.

Wait, that's Matt's arm.

So as not to disturb the person, in case it wasn't him, she rolled over and confirmed it was Matt. As she listened to his steady breathing, she realized with his manly features relaxed, only the dark stubble marked him as a man. Otherwise, right then, he appeared so innocent she would have thought him a boy with his peaceful demeanor.

Last night's dream seemed so vivid. In it, she was her mother's mother, Josephine. The crisp scent in the air, the lack of cell phones, and eating freshly cooked meals were so tangible that even now, Jennifer could recall days from that dream as if they were her own memories.

As if requested, an image of standing outside at nine years old and throwing things at the neighborhood boys as the girl group fought against them passed before her eyes. The leader of the boys' team, Melvin Jones, taunted her through high school; she wondered where he was now.

Oh, please! That was just a crazy dream. Melvin Jones isn't real.

Nothing in that dream added up anyway. Her grandmother, her sweet, loving grandmother, the terror of Cherryville? Please! Sure, her grandmother even now loved pranks, enjoyed motorcycles, and hung out with a younger crowd, but she wasn't that much of a trickster.

Jennifer couldn't deny some truths her mind maintained. As the youngest of fifteen, and only a half-sibling, Josephine embodied the baby gets away with everything rule—that part was true. She got whatever she wanted and not just needed.

Just a dream, she reminded herself, but it felt so real. It gave Jennifer sympathy for Belinda. Last week, Belinda dreamed Jennifer had re-arranged their dorm furniture. Belinda was angry at her for the entire day.

And this dream was like that. It felt so real, so solid and substantial—like Jennifer lived her grandmother's early life.

The oddest part of the dream was her grandfather. Jennifer didn't remember Richard Lee. All she had of him was an old baseball Braves cap from when they played for Boston, not Atlanta.

"What are you thinking about?" Matt asked, touching the center of her forehead.

"My grandfather. He passed away when I was a toddler," she answered.

"I'm sorry," Matt said.

"I didn't know him. There's a picture of him on the shelves in the living room, holding me as a baby… I dreamed of him… and my grandmother. My grandmother has a story of how they met. It was a harvest festival, where they literally raised barns or brought in the wheat."

She waited to see if he had any questions. He brushed a strand of her hair off her face, so she continued, "In my family's case, they had a peanut farm. Family and friends, basically the community, traveled from homestead to homestead, working hard all day gathering the crops, and dancing and celebrating late in the night. The men and kids would work the farm, while the women-folk would make grand meals."

"Go on," he said when she paused.

"Anyway, the story I heard is she got away with everything, including not helping with the food. She used her younger nieces and nephews to avoid manual labor, entertaining them with hide-and-go-seek. Her older brother, Frank, was angry because she left the laundry hanging out where everyone could see his, you know, underwear. He'd brought my grandfather. That's how they met, her hiding in a hayloft.

"In my dream, it happened differently. Josephine, my grandmother, hid a frog inside a picnic basket. When Frank proposed to his girlfriend and reached inside to get the ring, the frog jumped out, causing the girl to scramble away, knocking over the picnic basket and losing the ring. When my grandmother tells the story, she makes it sound like she was innocent and her brother was unreasonably angry. Anyway, both stories end the same way. She hid in a hayloft, and my grandfather found her there."

Gently, Matt touched her nose. "You dreamed of an event in your grandmother's life and then added details?" Matt asked.

Raising her eyebrows and looking toward the headboard, she said, "Yeah. I guess I turned it into my own twisted story." She bit her lip, then said, "Crazy, right?"

"A little. Sounds to me like you've been hiding your fun-loving side by studying too much. You need to relax."

"Thank you, Doctor Davis. Do I pay the receptionist on the way out?"

"I don't take cash. You can pay me by not studying today. We'll goof off, play games, and eat bad food. That should give you a temporary fix. If the dreams continue, we might have to find a more dangerous situation."

"More dangerous, like what?"

"I don't know if the ski slopes are open. White water rafting is out, water levels are too low..." He scrunched up his face and said, "What about those giant bubbles that you roll down the hill in?"

"Trying to kill me? Did you take an insurance plan out on me?" she asked.

"Nope. Trying to help you live a little before you implode from too much studying."

She grabbed the pillow from under her and smacked him on the head. "I'm fine. Maybe you should study more."

"Hey," he said, leaning on one side and tickling her ribs.

"Stop it," she giggled-talked while shoving him.

"Don't poke the bear," he said.

She froze. *The bear fell backward, a red claw running through its meaty flesh.*

She saw the realization in his eyes as his body went rigid and the playful atmosphere shifted.

Kissing her lightly on the forehead, he pushed himself up and moved away. The bed sheet fell away from him as he stood. He spent the night sleeping shirtless in his black sweatpants. Like a magazine photo, his skin glistened over his hard muscles in the light coming through the blinds. A drool-worthy image indeed.

In the doorway, he turned toward her with a mischievous grin, like he had a secret. "I'm going to make us breakfast. I make a mean omelet."

"I would love a mean omelet." Throwing her legs over the side, she sat up. Pink fuzzy bunny slippers waited in the corner. She barely remembered Matt purchasing them for her, yet that was only yesterday.

"What's wrong?" Matt asked.

"It bothers me that I can remember the dream last night, but I'm struggling to remember you buying me the slippers. That dream felt so real, Matt."

"Well, you did eat that steak raw last night. I'm not accustomed to watching any girl, let alone my girlfriend, eat a medium-rare twelve-ounce ribeye, followed by two fully loaded potatoes and a Mississippi mud-pie brownie. It was like being back in high school with my football buddies."

Embarrassed, she tried to remember dinner, and she couldn't. "I ate raw steak? I like my steaks torched with crispy black around the outside, charred, past well-done."

"And you downed a gallon of tea with the meal—that Southern-style tea. You know the type. The straw sat in the middle of the glass and didn't move from all the sugar. I chalked it up to you not eating much over the weekend or yesterday. And you pushed me during the run. Do you realize we ran ten miles, and that you're fast?"

Something about mentioning the run triggered a faint memory of passing a church. Well, there was nothing she could do about not remembering, so she ignored what she couldn't recall. It didn't matter anyway. She stood, noticing she was even dressed in soft pink pajamas. If she and Matt had done something, she hoped she'd remember, but whatever they did didn't involve sex, or she would be searching for her clothes right now.

Speaking of sex, even the sex in her dream seemed real—the feeling of touching and being touched. She shuddered, glancing through the door at Matt as he pulled out a carton of eggs.

What would it feel like if he touched her where no one had ever gone?

Focusing away from physical needs that crept into her mind, she said, "Let me help you make breakfast. I can start the coffee. I personally could use a strong cup."

Moving to stand in front of Matt, she placed her hands on either side of his face and kissed him. As she moved in, his eyes seemed to enlarge into saucers, and she wondered what she did that surprised him.

Keeping her chest touching his, she broke the mouth-to-mouth contact.

"Since when do you drink coffee?" Matt asked.

So that was what that look meant. When did she start drinking coffee? An odd thought occurred to her. She, Jennifer, didn't drink coffee. She, Josephine, Jennifer's grandmother, did drink coffee. The desire came from her dream. She wanted coffee because she dreamed her grandmother had drank it every morning since she was fourteen.

Regardless, it was too late to correct the mistake. "I usually do around holidays," she said. It was true now, at least. "Do you want some help making the eggs?"

"You're my guest. I will cook breakfast." He bent down and placed a feather-light kiss on her nose, hugged her, then moved over to the cabinet and pulled out a frying pan. She walked behind the counter, pulling out a bar stool tucked underneath the raised countertop.

His head disappeared into the refrigerator and reappeared with butter, tomatoes, and onions. "I don't need your help. It is my treat as a guest of my house. And, should you decide to stay one day, you know, shack up with me, I can take breakfast, and you can have lunch. We can make dinner together." He reached above him and retrieved a bowl from the cabinets. As he broke the first egg, he said, "Though, if you like, you can help clean."

Once he scrambled the eggs with a fork, he smiled, and the touch of mischief returned to his grin. "Wait here," he said to her. As he passed by, he caressed her hand. She watched him walk to the door at the end of the hall and knock. "Hey man," he called, banging.

"What?" came Doug's voice.

"Do you and Lauren want some eggs?" Matt asked.

"Sure, man, thanks."

When he returned to the kitchen, he stopped in front of the bowl. "Would you like anything in your omelet?"

"What do you have?" Jennifer asked.

"Good question, not sure." He returned to the refrigerator and pulled out various vegetables and deli meats.

Everything appeared yummy, and her stomach growled. How could she have eaten such a large meal last night and be so ravenous this morning? "I'd like a little of everything, please."

Matt held a knife, ready to slice-and-dice, and paused, glancing away from the ingredients to stare at her. "You're that hungry?"

An audible gurgling answered for her, and she relaxed her hand over her stomach. "Yeah," she said as an apology.

"My girlfriend has developed a healthy appetite. That gives me an idea. There is more in the freezer."

Facing away from her, he opened the freezer section and

placed frozen sausage and bacon on the counter. Turning on the hot water, he moved the bags into the stream, thawing them faster.

Doug exited the master bedroom and strolled down the hall wearing thick jersey material pajama pants and a plain T-shirt. The top of his light brown curly hair stood up at odd angles, and an unkempt beard covered his facial features. With his belly extending out, it was hard to believe that at one time, he was the star quarterback of Matt's high school.

Seconds behind him, his girlfriend, Lauren, a few inches taller than Doug, followed him. Her black hair contrasted with her extremely pale skin. A few ebony strands escaped from the loose bun on top of her head. Setting off the vibe, she wore a black T-shirt and shiny silk onyx boxer-like shorts with dark red acrylic fingertips and manicured toes.

Though Jennifer never asked, she assumed Lauren was the oldest out of this group. This was because, after this year, Lauren had one more semester to complete her master's in nursing. She didn't really smile, more of a thinker than a doer, and she never gave off helpful or friendly vibes—though nursing and then helping Matt pick out things for her suggested somewhere behind the goth appearance was a caregiver. Lauren asked, "I need some coffee. Jennifer, would you like some?"

Glancing at Matt, he stared up from the frying pan and winked at her.

Jennifer's parents weren't coffee drinkers. Stretching her mind, she couldn't remember a time when she'd ever tried it. Could she dream about an accurate taste of coffee after only smelling it? She wanted to find out.

"Yes, please," Jennifer answered.

As Lauren squeezed behind Matt to get to the coffeepot, he lifted the skillet off the stove and gave it a flip. The egg rose and twisted, like a pizza crust.

"Yeah, Matt should be a chef, but you better close your

mouth, Jennifer, or you'll catch flies," Doug said, sitting at the table. "He has some mad cooking skills. Lauren, make me a cup of joe as well."

Lauren placed a cup of coffee in front of Jennifer, then handed one to Doug. As she squeezed behind Matt, she said, "It's black. Black is healthier for your body, but we have sugar and creamer if you want it. And Doug is right. Your boyfriend cooks like an angel and cheats like a devil."

As she walked behind Matt, he stuck his butt out, bumping her some. "I did not cheat."

"Well, I call rematch," Doug said.

"Yes, rematch," Lauren echoed as she returned with some dark liquid for herself.

"Rematch for what?" Jennifer asked. While she listened, she absentmindedly took a sip of the drink. The bitter flavor was reminiscent of the stuff from her dream last night. Maybe she'd had it in the past, even a sip, and that was why her mind created the flavor in her dream?

Lauren said, "A rematch to a Risk game. Matt won, but there was no way he could have, the little sneak. I'm not even sure how he cheated."

Laying an omelet with all the works in front of her, Matt said, "I agree to a rematch, but only if Jennifer plays."

When he glanced at her, he smiled, and a cute dimple appeared on his left cheek.

"I'm game for anything new, but I've never played," Jennifer said, surveying the room. No one looked surprised. She sipped her coffee.

Matt threw some more egg batter into the pan. He said, "Well, it's easy enough to play, but it might last all day. Usually, we put on HBO or Showtime, and order pizza for lunch and dinner. Takes a day of insane playing."

"Sounds like fun," Jennifer said.

After Doug cleared away breakfast, the group of four played a heated game of Risk, which Matt won yet again.

CHAPTER 11

PETR

THE RAIN THAT HAD FOLLOWED PETR ON THE DRIVE TO Cherryville, North Carolina, came down in sheets now. Parked outside the tan brick building with a giant glass cherry under the sign, he watched for indications of the building coming alive through layers of water droplets. Beside him sat his briefcase of school papers. He had a separate satchel in the trunk with the research documentation and notes for today's hunt. That is, once the office opened.

Pulling out the grading key for the exam he gave on Wednesday, he prepared to use his free time to catch up with where he left off. He laid the paper over the first test and placed red dots on the missed questions.

Using her foot, a woman with a green umbrella closed the door on a gray Oldsmobile. She glanced in his direction, her oversized orange purse dangling under her arm. Then she ran for the door. As she balanced everything with one hand, her other pulled out a loop of keys from the bag. She fidgeted with the keyring until she found the right one and opened the door.

After placing the exams back into the briefcase, he listened to the rain, giving her enough time to settle into her surroundings. Minutes clicked by before he decided enough time had passed. Grabbing his keys, he made his way to the trunk.

Petr owned two vehicles. Both were sensible black four-door sedans that blended well with all the other cars on the road. If he possessed something that stuck out from the crowd, maybe someone would remember him, and he didn't want or need that. He'd rather fade into oblivion than for anyone to somehow discover his actual age. Though he doubted anybody could guess or even postulate the number of seasons he had lived.

Refusing to show how much he hated cold, wet rain, he walked at a steady pace into the gray interior. Unlike most government offices, this one lacked the usual metal detector and police officer ensuring you had no firearms. And more like a medical building, a kiosk slightly above eye level mounted on painted cinderblock listed each department's location.

In the glass's reflection, his auburn hair curled wildly in different directions, and other than shaking his head to remove as much water as possible, he ignored the disheveled mess. The moisture and the cool weather chilled him, but he'd survive.

Once he located the right room, steps away from the marquee, he entered the records office. The area reminded him of a library, which he was happy to discover. Some record offices stored the information digitally, while others kept files sorted in vaulted rooms. In both cases, he'd have to check out anything he wanted to view—all of which extended the hours he spent researching and left a paper trail.

A woman sat in the middle of a circular booth with tall counters. She had short salt-and-pepper hair and cat-rimmed glasses. She leaned close to a computer screen as she typed away. Between her and rows of bookshelves and filing cabinets were vibrant primary-colored chairs surrounding round tables.

At a workstation, he placed his research material on the surface. The folder he pulled out opened to the large picture of Jennifer. From the two-dimensional image, she stared back at him with her mesmerizing green eyes, and for a second, he lost himself.

Was she flirting with me when we met?

Behind the photo, in bold letters at the top, was Jennifer's parents' information. Taking the sheet of paper with a header reading Jacob and Pauline Wright, he approached the record keeper's desk. She sat with her back straight, still only an inch away from the screen, her fingers flying over the keyboard, and she ignored him.

Typically, small record offices asked more questions than one in a big city. As he waited, Petr hoped this wouldn't be the case now. He made a slight noise, drawing her attention. Her glasses must have been bifocals because she pushed them down to the bottom of her nose, but the rest of her body stayed rigid.

"Yes," she said, her voice scratchy like she smoked, though he detected nothing over the scent of old documents.

"Thanks, I could use some help. I'm looking for marriage licenses?" he asked.

She stood, simultaneously pushing her glasses up her nose and kicking her chair backward. Pointing in different directions as she talked, she said, "Over there are our marriage licenses. Over there, we have birth records. Behind you, we have the census data. As you can imagine, we have more census data than anything." She turned around to look at the bookshelves beside the wall. "And the death certificates are over here. Oh, and if you're curious about our old papers or the ramblings of our historical society, those are over there.

You may make photocopies," she added, pointing to an ancient machine. "However, the prints are ten cents each. The books aren't allowed to leave." She sat back down. "We close at six p.m." And she started typing again, with her neck uncomfortably pushed forward toward the screen.

He ran his hands through his hair. They came back wet, so he dried them on his jeans. Deciding not to get caught without enough time to finish, he returned to his table, dug for his cell phone, and set an alarm to let him know when to clean up. Then he headed to the marriage certificates and started his search...

Hours passed as he made headway into Jennifer Wright's lineage. Her parents, Jacob and Pauline, lacked siblings, and both were born and raised in Cherryville, North Carolina, a few blocks from each other.

Jacob Wright worked as an architect in an office close to this building.

Pulling out a copied picture of her father he found in his senior yearbook, he compared his headshot to Jennifer's photo. The black-and-white photo didn't show eye color other than a lighter gray tone, indicating a paler shade, and his hair might have been fair, but he wasn't sure. Nothing in her father's face reminded him of Jennifer.

Her father's mother, Meredith Beasley Wright, passed away from breast cancer before Jennifer was born. She was also a native of the area, and Petr quickly found her family records. Lucky for her, she came from a large family with many brothers and sisters.

On Jennifer's photo in red pen, he made the symbol '-/+//.' The symbol represented Jennifer's paternal grandmother's line came to a search end. Meredith Beasley Wright had too many siblings to continue hunting for a dragon in that family.

However, with Jacob Wright's father, Stewart, he lost the trail. First, he wasn't born in Cherryville, and in this library, there was no record showing he still lived in the area. Tracking him down would require more work on his part.

So, he moved on to Jennifer's mother. Apparently, her mother had local fame at one time. He found a picture of Pauline Lee in the local paper as she won a regional beauty pageant. Glancing at it now, he saw why. Crystal green eyes, bright white, classic, perfect smile; her mother could have been a model. He made a copy of the article as well and laid her image down beside the one he made of Jennifer.

The similarities were obvious. Jennifer's features matched her mother's more than her father's. Compared to Jennifer, her mother appeared thicker, not fat, just with more width. However, it was more than that. The eye shape and structure were identical, yet the glint in Jennifer's seemed more calculating. He would never express this out loud, but Jennifer's features made him consider her intelligent and her mother more accepting. Like inside Jennifer's head, she contemplated an answer to every question ever asked.

Petr imagined himself sitting outside a small house or in the woods, doing nothing more than talking. He'd ask Jennifer questions and patiently wait for her answers.

Long legs might tempt him to bed, and her smile cause him to kiss her, but her wit would keep him entertained for generations.

Could I be overthinking Jennifer Wright? What was it that Matt said about her? Oh, that's right, she wants to be an architect. Perhaps she took her physical appearance from her mother and had her dad's intelligence?

Regardless, the longer he stared at the 2-D image of Jennifer, the more he wished he had met her before Matt did.

Sighing, he ran his hand through his hair, happy it finally

dried. In front of him, the image of Jennifer's mother, Pauline, smiled back. He located Pauline's birth records, with both parents named Richard and Josephine Lee. After more searching, he retrieved their marriage certificate.

Unfortunately, he also found Richard Lee's death certificate. He perished from injuries sustained in a car accident. Because of how he died, he could still have a dragon in his ancestry. Hunting for Richard's family, he discovered an article about him and his younger brother, Eli Lee. Standing side-by-side after winning a fishing tournament, they looked identical. With the red pen, he marked '+/-//' on Jennifer's photo to indicate the end of research in the Lee family.

But his luck ended again with Jennifer's grandmother, Josephine English Lee. At first, when he found that she was the youngest of fifteen children, he picked up his red marker, held only inches from the paper, when differences in the two censuses sitting to the side struck him.

The older of the two listed David English and his wife, Carolina. The second listed David English and his wife, MaryAnn. So, the man had two wives and fifteen kids between them. His pen froze above Jennifer's photo briefly before putting it back down.

David English, for sure, wasn't a dragon line, but what about MaryAnn English?

The alarm on his phone beeped, and he swiped it off. Leaning back, he stretched and sighed. With his eyes shut, he imagined Jennifer Wright in a white gown, laughing at something witty he said. Her head cocked back, and for a second, he thought he recognized the perfume she wore. The scent reminded him of a walk in a lavender field, fresh and clean.

"Petr, it's taboo to pursue your great-nephew's girlfriend. She is off limits. She is Matt's girlfriend," he whispered, opening his eyes, gathering his files, and returning the borrowed documents.

Though the faint lavender fragrance lingered.

As he placed the last document back on the shelf, the phone on the table vibrated. The woman behind the counter lowered her glasses and glowered at his stuff, then at him.

"Sorry," he whispered under his breath, hurrying to answer. By the time he reached it, the phone stopped ringing. He didn't recognize the number, so he placed the phone in his pocket.

The cell dinged almost immediately, and he pulled it out. The same number that called had left a message. The message read:

> PETR, YOU ARE THE CLOSEST TO THE DRAGON SHIFTER, AND BECAUSE THEY ATTEND SOUTH HOLT UNIVERSITY, YOU'RE THEIR BEST HOPE. I CAN'T TEXT YOU THEIR NAME OUT OF FEAR THE IMMORTALS WILL FIND IT. MEET ME TOMORROW NIGHT, 7:30 AT THE CHERRYVILLE RESTAURANT, MAMA'S HOME COOKING, AND I WILL TELL YOU THE NAME OF THE DRAGON SHIFTER. YOU WILL LIKE THE BUILDINGS. —THE WHITE JAGUAR

This person used English, his real name, and knew his current location. He surveyed the room, finding only the woman behind the desk. She still sat up straight, her eyes inches from the screen, her fingers pecking away. Approaching her, he cleared his throat to get her attention.

"Excuse me, is there a hotel nearby? I didn't finish my research and will need to return tomorrow."

"With the quilting circle in town, there won't be a room available here or in White Pines. You'll need to head toward Interstate 74, toward Charlotte," she responded without glancing at him.

"Thank you," Petr said before he left the records office. In the hall, he dialed the number on the text. After a quick ring, he received the message, "The number you have called has been disconnected and is no longer in service. If you find this call in error, hang up and dial again."

Sighing, his eyes roamed the parking lot, hunting for anything strange.

Nothing. No one paid him any attention in the cold, foggy rain. He guessed the caller was nowhere around.

As he placed his documents in his car, he considered hunting for a hotel. If he couldn't find one he'd drive home, and return tomorrow. He had a White Jaguar to meet.

CHAPTER 12

MATT

WEDNESDAY, THE DAY BEFORE THANKSGIVING, JENNIFER'S parents expected Matt to bring their daughter home. Except, sitting in his car outside her dorm, she didn't answer the phone.

How could he bring their daughter home if she never showed up?

This wasn't like her. She always rose early since he'd met her, even on weekends. Last night, he dropped her off at her dorm before nine.

If this was a normal school week, he'd ask someone to knock on her door and wake her up. But glancing around, he saw no one. Not a single person.

Not sure of his next actions, he dialed again. This made the tenth time calling—not like he was counting or anything.

Finally, "Hello," Jennifer said.

"Jen, where are you? I'm outside your dorm waiting. We have to meet your parents. Did you forget?" he asked.

Instead of answering right away, she paused, then said, "Okay."

"Okay? Why the delay? Please don't tell me you were

studying and time got away from you. Do you need me to come upstairs and help carry anything down?"

Jennifer didn't answer, so he added, "I believe you told your parents you would leave here at eleven. As it is now…" Glancing at the clock, he continued, "It's already eleven. We won't be there until twelve by the earliest, and that's without stopping. And I'm not taking a 'no' at eating lunch at Barney's Burgers. I want to see you eat the five-pound challenge. Call your parents and tell them we'll miss the two-p.m. matinee. We'll have to go to the one at four."

As he waited for a response, he thought about yesterday. While they goofed off, Jennifer's parents called five times. She answered several texts as well, almost like a check-in to her parole officer instead of her mom and dad.

Interrupting his thoughts, she said, "Thanks for the offer, but I don't need your help. Plus, to let you in, I'd have to go downstairs, anyway. I'll be down in a second. Let me grab my things," and the line went dead.

No bye. No see you in a second.

Minutes ticked by, and no Jennifer. He debated calling her again when the door to the dorm opened, and someone exited wearing shorts so high that the white pockets hung out from the bottom. He ogled her body, starting at the bright red, open-toed heels that seemed to flag his eyes and allow his lazy gaze to drift upward to long, silky legs. Further up, a white tank clung to her skin, almost as if the material molded to her curves.

This girl was smoking hot, but with the temperature being so cold, she obviously wore the wrong outfit to grab attention.

The way the girl walked with her hips swaying confidently held him captive, like a snake mesmerized by a charmer.

A gust of wind blew away the loose blond locks from her face, revealing—Jennifer!

He gawked. How did he miss the green duffle bag under her arm?

As his innocent Jennifer pranced in the November chill, she teased, nothing like her normal busy pace. Grabbing the handle on the door, she swung it open, stopping in front of the side mirror to admire herself. She pressed her bright red lips together and puckered while checking herself out. The cool wind breezed into the vehicle, bringing a scent of rose perfume.

"Sugar, you better close your beautiful mouth, you hot bag of maleness," Jennifer said with a strong Southern accent—one that she hadn't had last night or ever since they met.

In an exaggerated motion, she slung her body into the truck's cab, giggling as she sat. Facing him, she placed her hands on either side of his face, forcing him to look at her, and plastered a kiss right on his lips.

"Goodness gracious, Matt, yer better lookin' than I remember."

His girlfriend rarely, if ever, had a Southern drawl to her words. Sure, there were occasional phrases, like *fixin'* or *wound up,* that held the accent. And, of course, she used toboggan to mean hats and not sleds and said oil as one syllable.

She didn't, however, call him *Sugar* or say *goodness gracious.*

Biting her lower lip and batting her lashes, she glanced at him several times.

Honestly, she reminded him more of the girls he dated in high school and not his girlfriend, Jennifer. He rather liked the nerdy girl. Was she doing this unintentionally because that was what she thought he liked? After all, Doug had teased Matt by telling Jennifer about all the different girls Matt had dated before her. Perhaps she thought she needed to use the same techniques?

Or was this an elaborate joke that Doug encouraged her to do?

"My dear Matt, aren't you taking me to my parents' house so we can retrieve my brother?" she asked, gently touching his hand while leaning toward him.

"That's just it, Jennifer. I'm meeting your parents." He gripped the steering wheel.

"I know. I remember." She smiled.

"No, Jennifer. I can't take you to your parents with you dressed like that in November. Maybe if it was summer, but even then, I would not feel comfortable. I want your parents to like me, not think I'm corrupting their daughter. Even if I just say hi for a second before we leave, I want them to like me."

Slowly, Jennifer inspected her outfit, leaning over some as if to comprehend the full image. As she did, her face grew pale, followed by her cheeks turning red. She crossed her legs and folded her arms over her chest.

"Is that Belinda's?" he asked. He seemed to remember seeing the outfit on her once or twice.

"Yes, I believe it is," she said, the Southern accent missing from her words. "I had no clean clothes. When we go to Barney's, I'd like to stop at the store next door and buy something else."

"Okay," he agreed.

"Can we leave, please?" she asked.

"Not until you buckle up," he said.

She grabbed the buckle and fidgeted with it, not latching it. "Help, please. I can't figure out how to extend the loop."

"Are you thinking of a lap belt?" he asked, puzzled. His dad liked old cars. He'd seen a few in car shows with similar seatbelts to what she described, but most of the antique vehicles had been updated with a three-point harness.

Closing her eyes and pinching them shut, he thought he caught moisture at the corners. Was she trying not to cry?

"Yes. I was thinking of the ones that go across your lap. That's what they had in my dream," she admitted.

Frowning, he said, "Hold on." As he leaned over, a whiff of rose assaulted him. "Is that Belinda's perfume?"

"Yes."

Once he sat up and left her personal space, she opened her eyes but didn't make eye contact, intensely staring out the window with a look of concentration pressed on her features. "Are you okay, Jen? Is that sickness coming back? Do you need to rest?"

"Let's just head out. I have to go home, regardless, and we told Randy we would take him to a movie."

Glancing in the rearview mirror and around the area, he maneuvered the truck out of the dead-end and toward the road.

"Let me turn on the heat." As he reached for the knob, she moved her leg away. The movement was subtle. He smiled at her despite her hesitance. Her stern face stared straight ahead.

There had to be something he could say to get rid of that sour appearance. He had an idea and said, "So, the bet last night… You currently owe me a movie of my choice for wiping your dictatorship off the Risk map. What did you call that army of yours again?"

She whispered, "The butterfly shadow alliance."

"Well, the ninja furry kangaroos beat you, so you owe me a movie."

"You only won because you had New Zealand."

"True. But I can win from other countries as well. That's not the point. I want to go double or nothing."

This sparked her attention, and her arms fell away from her chest. Not meaning to, he glanced at the swells of her breasts. In his defense, it was hard not to. She didn't act like she caught him, so he continued, "Yes, I'm offering you a chance to redeem yourself."

"I need terms, Matt Davis."

"Jennifer, are you wearing eye makeup?" he asked.

"Yes," she answered as the scowl returned, and she folded her arms across her chest.

Trying to keep things light, he said, "You're beautiful either way, but I like you best as you, without makeup." Hopefully, this deterred any of her attempts to act like the girls he dated in high school—in case that was the reason for this costume.

This time, she relaxed as her eyes and shoulders seemed to soften, and she grabbed his hand that rested on his lap.

"Are you okay?" he asked, needing a response.

She sighed before answering. "I think so… I'm sorry, Matt. I shouldn't have dressed this way to go anywhere. It's these dreams. I had another long dream that seemed real—like I was that person. Incredibly intense, over-the-top dreams that start when I'm the person as a toddler. Stranger still, I can recall everything about their life, their friends, subjects they liked in school, even their values. The person in my dream needed to have male attention." She let go of his hand and pointed toward her outfit. "Apparently, they wanted to be loved, really badly."

She laughed, but he wasn't sure why.

"What's so funny?" he asked.

"Didn't you mention me wearing sexy pajamas the other day?" she asked, holding her arms out. When he peeked at her, she added, "Get your fill." This time, she snorted, causing her breasts to bounce. And he watched, as requested.

A car honked at the same time Jennifer demanded, "Hey, Matt, eyes back on the road!"

Chuckling, he waved sorry to the vehicle beside them. "I really thought… So, the outfit has nothing to do with Doug's comments… about the girls I dated before you?" he asked.

She blinked several times, like she was replaying what Doug had said. "No. My outfit has nothing to do with last night other than the dream."

"So, the attire was meant to grab male attention?"

"Yes," she said.

He checked her out again, carefully taking his eyes off the road for a long second. He wanted her to comprehend what he did—that he appreciated her as a woman as well as a friend.

He avoided fawning over her beauty or drooling all over her body. He treated her like anyone else and called things as he saw them. Calling her beautiful or saying she looked pretty wasn't the same as deliberate, meditated observation. By taking the time to really look at her, he showed her he thought about his words.

Their sacred time together was spent doing things and building memories—the important stuff. The sex would happen in its own time. Yet, maybe he had neglected letting her know how sexy she really was. After all, she had spent a few nights in his bed, and all they'd done so far was kiss.

As he focused on the traffic again, he said, "It works, Jen, but men notice you without a skintight outfit. You are beautiful enough to wear baggy clothes and get attention from men."

"Thanks."

He changed the subject and said, "So the bet, if you can out-eat me in the Barney's five-pound challenge, I'll pay and let you pick today's movie."

"And if you win?" she asked.

"Hm, I hadn't thought of that. My plan was to see if you could eat as much as a guy. Do you know you ate a whole pizza last night? I thought girls were concerned about their figure?"

At this, she stared down at the outfit. Though her cheeks gained a warm glow, she continued like nothing was wrong. "Before I agree to this idea, what is your price, Matt?"

"When my mom went out of town for work, my dad would take me to a double feature at the movie theater. Let's call this a day of excess. We'll attempt the five-pound meal. If I win, you pay for lunch and both movies. If you win, I pay for lunch and both movies. Not only that, if I win, horror and action, and if you win, whatever movies you'd like to see."

"Fair—"

"Better than fair. I'm giving you the opportunity for not one but two movies. I call that an improvement."

"Well, when you put it that way, I'm not sure I could say no. Plus, I'm pretty hungry. I believe I'll beat you. Though, conceivably not in these shorts. I'll need something baggier, I think."

Matt laughed. The idea that the girl sitting beside him could out-eat him excited him. Beyond a doubt, he found her body attractive, but he enjoyed the banter, and for once, he could be himself. He hadn't fathomed there were girls like her—his special, wonderful, rare bird.

CHAPTER 13

JENNIFER

THE MOVIE THEATER, SET ON A SLIGHT HILL, OVERLOOKED THE town of Cherryville. Night settled all around, yet Jennifer easily made out everything as if it was still daylight. Beside her, Matt slurped on the last of his drink while holding the door open to allow others to leave. He waited on her brother, Randy, whom they picked up to join them after she won the Barney challenge and, to everyone's surprise, also ate an apple pie.

Her gaze turned toward the strange, overpowering orange reflection caused by the sodium streetlights. For some reason, the streetlamps bounced off the parked cars like spotlights, in the exact opposite of shadows. Not that shadows ceased to exist on the other side; they did. Just that all the metal surfaces, and some non-metal, became like mirrors, coating the pavement with brilliant orange swirls, like an impressionist artwork by Leonid Afreronov. It was beautiful, but it hadn't rained, so there was no reason for the reflections.

Interrupting her observations, Matt's arm passed in front of her as he threw away his fountain cup. "Well, that was wholesome," Matt said seconds before he put a sticky hand into hers.

"I liked it, and what is on your hand? Eww." She pulled her hand away. The yuck coated her palm.

"Sorry," he said, wiping his fingers on his jeans. Turning, she left Matt and moved to a nearby trash bin.

Matt stood close by the door, watching as each individual left. She assumed he was waiting for her brother. Randy had yet to join them, still somewhere in the theater talking to a friend. She searched her purse for a wipe. Finding one, she cleaned off the gunk.

As Randy strolled out, he said, "I would have rather seen the other movie." In his hands, he held the giant bag of popcorn. He grabbed another handful and chewed.

They joined her around the trashcan, reminding her of a scene from *Rocky*—minus the fire. Her brother had grown and now stood her height. Facing her, he turned the bag upside down to show her he finished the popcorn, then wiggled his eyebrows, releasing the emptied container into the trashcan's dark depths.

Earlier, when Matt bought the popcorn, she told Randy he couldn't eat all of it. He proved her wrong. She fought the urge to laugh at his antics, but wanting to be a good role model for him, and a little bitter that she misjudged a teenage appetite, she gave Randy a stern look.

After handing Matt a wet towelette, she dug in her purse for another for Randy. Matt wiped off the filth, wadded the material, and threw it like a basketball into the wastebasket.

Acting very much like a teen boy of fifteen, Randy said with a whine in his voice, "Can we grab something to eat now?"

Hungry? How could her sibling be hungry? When they arrived at her parents' house with only seconds to make it to the four p.m. movie, he had a hamburger in his hands. Jennifer quickly introduced Matt to her parents and shoved Randy, food in hand, into the truck. Before the first movie,

Matt bought him a chocolate bar and a hotdog, and in between the shows, some candy.

Matt answered while Jennifer intentionally made condescending eyes at him. "Sure," Matt said.

A smile crossed his lips as Randy's blond hair fell into his face, almost covering up his blue eyes.

"No," she demanded, crossing her arms over her chest. She found another wipe and offered it to Randy. He refused, but she insisted, shoving it toward his face.

"Come on, Jennifer. You can pay. I'm sure Mom and Dad won't mind. After all, Matt paid for everything so far," Randy begged. "I'm hungry." But he took the wipe and started rubbing his hands.

When he finished, he dabbed the corners of his lips in a mock display of obedience. Then, with a sarcastic smile, he bowed. If someone other than her had seen it, they would have thought him charming or polite.

She knew better.

Tapping her foot, she leaned back. "No, Randy. Let's go home!"

"Come on, Jennifer! This is so not like you! You're even standing like Mom when she's angry. With Thanksgiving tomorrow, Mom would be angry at me for messing up the kitchen, so you know I can't eat when we get home!"

A person coming out the door that she recognized from church hastily stared at her before pointedly turning away. Jennifer frowned. His argument about her mother and the kitchen was accurate. Since her parents redid the kitchen, her mom was obsessed with keeping the countertops pristine.

Matt stepped between them while she weighed Randy's words, and patted her on the belly. Matt said, "Well, of course, your sister is not hungry. Did she show you the shirt she won from Barney's? After finishing the Barney Five hamburger, I told her she couldn't eat the apple pie, and she proved me wrong. That's why I paid for you as well as her. I'm only sorry I couldn't talk longer to your parents."

For emphasis, Matt rubbed her tummy. "I will never bet against your sister's never-ending stomach again."

Randy started laughing and tossed the wet wipe. "Are you saying my sister did the Barney challenge?"

"Yes." Matt's voice simultaneously held shock, surprise, and fear.

What was the big deal? With everything Randy had devoured since they picked him up this afternoon, he made the Barney challenge look like a kid's meal at a fast-food restaurant. In the last few days, she experienced hunger that didn't want to go away, no matter how much she consumed. Staring at skinny Randy, she could blame it on genetics. Besides, when you were famished, you ate.

Right then, her stomach gurgled, and she was glad Matt hadn't left his hand on her tummy. Defensively, she said, "Please, Matt. I've just been hungry."

Randy's eyebrows rose, lost under his hair. "Well, that does explain why she isn't starving. Didn't a guy die from eating all that hamburger last month, like it stretched out his stomach?"

Where did her brother come up with these stories—the Internet? "What? That's not true. You eat more than I—"

"I don't know. They wouldn't give your sister the shirt until they played back the video of her swallowing every bite. They accused me of helping her by eating some of it, but man, I didn't. That's why she has on the overalls. It allows her stomach to stretch," Matt said.

Randy surveyed her. When he finished, his face held that shocked, surprised stare that he faked so well, and he said, "That's sick, Jennifer. Do you have an alien living in your stomach? I read about some worms you can eat that keep you from getting fat."

The image of her hand, red and scaley like an alien's, flashed before her. She shoved the thought far from her mind.

Well, if the defensive approach didn't work, maybe she should try playing the victim? "Wow. First, I let you join us for the movie. I won the right for you to go at great personal suffering." She placed her hand over her belly. "I sacrificed my body to fit all that food into my guts. And now, you want to hijack my date even more by us taking you out to eat? You even accuse me of being an alien. Besides, look at the time. No one will be open anyway."

Randy came up behind her, placing his arm around her shoulder. With each breath, she smelled some kind of shaving cream. He was growing up, so she should expect him to care more about his hygiene.

Tapping her on the back and resting his weight on her, Randy said, "You know, I'm your chaperone. This way, Mom and Dad will have someone making sure nothing happens other than good old-fashioned fun. I should get Mom to pay me. Plus, it's only right you take me out to eat. And I can find a place that's open."

Shoving his hand off her shoulder, she faced her brother. "How is it only right?"

Before he could answer, Matt maneuvered between them, pushing Randy out of the way so that he stood beside her. Taking possession of her hand, he rubbed her fingers. Then he guided her toward the truck. "Jen, it's okay. I don't mind spending more time with Randy. He reminds me of me when I was his age. Besides, I always wanted a younger brother. I'll pay."

Glaring around Matt at Randy, she said, "You only want to spend time with him because you don't have a brother."

Laughing, Matt gave a slight gentle jerk to bring her attention back to the path in front of them. "Good, it's decided. Where would you like to eat, Randy?"

"How about Mama's?" Randy asked.

"Sure," Matt responded. "Jennifer, would you please give me directions?"

She pointed straight ahead, almost directly in front of them. "It's just across the street from the courthouse."

As she pinpointed the location, she caught sight of a set of stairs leading to one of the old storefronts. It reminded her of the dream last night. The sign over the door with a glaring neon toothbrush clearly indicated that a dentist used the building. But in her dream, it was a corner store, like a miniature food and drug store. If she compared the outside, she saw little differences in the brickwork and windows.

Hours had passed since this morning, and once again, Jennifer felt like Jennifer, but she hadn't when Matt picked her up. The woman in her dream, Jennifer's great-grandmother, MaryAnn, still lived. Though vivacious for her age, GG MaryAnn never seemed...well, wild.

Yet, in the dream, her GG cornered her great-grandfather, a widower more than twenty years her senior named David English. Sure, Jennifer knew her great-grandfather, David English, was much older than her great-grandmother, but that happened to someone else, not to Jennifer—until last night.

His age wasn't the only odd thing in the dream, Jennifer reflected.

In the dream, MaryAnn Collins English's earliest memories were of living in Kentucky with her mother and biological father, Robert Sowards. Yet, in truth, MaryAnn's mother was Mildred, and father was John Collins.

Robert Sowards never existed.

The dream didn't gel with reality. Once again, Jennifer's mind made up details that weren't true.

As Matt unlocked the truck door and she maneuvered into the cab, squished between Matt and her brother, she wondered how much of the local area her imagination recreated in the dream.

Her eyes fell on a giant oak near a graveyard to her right.

When it was a sapling, MaryAnn Collins climbed that tree's branches, hiding from her stepfather, who everyone thought was her biological dad.

Jennifer sat very still, stunned. Her subconscious had the ability to reconstruct a potential timeline for a town? Maybe Jennifer should become a writer.

Distracting her, Matt touched Jennifer's leg and leaned over. He whispered, "Are you alright?"

"I'm fine. Just wondering what this place looked like years ago. You know my kin are from here," she said.

"Really, cute city," Matt whispered.

"It is, and a nice city to grow up in. The Collins, my mom's side, had a law practice in town. My great-grandmother's father, John Collins, was the last lawyer in that line."

"Are you thinking of becoming a lawyer?" Matt asked, entering the restaurant's parking lot.

"No, but I might do a genealogy study over Christmas break and find out more about my family."

Matt smiled and parked the car. "I thought about that once, studying my lineage, but decided against it. I didn't see what I would gain from knowing, and how was I to know if what I found was even true? Like if I found someone who did something great, like the guy who discovered the vaccine for strep throat, or the guy who studied the plague, or, I don't know, a king—what good would it do me?"

Maybe Matt was right, and learning about her ancestors had little to do with her choices or destiny. Then again, what if she learned from their lives? Could she prevent herself from making their mistakes? Or what if some part of her could maintain all the knowledge they gained—could she start where they left off? What if the real reasons people became doctors, or picked certain people for their spouses, or decided where to raise their kids had to do with genetics more than environment? Perhaps her subconscious was trying to help her make the right choices by giving her dreams of her ancestors?

But what lesson was she supposed to learn—not to be promiscuous? She already had that down.

Matt opened the door, and the scent of steak caused Jennifer to forget about everything except food.

CHAPTER 14

PETR

The thought of accidentally running into Jennifer crossed Petr's mind several times Wednesday night on the drive to Mama's Home Cooking Restaurant. Would she interrogate him again, or if she were alone, would she flirt?

Part of him hoped for this seemingly random meeting with the only person who might recognize him. But the other half, his logical side, ascertained the possibility was slim.

With tomorrow being Thanksgiving, he didn't expect a crowd. Yet, he circled the gravel parking lot several times before he found a spot. Grabbing the folder beside him, he locked his car and approached the building.

The old nostalgic brick storefront held several small details from another time—dark green metal drains on the end of the gutters shaped like dolphins that he thought were made of copper; an iron doorknocker mimicking the shape of cherries, a constant theme in the town of Cherryville.

He searched for similar details wherever he went. His eyes instantly fell on the thick, hand-cut floor planks when he stepped through to a loud, bustling dining area. Above him, the walls were bare to the brick, and the ventilation was painted black with twinkling fairy lights.

The scent of Southern food, fried chicken and sweet fruit pies, filled the space, in contrast to the decorations. The room reminded him more of an Italian or Greek restaurant with the strong Tuscany décor feel, though the name spelled out home cooked meals.

While he contemplated the contrast and similarities in the atmosphere, a hostess approached. The uniform for the staff appeared to be casual, as the woman who greeted him with a large smile and a pencil behind her ear wore jeans and a 'Mama's' logoed T-shirt. She led him through a strange arrangement of tables and plants, all positioned at odd angles, he assumed, to isolate the visiting customers. Yet, the table she placed him at gave him more than ample ability to watch the front door.

Once she left, he glanced at his watch. Seven-thirty on the dot, yet no one approached him. He sought out anyone paying particular attention to him.

At a table to his left, behind an artificial Ficus plant, a blond man in his thirties glared at him. The person gave him an evil look, his eyebrows pressed together and shoulders tensed. When Petr caught the man's eyes, he glanced away. Not seeing any other potential contacts, he opened the folder.

You are taking more risks than normal, Petr. I almost think you want Jennifer to catch you, he chided himself.

What would she do if she caught him?

When the records office closed, he found an open coffee and dessert shop and waited for seven-thirty. He made use of his time by grading papers... only occasionally glancing at Jennifer's image.

The glint in her now familiar green eyes, with a touch of something mysterious, stared back.

The hunt in Cherryville had ended. Jennifer's great-grand-mother, MaryAnn English, applied for a birth certificate years after her birth, claiming home delivery. Somehow, the document failed to list any information on her mother other than a first name.

All of MaryAnn's siblings were adopted, but her father was easy to find, coming from a large family and being a local lawyer. Without being able to trace MaryAnn's mother, he could close this path.

Before a member of the waitstaff came to take his order, he pulled out his red pen and marked the image with the symbols closing her mother's line.

Surveying the room, he found no sign of the mysterious informant who knew his real name. He closed the folder and sighed.

To adequately search for her father's family, someone needed to visit a township in Michigan. But why would they? If the Nose arrived soon, they could sniff out the dragon. Until then, he'd keep a close—but distant—eye on Jennifer Wright for any strange behavior.

When the waitress returned with water, she smiled. "What would you like?"

"What do you suggest?" he asked her.

"Everything is wonderful because it's made with love, but I suggest the country fried steak."

"Please bring me a sweet tea and a country fried steak," Petr said, following her recommendation.

When the server left, he glanced around the room. The only other person eating alone, the blond guy to his left, glanced at him and stood.

The person wore a black leather jacket that hugged his large, muscular frame. Underneath, only the letter 'e' on his gray T-shirt peeked out. Reaching behind him, he pulled a trifold leather wallet from his jeans pocket and threw a few dollars on the table. He swaggered toward Petr, shoulders back, legs limber and fluid, in confident movements, reminding Petr of a boxer before a match.

As he passed Petr, he bumped him on his shoulder lightly.

"Sorry, man," he said as he continued to move toward the cashier. The man then left the building.

By the time Petr finished his meal, he'd given up hope of seeing Jennifer and meeting with the White Jaguar. Taking the check, he handed it to the woman behind the cash register, along with his credit card. As was his custom, he grabbed a toothpick from the dispenser and placed it in his mouth.

The woman made idle conversation as she typed the amount into the machine. "How was your meal?"

"Delicious," he responded, staring at the pictures behind the wall, attracted to an in-sepia image of this building with men carrying large bags of grain. His suspicions of this once being part of a larger market were correct, and now, when he stared at the floor, he made out scratches where heavy loads carved grooves into the wood.

She glanced at the ticket as she handed back his credit card and said, "The country fried steak is my favorite."

Petr prepared to say something in return as he placed the plastic in his wallet, but cool air from the opening door brought in a scent of lavender. Automatically, his pulse raced, knowing beyond a doubt who entered. Listening before turning, he recognized the footsteps of two other people with her, and to his delight, her heart sped up. His mind already concluded her reaction was to seeing him. He swallowed. Anything he intended to say to the cashier was forgotten as all words died on his lips.

He faced the front, and his eyes locked with Jennifer's before noticing anyone else. Beside her, Matt held her hand, a giant grin smeared across his face. Behind her, taller than he expected, he recognized the other person with her as her brother Randy.

His eyes drifted to Jennifer again, drinking in the details. Her hair, pulled back in a ponytail complemented her facial structure. She wore a simple yellow T-shirt under baggy black overalls, with black running shoes.

"Dr. Smith. I didn't expect to see you here," Matt said.

Unfortunately, Petr feared someone might notice how long his eyes stayed on Jennifer—if they hadn't already—so he forced them on Matt.

With his toothy grin and usual jovial demeanor, Matt let go of Jennifer's hand and held it out for him to shake. Stepping forward and returning the smile, he shook his hand in greeting.

"Matt, I'm surprised to see you as well. I was driving through, and someone suggested I stop and try the country fried steak. They thought I would like this old building storefront." Nodding to the surroundings, he continued. "I must say, I'm glad I took the time. I'm about to head back to Charlotte. Are you having a pleasant fall break?"

"Yes, I am," he answered.

Petr released Matt and, out of politeness, offered his hand to Jennifer. The instant they touched, static electricity jumped between them. In a jerky motion, Jennifer pulled her hand back and softly whispered something almost inaudible that sounded like "fruida."

The word *"fruida"* in Dragon meant spark.

Petr took two steps back, but his eyes stayed locked on those emerald green eyes, the same color as his deceased friend Spring's.

"Sir." His waitress rushed forward, holding out the manila folder. How could he forget the evidence? Now his heart pounded, beating loud enough that others surely could hear it! He hastily grabbed the envelope with Jennifer's name clearly written on the cover.

"Hey, Jennifer and Randy, tell your mom I said hi," the waitress said, staring between Jennifer and him for a second, and he realized his server had seen the name written on the outside. He wondered if she had opened it and saw all the condemning information.

"Thank you," Petr said to the woman, tucking it under his arm to hide the contents.

"Well, you're welcome," the server said, but the words came out like a question. Soon, though, she shook her head while heading back to the tables.

The boy, as tall as him, bounced and jumped, pushing past Jennifer blocking his view of her. Randy regarded him as if he were a circus clown and said, "Wow. This is one of your college teachers?"

Shrugging, Matt introduced him by saying, "Dr. Smith, this is Jennifer's brother, Randy."

Despite Randy's height, Dr. Smith greeted the boy by patting him on the back. The gesture seemed like the professor thing to do. Even without the birth certificates or census tucked under his arm, beyond a doubt, Randy and Jennifer were genetically brother and sister.

A boy with a blue baseball cap at a nearby table stood, waving his arms. The teenager shouted, "Randy!" Seconds later, an adult chastised the youngster.

"See ya." Randy left the group and headed over to the person who called out to him.

"Sorry. That's his best friend, Greg. They've been best friends since they were five. I apologize he disappeared so quickly."

"No, it's all right," Dr. Smith appeased her. "I need to head back to Charlotte, anyway. I haven't finished grading the tests or term papers." He crossed his fingers. "I'm getting close."

"Well, it was good seeing you," Matt said in farewell.

"You as well. I hope you both continue to have a great fall break and a happy Thanksgiving." Petr took the receipt from the cashier. Before walking out the door, he made eye contact with Matt and then Jennifer. "Enjoy your meal."

Once outside, he practiced breathing to calm his heart. Each exhale brought a white puff into the chilly night air. He recognized adrenaline, followed by the euphoria of dopamine, circling his brain. Very few things had energized him in such a way in years.

He felt alive!

Pulling the key from the fob, he unlocked the car door. For the first time, he was almost caught investigating.

What if the waitress told Jennifer?

Being so old, he could no longer tell someone's age, but if he guessed, there was at least a ten-year age gap between the women, suggesting they had different friend groups. Presumably, they didn't know each other well enough for her to tell Jennifer or her mother about the folder.

Then again, if she did, he could say it was for one of her professors. When he returned, he'd pull up her classes to have his alibi ready if she asked.

Sitting in the cold car, he laid the folder on the seat. Blowing in his hands, he tried to think past the adrenaline-induced euphoria, but the chemicals blocked his logic.

Fruida, a Dragon word, might have slipped from her mouth when she touched him. Then again, perhaps he read too much into what he wanted.

Why? Why did I want her so much to be the dragon?

"Because I want to get to know her," he admitted.

But, if she is a dragon, she belongs to Matt. And even if she is not, she still belongs to Matt.

Glancing up, he noticed a white piece of paper sitting on top of the dash. Strange that he didn't remember leaving anything there.

He pulled it down and unfolded the note. Written in black block-style lettering, the note read:

> SORRY I COULDN'T MEET WITH YOU, DR. SMITH.
> IT WAS TOO RISKY. YOU ARE BEING WATCHED.
> —THE WHITE JAGUAR.

Someone in the dragon world recognizing he ate a dragon's heart wasn't that uncommon—they could smell it. But what if the person spying on the place's actual target was Jennifer or Matt? Glancing at the restaurant, he wondered about their safety. Were they okay?

If Jennifer said a dragon word, she could be the dragon. Anybody capable of identifying him could sniff out a dragon shifter.

Except, Jennifer had a brother, something so rare he'd only heard of two families in his long life that had siblings so close together. It had never happened among his sister's descendants—there had only been single births until Matt.

Plus, Petr narrowed down her lineage and eliminated fifty percent as not having a dragon ancestor. He doubted again that she was the dragon shifter.

Was he making smart decisions? If it was someone other than Matt and Jennifer who could be the dragon shifter, would he decide differently and just ask them?

He didn't know for sure, but he thought his decision would be the same.

Glancing around the parking lot, he searched for someone watching him. He couldn't find anyone, but his neck tingled, indicating they were there, in the shadows, waiting.

Picking up the folder, he opened to the picture, staring, and traced her face. He shut it and slammed it into the seat, sighing.

"Obsessed, Petr?" he asked himself, running his hand through his hair.

I'm doing it for her protection and Matt's, he lied.

At this point, days after the awakening, he knew Matt wasn't the dragon. By now, the dragon shifter had dreamed of their grandparent and possibly up to their great-great grandparent. If Matt was the dragon, he'd remember Petr.

With Matt removed from the equation, only Jennifer and the rest of the campus could be the dragon shifter.

Was she safe?

With so many people around and being with family, she

should be safe, dragon shifter or not. The Immortals would wait to get her alone. Until the Nose came to town and confirmed the dragon, Petr would watch her closely—from a distance.

Petr turned on the car and contemplated waiting for them to finish eating. He could follow them to see where Jennifer and Matt went next and ensure they were safe.

You just want to know where she goes, Petr. Stop it! Matt's girlfriend! She is not for you. You love your family too much to interfere with Matt's choice. Plus, if this person following you finds them, they might figure out how you are related to Matt. Best not to get the Immortals anywhere near Matt.

Decision made, he navigated the car to the interstate, checking his review mirror for someone following him.

CHAPTER 15
JENNIFER

...The crazy vixen, Mildred, wore the pink nightgown with lace and thin straps again. "What did you say that outfit was called? I like it. It falls off your body rather nicely." I took a seat on the chaise lounge. Mildred followed me, holding my nightly dose of the concoction for whatever might ail me.

"A chemise," she said, shoving the tea into my hand. I sniffed a hint of rose and mint—possibly a green tea.

"You expect me to drink this without knowing what it is?" I asked.

"Guess! It's not any fun if I tell you," she demanded, tugging her gown's strap back onto her shoulder.

"Make it worth my while," I said, staring at her body, not her face.

"You want an award? Take a sip," she said, her voice all sultry with a hint of promise, her hand toying with the strap, teasing that she'd remove her clothing in exchange for obedience.

I did as requested, knowing perfectly well where this would lead me...

• • •

As a morning person and driven by the aroma of a scrumptious roast pig, Robert Sowards sat straight up in bed. Glancing around his Manhattan apartment, things didn't add up. His wife, Mildred, bought this hideous painting from one of 'her' plays—where was it? And the woman who cleaned his room always had a paper sitting on the corner of his table. It, along with his furniture, was missing.

His first thought was that his friends had played an elaborate hoax on him. When did he swindle the guys last? Did Danny or Tony retaliate for something he did? Payback of some type? He guessed they slipped something into his nightly mint tea and carried off his slumbering body. That was something they would do. He'd never noticed an unfamiliar taste since no two drinks were ever the same. Mildred added different medicines to create the perfect healthy cocktail.

Well, best to search the area and find the bathroom before he resorted to using the window.

The brown furniture decorating the room lacked style, being both plain and average. The mirror above the vanity, though, had crisp corners instead of fading, like his antique piece he kept for luck.

His breath caught. A reflection of a young woman, one that he recognized, stared at him from the mirror. She moved, and he moved.

Touching his face, he traced where the outline of his beard should be. Soft, delicate fingers almost tickled the smooth skin. Fearful of what else might have changed, he searched in his pants for the ultimate test of his maleness, but Fredrick was missing.

As he stared at the odd girl, he said, "What a dream I'm having! I could use some giggle water!" A woman's trill replaced his deep voice.

The colored photograph in the mirror's corner held the same face he noticed in front of him. He pulled it off, trying to remember the name, and he wondered about her relationship with the other two people in the picture.

"I have the heebie-jeebies," *she* muttered and frowned as *she* grabbed a handful of her breasts. "This is the bee's knees; I'm a hotsy-totsy girl."

Taking the photo to study, she collapsed on the bed.

There were clear memories of shaving every morning. Faint recollections of playing with dolls in the corner and crying when she broke the family heirloom vase.

He focused on that remembrance. On their first wedding anniversary, the long-necked vase held twenty red roses for Mildred. As the artistic decoration shattered again, so did the illusion of Robert Sowards.

Breathing deeply, Jennifer distinguished between two memories—one of Robert Sowards' life; the other, her own. She wavered at the complexity of untangling the two sets of memories. It was like she had two timelines. One timeline held her personal life experience. The other experiences belonged to Robert.

In one lifetime, Jennifer remembered being a boy named Robert, growing up in a small building, like in *Little House on the Prairie,* only smaller.

In the other period, when she was about the same age, Jennifer relived being a girl attending church with her mother and watching cartoons with her brother, Randy.

Jennifer recalled fishing with Robert's buddy, Ruddy Belcher. At the same age, she thought back to having a contest with Randy at the local pool for who could hold their breath the longest.

And just like that, she was Jennifer Wright, not Robert Sowards.

"Wow," she said, grabbing her forehead, expecting a headache, and dropping the picture.

The man had the same name and appearance in her two dreams, the one last night and the night before, yet two different personalities—one hateful and bitter, and then in last night's dream—interactive and jovial.

"Wow," she said again, running her hands through her hair.

Last night, the young Robert lived in New York and married a wild flapper babe with sexy gams.

The first time he viewed Mildred, his heart stopped from love at first sight. True to the flapper world, she wore a knee-length dress that glittered and curled her auburn hair under, which accentuated her sultry painted eyes. Batting her eyelashes, she asked him for a light. She held a long black cigarette in a cigarette holder. Until then, Robert had never considered dating, spending his time focused on making his fortune.

The wild woman, Mildred, took him to a speakeasy and whispered seductive words. Jennifer couldn't help the attraction and remembered how Mildred's curves perfectly matched his fingers.

Was she attracted to girls now?

As an answer, her mind's eye showed her a memory of Dr. Smith at the restaurant.

Was that last night or the night before?

The memory was fuzzy, but not his blue-green eyes. They pierced Jennifer's soul and made her feel more naked than if she had taken off her clothes.

Had he known what she was thinking when she saw him? How she wanted—regardless of not really knowing him—irrespective of her personal morals—him beneath her, his hands on her breasts, demanding their mutual pleasure.

She shuddered. Hot and thick desire coated her skin like a layer of electricity.

Well, that confirmed it—Jennifer was not into women.

She breathed out, her body too hot. She needed to leave her room, walk out into the cold, and cool off.

Instead, she opened her window and stood there, the sun

hitting her face, and she tilted her chin to soak up more rays as the nippy breeze relieved the tension—for now.

Staring around the neighborhood as she shut the glass, she spotted a bright red sports car. Around the family sedans that littered the other driveways, it stuck out. Shrugging, she locked the window—the Wilson's next door must have an out-of-town guest.

Lust gone, she wondered why she'd dreamed of Robert Sowards.

Turning on the computer sitting on the desk, she hoped to find an answer for what her mind had invented. Her crazy dreams added too many details not to be based on a random fact she learned in school. Perhaps Robert Sowards was involved with the Rockefellers, Carnegies, or Vanderbilts?

Expeditiously, she found a reference to the October 29, 1929 stock market crash. Black Tuesday, which brought about the Great Depression.

Since Robert Sowards was obsessed with striking it rich in the stock market, she guessed that could change his outlook on life between the two dreams—hope lost had horrible impacts on people.

What was she doing? Why would the stock market impact her dreams? She wasn't currently learning about the Roaring Twenties. Her class was focused on the eighties. Matt was right—she'd studied herself into an imaginary stupor.

Still wondering if her dream held any truth, she searched for Robert Sowards and found a golfer who didn't resemble the man in her dream.

The wonderful scent of sugar-coated ham distracted her from her hunt, and her stomach rumbled. She inhaled, her fingers hovering over the keys.

How did she forget Thanksgiving? The blessed day when her family visited.

An image of her hugging her great-grandmother, Mary-

Ann, flashed before her eyes. If that vague recollection was correct, the Grands arrived yesterday.

"The Grands" was an affectionate name for the collective group of her great-grandmother and her grandmother. The nickname developed when they moved to a retirement community called Grand Bahamian. Randy noted that the grandly older people now had their own spot of paradise. A place that didn't allow people under fifty-five for visits longer than two weeks. For some reason, Randy thought it highly unfair that he couldn't live with his grandparents over the summer. Over time, the name developed into one of affection.

Though their paternal grandfather also lived in the same community, he didn't get lumped into the Grands' term, and Jennifer wasn't sure why. Maybe her grandfather didn't like the nickname. He always came across as more refined and collected—not wild and playful.

Dressing speedily in the yellow shirt and overalls, she ran down the stairs to the first room on the left. Knocking, she tried to control her breathing.

What would she do if the dreams were true? If they weren't, she'd suggest hang gliding to Matt. That should scare the dreams away.

"Who's beating on our door like it is a piece of dough?" one of the Grands said. "I'm a-comin'." A shuffling sounded seconds before the door cracked, and the scent of vanilla and sandalwood oil assaulted her nose like when she had visited a candle factory on a school field trip.

Jennifer was staring at her great-grandmother, MaryAnn, wearing a brown dress with white flowers, her silver hair in a top-centered bun. Much shorter than Jennifer and slumped with age, she greeted Jennifer with bright, sharp eyes.

"Now, what has got your panties in a wad?" MaryAnn asked.

"May I talk to you and Grandmommy?" Respecting their privacy, Jennifer waited for permission to enter.

MaryAnn stepped out of the way and, with a hand motion, allowed Jennifer to pass into the room.

Her grandmother, Josephine, brushing her silver hair, walked out of the ensuite bathroom, leaving the light on over the medicine cabinet. Taller and weighing slightly more than MaryAnn, her facial features and green eyes had passed to Jennifer from her mother's line. Josephine wore a blue dress that hung just past her knees and cowboy boots, and she smiled with her entire face at Jennifer. "What do you want to talk about?"

"Me," Jennifer said and ran her hands through her hair. "I mean, you."

The Grands shared a quizzical glance. Josephine sat in the rocking chair, placing the brush on the nearby nightstand. Simultaneously, MaryAnn moved to one of the twin beds, taking on a businesslike demeanor.

Choosing the carpet, Jennifer lowered herself to the ground.

"I'm old, dear. You'll have to be slow because you've already confused me," Josephine said.

"Is anyone in our family psychic?" Jennifer asked.

"Why do you ask, dear?" MaryAnn responded.

Jennifer checked the clock on the wall to her right. It ticked and tocked twice before she answered. "Because..." Jennifer paused, gathering courage. "I have strange dreams. They seem so real."

"Oh," said Josephine. "Well, tell us your dreams. Maybe we can interpret them, like Joseph of the coat of many colors."

Trying her best to describe her experience, she said, "Well...The first dream seemed real. Like an event I watched. A handsome man walked this girl down an aisle. She married someone else, though, not him.

"The next day, not in the dream, but with Matt at a restaurant, I met a man who looked just like the person in my dream. Not the one who married the girl but the one who escorted the girl to the groom. He turned out to be one of our college's professors."

"Jennifer, are you sweet on one of your professors?" MaryAnn teased with a smile. "I'm not sure that new beau of yours will like that. I would keep this dream to yourself."

Shaking her head but glancing away from the Grands, Jennifer said, "No, I just found it odd that I hadn't met him but dreamed of him *and then* met him." Jennifer continued, "Then I dreamed about Mom and Dad meeting. In the dream, I was Mom. It was very bizarre. Then I dreamed about you, Grandmommy. I was surrounded by a large family on a farm."

"You knew I had a lot of brothers and sisters," Josephine responded.

"Did you meet Granddaddy in a hayloft? He was visiting one of your brothers. You had played a prank on Frank, and he wanted to throw you into a creek? I dreamed you were sitting in a hayloft hiding. Granddaddy came up and told you what beautiful eyes you had?" Jennifer asked.

"Yes," Josephine responded. "But Jennifer, that was your grandfather's favorite story—how he met his troublemaking wife. He was the handsomest man I ever did see, romantic as any, I reckon. But once again, your mom knows the story. She probably told it to you."

Jennifer placed her hand on MaryAnn's leg and quickly added, "The other night, I dreamed of you, GG. You were in Kentucky. Your dad was a coal miner named Robert Sowards. Your mother, Mildred, left him to be with the pastor, John Collins."

MaryAnn's face turned white, and her right hand trembled. Josephine, with a bright smile on her face, glanced at her mother. "Momma, Papaw Collins was a nice man. Always gave me candy from his pocket when he visited."

MaryAnn stayed quiet, staring at a spot on the floor, face still pale.

Smiling, Josephine turned her attention to Jennifer. "No, Mom's dad was John Collins. So there, it's settled. Your dreams are just dreams."

A heaviness settled in the air, and the scent of bitter vinegar caused Jennifer's eyes to water. Meanwhile, MaryAnn's breathing changed, becoming shallower.

Jennifer focused on MaryAnn, on the uneasiness in her face. It was true! Her dream was true!

"No, she's right," MaryAnn whispered under her breath. Her attention focused on something beyond the ground. "My dad's name was Robert Sowards. He lived in Kentucky."

If that dream showed her an actual event, could Dr. Smith be Petr? But that couldn't be true—a castle inside a volcano? No, that was too much like a fairytale to be true.

No one said anything for a few seconds. All eyes focused on MaryAnn, so she continued and said, "I never told anyone. I never even told your father. I just didn't see the point, and it was so many years ago."

Her ears burned. Where could a city like that even be? When did that dream take place?

It didn't. You're being crazy. Grab ahold of yourself.

Touching Jennifer's hand, MaryAnn said, "I don't even know what happened to Papa. I've wondered all these years. Did you dream about what happened to him?"

Jennifer reflected on her dreams as she glanced past the bed and out the window. "No, I don't know what happened to him. His personality changed. In the dream of your life, when you were a kid, he worked as a poor coal miner. In the dream last night, he worked at the stock market, living in New York, and he was wealthy and looked forward to being a parent."

Moving from the chair, Josephine snuggled up to her mother, placing her hand over hers. "Momma, Grandpa John wasn't my grandpa?"

If that dream was real… An image of a six-inch red snout, a claw, broken black wings…

Because one dream was true, didn't mean the other dreams were true.

Turning toward her daughter, MaryAnn moved a strand of hair behind her ear. "No, sweetie." Then, facing Jennifer, she said, "All that was long ago, my dear Jennifer. I can attest that what you have told me about my life is true. So maybe you are the family's first psychic." MaryAnn wiped a tear trailing down her cheek and smiled. "When did these dreams start?"

"In the woods, camping a few nights ago," Jennifer answered.

I'm not a dragon. I'm not a dragon!

They continued to stare, so she added, "I just want them to stop." She decided not to mention the dream of turning into a dragon or waking up on top of the bear. She left out the liquor as well. Jennifer's family were Southern Baptists; they still equated alcohol with wickedness.

Josephine said, "Well, Jennifer, we are a very logical family. I'm sure there's a reason. We just have to find it."

Yes, logic. Use logic. Don't let them see you panic!

Josephine stood up and walked to a dresser in the room's corner. She grabbed her purse from its surface and began digging. As she searched, the scent of mint combined with the vinegar and chocolate made Jennifer want to gag.

Pulling out a small flip pad and her cell phone, Josephine placed the pocketbook back on the dresser. After Squinting at the notepad, she turned toward Jennifer. "Hmm, where are my glasses?"

The cluttered yet clean room left few places to hide glasses. With something to do, Jennifer stood and searched the vanity. She found the pair in the bowl of knickknacks and handed them to her grandmother.

"I'm going to text an investigator. I used him to help me find Carla when she went missing. Carla and her silly ideas."

A few years ago, Carla, Josephine's niece, upped and moved to California, telling no one. Carla's dad, Josephine's half-brother, had passed away, and Josephine took it upon herself to protect her half-sibling's children.

"Eureka! And there. I have my French investigator, Pierre, looking for a plausible reason for your strange dreams or someone with a similar gift." She typed a little longer. "And now I'm asking him to find..." She pulled her glasses down her nose. "Jennifer dear, what was that man's name, my...grandfather?"

"Robert Sowards spelled S-O-W-A-R-D-S," Jennifer answered.

Find a logical reason, Pierre. I don't want to stick out! I just want to have a normal life!

Her grandmother started typing again. "And now I have Pierre looking for Robert Sowards. If anyone can find him, he can!"

Josephine returned to her mother's side and sat on the bed. "So, tell us, Jennifer, if you can remember the details of your own life, how are you?"

"I'm fine, Grandmommy," Jennifer responded.

"Not good enough, dear," MaryAnn countered. "Tell us about this Matt person."

"Not much to say." Jennifer paused, then continued, "He is tall, smart, and fun to be around."

"When did you start dating Matt?" Josephine asked.

"I—" Jennifer hesitated, not entirely sure. She vaguely remembered the scent of coffee and friends surrounding them, but that couldn't be the beginning of their relationship. If other people were around, how could it have been a date? "I think it was a few months ago." The grandmothers turned and stared at each other.

"Jennifer, what did you do yesterday?" Josephine asked.

"I think I went to Matt's apartment and watched TV, but it could have been the day before."

"So, details are no longer clear," Josephine commented.

"They're there, but it just takes longer to remember them. By the end of the day, everything is back to what it was like before I started having the dreams," Jennifer answered and glanced away.

"What about last weekend? Your mother told us you went hiking and came home sick. She said that's how she found out you had a boyfriend," Josephine brought up.

"Oh yes," MaryAnn agreed. "I believe she had a company run a background check on Matt." MaryAnn laughed.

Josephine said, "Matt passed the inspection and the investigation."

Nodding, MaryAnn said, "Maybe that's what's wrong, dear. I've heard sicknesses and blows to the head can sometimes give people strange abilities." MaryAnn leaned over and inspected Jennifer. "Can you see auras? Can you see the dead?"

Josephine laughed.

Only dragons.

"No," Jennifer answered.

Standing, MaryAnn said, "Well, if there is one thing I have learned in life, it is this: no matter what happens, it will be all right. It has no other choice. You can live in misery or just enjoy each moment." Turning toward Josephine, she added, "I was upset that I only had you and couldn't have any other children. I thought it was a curse. Then, one day, your dad died. I decided life was too short to worry about what you cannot control. I am proud to say I am a much happier person now." An infectious smile touched her eyes.

Directing her comments to Jennifer, Josephine said, "Now, young lady—you should get yourself ready and shower and pretty yourself up. You can't catch a bee without honey, so sweeten yourself up." She walked over to the door and opened it. Pointing toward the hall, she said, "Whether this boy or the professor sets your heart up and your toes a-curlin' is no different. Enjoy your life and get out of our room. The older you get, the more war paint you need, and I need a bunch."

"Thank you," Jennifer said.

I'll use logic.

GG could be right—maybe my dreams are the result of the flu or sickness. A new gift, yes, a gift, not a curse.

As the door closed, some of the weight she carried dropped off now that someone else knew, yet a new weight rested on her shoulders. How much of what she dreamed was true? Could Dr. Smith be Petr?

Could she be a dragon?

CHAPTER 16

JENNIFER

A SMALL BASKET OF ROLLS SAT BETWEEN JENNIFER AND MATT IN the truck cab. Matt pulled into the parking lot of an older, well-maintained, two-story Tudor. They had an uneventful lunch at her parents. And now it was time to have dinner with Matt's.

"Let me get this straight again—the guy who is taller than your dad and older but bears a striking resemblance to him, is your dad's dad?" Matt asked.

"Yes. He probably wants you to call him by his name, Stewart," Jennifer said.

"And he lives in the house next door to what you call the Grands, but they aren't related, just friends?"

"Yes, just friends. They do things together, travel, go on vacations. They have a lot in common. Well, Granddaddy likes history more than them, but they support each other, hang out, stuff like that." Jennifer leaned back. During the forty-five-minute drive to his house, they talked about her family.

"Did you know your GG, the older of the two Grands, had a motorcycle?"

"Yes." She laughed. "Third time you told me, Matt. I

know it's weird to see a seventy-year-old talk bikes and cars, but she drove it around when I was a little girl. In my childhood, it was perfectly normal for old women to have bikes...I wanted to ride on the back. My mother wouldn't let me."

"And your GG went to Manhattan to see one of the two 'The Wall' shows Pink Floyd did?"

"Yes. She told me all about the plane crashing into the side of the wall." Jennifer leaned against the headrest. Apparently, Matt liked her family.

Taking a more intense tone, he said, "She warned me about you."

Sitting up, she turned to face him, his hand on the steering wheel. "What did GG say?" she asked.

"She said you were special and to be careful."

"What? I'm sure they're just trying to protect me from you."

"No, it was the other way around. She said to watch to make sure you don't hurt me by breaking my heart."

How could I hurt Matt? she wondered.

Patting her leg, Matt said, "Anyway, my part is done. I think they like me. Now, it's your turn."

"Hey, this was your idea. I wouldn't have minded dating and waiting for a few years before we met each other's parents," she said.

A deep, rich laugh bellowed from Matt's chest. "Right before we get married?" he asked sarcastically.

Tilting her head, she said, "I was thinking more like after we had kids."

Moving her chin closer to his, he whispered, "Is that right?" The initial touch of his lips was feather-light, and she closed her eyes. As the kiss progressed, he grabbed her shoulders and tugged her body, molding her against his chest as much as he could while sitting in the truck's cab.

Gently, she pushed on his pecs, regaining her breath from

such a needy, passionate action. For sure, the man had serious skills. Yet something was missing.

Giving credit where credit was due, she said, "Wow, Matt. That, wow. You can kiss."

Bright, twinkling eyes met hers, and he said, "Thanks! Ready to meet my parents?"

"Bring it," she said, then looked out the window. The uniform lawn resembled a green carpet. Even the plants gave off the appearance of perfection, with perpendicular rows of shrubbery that seemed like copies of one another.

He said, "Yeah, Mom and Dad are a little lawn crazy. They have this Zen yard thing going on. There's a pond in the back with a bridge and everything. If it weren't dark, I would show it to you. Maybe later?"

"Sure. Do your parents live on a golf course?" Jennifer wondered.

"No. Why do you ask?"

"It just seems like one of those houses you see on the golf course. Look how perfect your lawn is. Mom is lucky if she can even get Dad outside to mow the yard. Usually, Randy does it."

Matt said, "I don't have a brother or sister, so the duty would have been mine. Mom and Dad hire a lawn company. Still, my parents find it relaxing to maintain the yard. Mom calls it peaceful." He glanced around at his house, then said, "Randy seems pretty cool."

Before she could answer, Matt opened the door and jumped out of the truck. Not waiting, Jennifer maneuvered out of the cab, grabbed the basket, and met him at the walkway to the front door.

She said, "Because Randy is so much younger than me, it's almost like being an only child. Mom said they thought about adopting before Randy came along."

Gliding over the stone pavement with thin patches of grass between the stones, Matt led her to the entrance. Small lights placed in different locations accented the architecture perfectly. There was even a small dog statue and a colorful fall flag.

Matt fidgeted with his hands, not making any effort to grab a key. Finally, he said, "Gung-Gung, my mom's father and my only living grandparent, well, Gung-Gung..." He shook his head and added, "Oh, never mind. First, you have to meet Gung-Gung."

Jennifer smiled. "Who?"

"Gung-Gung. Gung-Gung is what I call my grandfather," he continued.

"Oh, you mentioned that at lunch. Your grandfather, who was born in Germany, but raised in China, but then met your grandmother in India?" When he nodded, she said, "Thank you. I was a little lost. Never mind, I'm still lost."

"Just know my mom and Gung-Gung have lived in many places around the world. For all purposes, they are as American as apple pie. But, pre-warning, he can be strange but loveable." Matt pulled the key out of his back pocket and unlocked the door.

"I meant to ask, where are your aunts and uncles?" Matt asked, cracking the door.

"Both my parents are only kids. It made for great Christmases," Jennifer said, peeking past him into the dark opening.

"I can imagine. Are you ready to meet my family?" Matt asked.

"Yes," she said as he used his left hand to completely open the door and placed his right on the small of her back.

The area was dark, so the first thing Matt did was switch on the lights. As Jennifer surveyed the massive two-story entranceway, Matt bent over and took off his shoes.

"Right," she said, placing the red basket that once held bread on the entrance table. Matt's mother had sent the extra food as a gift. Taking her cue from him, she removed her shoes and tried not to gawk. The off-white walls were framed by dark wood archways, matching beams, and hardwood floors. Where she stood, the ceilings rose two stories, but off in the distance, she saw a hall with at least nine-foot-high ceilings, maybe even twelve. Bright decorations and furniture offset the building's natural colors.

Despite the dark flooring, she didn't find a dust bunny in sight. The house reminded her more of a magazine shot than a home. Inhaling, she picked up a trace odor of cranberry spice candles or a spray. She expected to smell freshly cooked food and wondered what they were eating for dinner.

"Are you sure your parents are here?" she asked.

"Yes. Hold on. Mom doesn't like loud noises. She says it's tacky." He walked over to the entrance table with a mirror over it. Opening the drawer, he pulled out a doorbell. As he pushed, a muted ring sounded in one of the rooms upstairs. Matt placed it back into the drawer.

When he joined her, he wrapped his arm around her back. Leaning over, he whispered, "It's how I say, 'Mom, Dad, I'm home.'" Matt slid his hand from her back to around her waist.

Seconds later, an elegant woman in a long white flowy dress descended the stairs, followed by a towering bald man. She stood before them, glancing briefly at Jennifer, then focused on Matt. "Matt, you are back," she said. Almost as tall as Jennifer, she had darker skin, brown eyes, and black hair. Her features were more handsome than beautiful.

Matt's dad, towering over everyone in the room, put his arm around his wife and kissed her forehead.

Nudging Jennifer closer to his parents, Matt said, "Jennifer, this is my mom, Maria, and my dad, Andrew."

The man, built like a retired weightlifter wearing a sweater over thick muscles, stretched his hand out in greeting. As she took his offering, his eyes narrowed as he squeezed. Exactly four shakes, and he released her. His voice much deeper than Matt's, he said, "Hello. We are glad to meet you and have you over for Thanksgiving."

"Come, let me show you around the house," Maria said, placing a firm grip around her back.

They didn't make it very far when a man with thick gray hair shuffled into the room, slowly edging toward them without lifting his knees or glancing away from the floor. He wore an all-white button-down oversized shirt that hung halfway down his legs. The outfit reminded her of something worn in a Kung-fu movie from the seventies.

He stopped in front of her, head bent low. "Ah, you must be Jennifer," he said, and she heard an accent but couldn't place it. Without warning, he brought her into a hug. She tensed.

As he backed away, Jennifer saw that Matt inherited his eye shape. Gung-Gung kept a firm grip on her shoulders and said, "Matt, you keep her. She has dragon in her. She is a good one. I smell it."

Jennifer had an image of red-clawed hands, and she froze at his words, unable to move or look away.

Matt grabbed her hand and pulled her close as if he understood her discomfort. He said, "Uh, Gung-Gung, this is Jennifer. Mom, I'm going to show her around the house."

He led Jennifer left. As she climbed the steps to the second floor, she studied the images lining the wall of Matt at different ages, from a chunky baby to a long-haired teenager and ending with a strapping jock.

At the top of the stairs, he directed her down a white hallway with white carpet. They passed rows of photos of Matt at school dances, each with a different girl on his arm. Sometimes, if she stopped, he'd join her and give a name or say something like, "We only went out once."

When the photos ended, she said, "You were quite a lady's man there, Matt. Did you have a black book?"

Matt laughed. "No. It was red." He paused for dramatic effect. "After all, red is the color of love."

Laughing with him, he stopped before one of the closed doors. He blushed with his hand resting on the handle and said, "This is my room."

As she passed him, she surveyed the area. The aroma of tropical flowers covered fainter odors of new carpet, paint, and possibly dirty workout clothes. She searched for a candle or a wax warmer but didn't find one. Trophies sat on the shelves. Books were scattered haphazardly in a corner. Video games littered the floor around a desk with a computer. The huge blue comforter twisted at odd angles under giant decorative pillows, making this room appear like the first lived-in area.

Perhaps Matt and his family only lived in their rooms, which made her wonder about dinner. She asked, "Are we eating? I didn't smell any food when we arrived."

He laughed. "Just like you to think of food. The only girl I know who can out-eat me. Mom does the catering thing and doesn't like a house to smell of home-cooked meals; something about the scents lingering in the home. She told me we're having Chinese."

The doorbell rang.

"And that would be our meal," he said as he plopped on the bed. "So, what do you think?" he asked as he waved around his arms to show off his private living space.

Catering on a holiday must cost a fortune, she thought, but said, "Your room looks like a guy's room." Taking a spot on the carpet, she sat with her legs crossed.

Matt grabbed a pillow off his bed, tucked it under him, and lay on his belly, facing Jennifer. "I am a guy, so I guess that's good."

"Your parents' house looks like something out of a magazine. If we had gone to your house first, we would have never gone to mine."

"Why? Your parents' house is friendly and fun. My house looks nice, but I've never been allowed in most of the rooms. I grew up in my bedroom, outside, or at one of my high school friends' places."

"I don't think my parents would let you into my room. Growing up, no boys were allowed in mine. Not that I ever tried. And after seeing this, there is no way I'm showing you my room."

Matt smiled. "You're the first girl I've allowed in here. That makes you even more special, in case you were wondering. And as far as seeing your bedroom, I like a challenge, so I'll see your digs soon enough." A mischievous smile, showing a dimple, lit his face.

Recovering, he changed the subject and said, "Oh, about Gung-Gung. He has some interesting beliefs." He sat straighter on his bed and crossed his legs. He rested his pillow on his lap. "Gung-Gung believes we descended from dragons."

She imagined a red arm, and quickly forced her thoughts away.

There is a logical reason. I'm not a dragon, she told herself.

She covered her distraction by moving to make herself more comfortable.

"I mean it, Jen. He believes one of our ancestors was a dragon. Not just any dragon, but this dragon called Futs-Lung. The smelling like a dragon, that's a compliment. I hope that didn't offend you."

Not glancing at Matt, she noticed pictures of a beach party on his nightstand. In one photo, Matt stood making faces, a group of his friends gathered around him. She said, "No. It's fine. But being called a dragon is something I will remember."

"So you say, but you forgot when we had our first date when your mom asked."

"Ouch. It's these dreams. I remember now. It was that

coffee shop near my dorm. But I'm not really sure that counts. We had five or so people with us."

"It counted." A few seconds later. "Have you tried sleeping pills?"

"For my realistic dreams? Not yet, but I like that idea."

"Maybe we can get some before we head back to campus." He reached behind him on the bed and threw a pillow at her.

It didn't hurt when it hit, but she pretended to be knocked out, landing on the carpet.

Matt moved off his bed. "Come on, girlfriend! It's time to show me your football moves! To the game console!"

CHAPTER 17
MATT

ONE OF THE ODDEST THINGS ABOUT LIVING IN THE SOUTH THAT even Southerners never seemed to grow accustomed to was mowing the yard in the fall.

Friday, the day after Thanksgiving, Matt pushed Jennifer's parents' doorbell and waited. He faced the house across the street and observed a man with a few strands of silver hair, a white wife-beater shirt, and a beer gut driving a riding lawn mower around forest-sized trees. At first, he wondered why, since grass didn't grow in the cold, but then he noticed the trail of missing leaves where the man passed—clearing the fall foliage, modern style.

The house across the street was on a corner lot. The road that poured into Jennifer's parents' street beside it. He ran his eyes down the rows of older two-story colonials, finding dwellings with stains on the roof and chipped paint. Not that the properties weren't maintained, but the differences in the details between his childhood location and here spoke volumes—untouched versus lovingly worn. He'd not noticed until Jennifer mentioned it last night.

And then, an oddity caught his eyes. A bright red Lamborghini Huracan, which he estimated to cost at least the amount of the nearby buildings, sat parked on the road a few lots down. With Thanksgiving so close, the owner was probably visiting family. Still, the sexy car would draw anyone's attention.

Someone tapped on his shoulder. "Matt," Randy said.

Forcibly, Matt closed his mouth as he turned to greet Jennifer's brother.

When he found out she had a sibling, he pictured a male version of Jennifer. Lucky for him, his imagination was wrong, and the similarities ended at the nose and the eye shape. There was just enough in common to know they were relatives and not enough to call them clones.

Randy ushered him into the foyer, and Matt took the opportunity to observe more differences. For instance, uneven patches of a blond beard scattered along his square chin. Soon, the fifteen-year-old would be shaving. Already, he stood close to his sister's height. Based on Matt's experience, Randy's super growth spurt should be happening about now. In time, this kid would stand eye-to-eye with him.

Randy was pale, while Jennifer had warm, coppery skin that most people called olive, which was rare in a blond and something he found attractive. And then there was the eye color: Jennifer's an intoxicating green, and Randy's an ice blue.

Jarring Matt out of his thoughts, Randy poked the bag. "Hi, Matt. What's in the bag?"

With the candy apple red vehicle outside, Matt had forgotten about the present. Now, he held it up like a prize. "Your sister said she's been suffering from bad dreams." He shrugged, lowering the grocery store items back by his side. "I picked her up some sleeping pills. I didn't get her any cough syrup, but I know a lot of people use that too."

Randy shrugged and said, "I guess so, but I can't see Jennifer putting anything into her body to help her sleep. She fusses when I drink energy drinks and says they're unhealthy.

I think she's still in her room. Let me get her down here for you," Randy said. Taking two steps at a time, he ran up the stairs to Matt's left.

Soon after, Matt heard three light knocks.

Matt surveyed his surroundings. Sure, he was here yesterday, but at the time, he was too nervous about meeting her family to pay attention to the area. After talking at his house last night, he was curious. So now, as he waited, he inspected her home.

One of the first things that Jennifer mentioned to him was that her father was an architect and had designed their residence. Standing on the herringbone pattern raised floor, he stepped down into the sunken living room and onto the yellow carpet.

Although he knew nothing of architecture, he assumed that sunken rooms and this particular shade of carpet weren't a current trend.

Around him, the wood paneling on the walls held small glimpses of Jennifer's childhood. He passed a couch on his left and a bright oversized window on his right. His one goal was to take in the pictures on the wall around the television. Several chunky baby Jennifers stared back at him.

This time, he heard three heavy pounds on a door from upstairs, drowning out the television, and Matt focused behind him on the staircase. It sounded like Randy used his foot to knock on the door. "Jen, it's lover boy," Randy screamed.

So now he was lover boy. He liked that, the grin his friends called wicked on his lips.

"And touchdown," the sportscaster enthusiastically chanted, followed by erupting cheers. For a second, he recognized the uniform of the Cowboys football team before the camera focused on someone in the stands wearing a giant sombrero. He forgot about the football game as he slid over to the other side and found an interesting fall picture. A country scene with a bright-eyed baby wrapped in a denim blanket surrounded by hay bundles. Next to the baby stood a toddler with braided pigtails. She definitely jutted her chin at the camera, a piece of straw dangling from her mouth.

"Mom likes that picture," Randy said, standing at the bottom of the stairs. "Jennifer is up. She'll be here in a few seconds. Lazy head was still in bed." He twisted his mouth and shook his head in shame before grabbing a football on the loveseat.

"Want to join me watching the game?" he asked, jumping over the back of the long couch and landing almost in a lying position.

"Do you play?" Matt asked, sitting in the single armchair, curious as he followed the ball Randy tossed and caught repeatedly.

"Every sport I can. My favorite is football… or track...Never mind, I like them all, but Mom limits me to two sports a year."

"What sport are you doing now, then?" Matt asked.

"Football in the fall. Track in the spring," Randy said as the ball landed perfectly in his hand.

"Football for me, but I hurt my arm in practice," Matt said as someone in his peripheral vision entered the room. He assumed it was Jennifer's dad, with their legs spread apart and their hands in their pockets. "When I was offered a scholarship to play ball, I turned it down—"

Jennifer cleared her throat.

Shocked, in the most non-sexual way, Matt's eyes gravitated to her feet, where she wore shiny black rain boots. Oversized brown pants hung loose on her frame, and he wondered if she had her hands in the pockets to keep them from falling off. Over that, a thick orange flannel shirt. Then, finally, her hair had a non-existent part, with strands randomly sticking up.

"Jennifer?" he asked.

"Yeah," she said, but her voice came out deeper than normal.

Pretending not to notice her clothing, he approached her and held the bag out. "I bought you some sleeping pills, two different kinds. I also bought some melatonin that the pharmacist said would help. Anyway, I thought you might try valerian. It's a root herb if a root can be an herb. I'm thinking if you can enter a deep sleep, maybe the dreams will stop."

Her eyes did that weird twitch thing he recognized she did the other mornings right before she started acting normal again. As she took the bag, she said, "Thank you, Matt."

"Jennifer?" Randy's head peeked out over the top of the couch. "Are you wearing clothes from the hamper?"

Her cheeks brightened to pink as she stared down at her outfit. "Yes, I thought I would be comfortable."

"Those are Dad's clothes; Mom was giving them away. No wonder you look so stupid." He faced the television again and started screaming, "Go! Go!"

Matt caught the last few seconds as the Dallas wide receiver collapsed under the red-white-and-blue of the Giants.

Without asking, he knew she'd had another dream, and this time, it was about a guy based on how she dressed. He'd never heard of someone dreaming they were someone else to the point they woke up believing they were that person, but that didn't mean it didn't happen. He wondered if he bought her *Ride Along* tickets to the NASCAR racing experience and scared her if it would help fix the dreams—like it ended hiccups.

Jennifer tapped him on the shoulder. "Why don't you watch the game with my brother, and I'll pack up? I'll be back down in a second." She handed him the bag. "I'm afraid I'll forget them, and I'm hoping they'll help."

Taking the medicine he bought her, he took over the armchair again and watched the game with Randy.

❧

At halftime, Jennifer, his Jennifer, reappeared downstairs wearing a gray shirt and jeans, carrying the green duffel bag. She hugged each family member one last time before they set out for the long drive back to campus, avoiding the interstate. Their conversation veered back to their easy banter that he'd come to appreciate so much. After a few hours on the road, they pulled up at a little roadside diner for an early supper.

The sun was fading by the time Matt parked in front of the dorm. He glanced at a group of students playing a spirited game of hacky sack around the cherub fountain. A few people trudged down the hill on their way to the library, weighed down by heavy textbooks. Everywhere he looked, students were chatting and laughing; the college throbbed with energy.

He leaped from his truck, determined to greet her before she opened her door, so he left the engine running. But once again, she met him in front of the headlights.

He couldn't stop staring at her. Jennifer looked stunning, her beauty magnified by the shadows that surrounded her. Her long hair cascaded down just past her shoulders, and her gray shirt clung to her curves in all the right places.

"Did you put the medicine into the green meanie?"

"Green meanie?" Jennifer asked.

"Yeah, the duffle bag."

She held it up like she was inspecting it, turning it around in her hand. "Interesting name. Yes. They're in there. Thank you again."

When he smiled his mischievous grin, he tilted the right corner of his lips toward his eye. He'd practiced this move in the mirror before, using his good looks as a weapon. Gently, he shoved the duffle bag down. "You're welcome. Listen, I told your mom I would make you call her. So…call your mom."

"Thanks," Jennifer responded as she pulled her phone out of her pocket and pecked on the screen. "Done. I sent her a message that I was fine and working on homework."

Without a word, Matt closed the gap between them, his hands reaching for her waist. He deeply inhaled the inviting aroma of fresh laundry, a hint of vanilla and lavender, savoring the intoxicating scent. In his arms, she gasped in surprise. Whispering close to her ear, he said, "I'll talk to you tomorrow."

In a normal voice, she responded, "Sure, but call. I have a report on the economics of 1987. I've been procrastinating. That's how horrible this evil report is." She held up three fingers in front of his face and counted down as she talked. "Three pages, double-spaced, typed, one-sided, and something else."

"Understood. Math homework. Due Monday. I haven't even looked at it."

They stood there momentarily, lost in each other's embrace, before he pulled back and looked into her eyes. They were a deep shade of green, like the leaves of a forest in springtime.

Willing her to be under his manly powers, he tilted her chin upwards toward his mouth and licked his lips. He continued to whisper, "Hey, have a good night. I won't call until Sunday so you can study. Lauren has promised to help me with math, anyway."

Jennifer smiled. "Alright. Besides, Belinda should be back, and she might want to hear all about my Thanksgiving and how you're already ignoring me. It'll be more believable if you don't call."

He loved that about her. She joked, made him laugh, and rolled with his play on words. Witty, brilliant, beautiful, perfect…and his.

Matt laughed. "Goodnight, Jennifer." Deliberately, he leaned down and challenged her lips. The pressure he applied was initially soft but more demanding as the kiss progressed. He made every ounce of his energy count. Not only so the event was unforgettable for her, but so that those around comprehended that he now claimed her as his girl.

When he finished, he walked back to his vehicle, stepping on the truck's ledge so that his head was above the door frame, and faced her. She stood, green duffle bag dangling, watching him, her fingers rubbing her lips like they tingled.

He smiled using the full power of the look he knew made girls melt.

Screaming over the top of the engine, she said, "That was good."

"I want you to miss me," Matt said.

The cute redhead, Matt didn't know her name, passed between them. She waved at Jennifer and said, "Hey," breaking the trance.

With others observing the kiss, he knew the news would spread, as he hoped. The small college would catch fire with rumors. As he pulled the door shut, Jennifer's roommate, Belinda must have seen the kiss because he heard Belinda ask, "Was that a kiss with Matt?"

"Goodnight, Matt," Jennifer said while waving goodbye. Belinda waved, too, a grin on her face.

Then he shut the door, and he couldn't eavesdrop anymore. As he backed away and drove down the street, in the rearview mirror, Jennifer and Belinda watched.

CHAPTER 18

JENNIFER

FROM DAY ONE OF WALKING INTO THE LIBRARY, JENNIFER FOUND a favorite spot: a lime green couch on the second floor close to the computers, balcony, and tables. Sitting there among all the books, she felt studious, like just studying in the area would cause her brain to expand and suck in all the information via osmosis.

When she glanced at Matt crouched beside her, she noticed his math book opened to the same page it was turned to an hour ago. Following the trail of his eyes, she found all his attention focused on the exit sign. Unlike her, she got the impression this area bored him.

Quietly, she closed her study material. Finishing the economics paper for political science yesterday had taxed her brain, anyway, and she was ready to leave. Yet, she, the studious one, couldn't be the weak link and suggest they leave first. So, she asked, "You're not feeling the learning vibes, are you?" Her knee grazed across his leg.

Making eye contact, he said, "Not particularly. I spent all day yesterday with Lauren studying."

"Do you feel ready for the test, then?" she asked.

"Sure. I memorized the derivatives. As long as I can

remember the geometry laws and the formulas, I should do alright."

Prying and hoping, she asked, "Do you have anything else you need to study tonight? You've had the math book open for a while now. You could study something else if you can't focus on math."

Without showing concern about keeping the volume down in a library, he closed his book, which produced a rattling sound that echoed off the walls. The table to their left held two students with their heads buried in literary works. They tilted their chins upward and glared at Matt. He shrugged at them, and they returned their attention to their studies.

He said, "Nothing else tonight. I suspect if I went to a different college, no one would care about studying, and the library might be used for entertainment as well as learning."

"It's the floor we're on," she said, glancing at the condemnation still on the other's faces, even though their noses were buried in books.

That could just be their study war face. She wondered if she looked that agitated when she concentrated.

"How so?" he asked, laying his hand on her leg, ignoring their censorship.

"Well, the floor below has all the people rushing to the library desperate for answers, not the regulars. Above us is all about wanting to hang out and talk, and it has meeting rooms. Who knows what happens in those rooms since the doors lock and have blinds? The fourth-floor lighting is horrible, so all the sleepers gather there; and lastly, there is this floor, the second floor, where all the serious studiers go."

"I think I belong on the third, then. Maybe next time, we should go and check it out." He reached down and grabbed his backpack, placing the overly thick calculus book inside.

"I guess this means you're done studying for the night," she said, keeping her voice neutral despite her hope.

Instead of agreeing immediately, he leaned against the seat, his face pointing toward the ceiling, and closed his eyes. "Yes. I'm done. Did you know that this building is sinking?" he asked.

As she surveyed the nearby column, it was hard to believe, but true. According to one of her professors, when they built the foundation, they didn't consider the material of the slab underneath. As time wore away the supports, combined with the weight of the books in the building, the library sank.

"I knew, but it still surprises me. You'd think the building's designers would learn from the Leaning Tower of Pisa since the cause is the same," she said.

"How so?" he asked.

"The tower's foundation hadn't settled when they built it, and over time, the tower leaned. I guess I figured, after such a well-known and costly lesson, every architect and engineer would consider the soil and the ground before building."

"That was very nerdy of you, but you're right. They should have anticipated an issue. I understood this library was built on a limestone foundation, and the water table is high. They said something about an underground river, but I ignored that part because I'm not sure what they meant and didn't need to know. Anyway, the limestone is being eaten away. We went over it some in my engineering fundamentals class." He yawned. "Oh, they also didn't factor in the weight of the books."

Personally, she found the information interesting and an incredible exemplification of what not to do. Fundamentals of building a structure should include considering the use and where the construction project will sit, and because the same event was repeated despite past examples, some poor person would make a mistake again. She planned on it not being her.

Matt interrupted her thoughts and said, "Due to the building one day collapsing, the college plans to tear this library down, but not in our time here. Sometime in the future. They don't want the ceiling falling on top of any students."

Possibly her first job would involve the construction of the new library, since the money wouldn't be in the budget until after she graduated.

Rehashing her earlier desires to maneuver him to leave, she asked, "What made you think of that? Do you have a test on it?"

"That, my dear Jen, is an interesting question, one that takes consideration and reflection. Let's examine the theoretical math. By sitting here, I'm contributing to the problem, especially with all my brain power weighing down the nearby columns, pressing deeper into the foundation. I think we should leave and potentially grab something to eat? Plus, I'm not sure why you like this couch so much. It hurts."

Trying not to laugh at his dramatics, she placed her hand over his and intertwined their fingers. Now, she needed to secure the idea of leaving and that it was his conception. To do that, she would say something opposite to what she really wanted. She said, "I'm not accustomed to you complaining about things, Matt."

Not a strong argument, but hopefully, it would do its job.

"Hm. Perhaps I'm not made for libraries. Or rather, libraries are not made for me. I think it's all the dust in the books." He pretended to sneeze, using his free hand to cover his mouth.

Without opening his eyes, he pulled on her hand so that she fell across his chest. She squeaked in surprise. Peering around the room, several people gave her the stink eye. "Matt, they're staring at us. We should be quiet."

Keeping his eyes shut, he patted her on the head while she rested on his chest. "Poor them, but you wouldn't know that unless you looked around the room." He corrected her and said, "Stop making eye contact with them. Leave the study animals alone. They might bite. It's like feeding the lions in the zoo, not worth the risk."

The patting turned into his fingers brushing her hair, sending pleasant tingles up her spine. He said, "Oh, all this geeky talk reminds me we're relaunching Movie Monday. Will you be avoiding us again now that you're my girlfriend?"

There existed on this planet people who could relax, cram, and make straight A's, but not Jennifer. Once, last semester, she gave into Monday B-movies at Matt's. The next day, she received an eighty-six on a test—her lowest grade in college, ever. How she wanted to go and hang out, to be a normal college kid. It tugged on her like a physical weight. But her grades, her parents' expectations, her scholarship, not to mention her own desires to excel and prove herself as not another dumb blond, kept her from even considering it. A few hours of fun could kill her hard work—at least for Jennifer.

"Probably. Matt, I love monster movies as much as any college student. I just need to keep my grades up."

He leaned down and kissed her head. "You are forgiven—"

"Forgiven for?" She pushed against his chest, sitting up.

"Not going to Monster Monday night. B-movies are our opportunity to unwind, but you can make it up to me. Say you'll go camping this weekend? Just the four of us."

"Who are the other two?" she asked, curious.

"Honestly, I don't care who else goes, as long as the two of us are together, but if you must know, Lauren and Doug," he retorted.

The image of the bear falling backward, her red talon piercing its flesh, flashed before her mind. How easy the tissue parted, like playing with playdough.

She gulped.

Could she camp and enjoy it after what happened last

time? Would she believe she was a dragon again? Or would this be a positive event in her life, and she would be facing her fears, ending the dreams forever?

"You need an answer right now?" she asked.

"No, you can tell me later. In the meantime, I have plans for us Thursday," he said, then yawned.

"What plans?"

"It's a surprise. Do you think you can pull away from the library long enough to go out to dinner?" he asked.

Quickly, her mind ran through her classes, reports, test schedules, and homework that might be due. "Only dinner? So I can study first?" she asked.

"Yes, only dinner."

"Sure, I think so."

"Good. I'll pick you up on Thursday," he said.

The room grew quiet. Someone turned a page. A few seconds later, a person slammed a hardcover book on a table, and all the evil eyes turned to that poor soul. Chewing on her bottom lip, she waited for Matt to make a move toward the exit, ready to leave but listening to his heart. His breathing became deep, his pulse even, and she knew he had fallen asleep.

She needed another tactic to get him to initiate leaving. Patting his chest, she sat up. She said, "Oh, that reminds me..."

Startled, Matt jumped. His round eyes darted around the room. "Sorry, Jen, I must've dozed off." Contorting his face in pain, he rubbed his neck and said, "These couches weren't meant for sleeping."

"No, because this area is for studying. But that reminds me. The sleeping pills are working. No dreams last night. Matt, it was wonderful. Thank you."

"Am I the best boyfriend ever?" he asked, fishing.

"Yes, of course you are."

"Well, then, now that is decided, let's go grab something to eat," he said but yawned.

Sometimes getting what you wanted required action. Done talking, she picked up the book that had been in her lap the entire time and shoved it in her backpack. When she went to swing the weight onto her shoulder, Matt stopped her.

"I got it, Jen," he said, reaching his hand out. She didn't mind if he carried some of her weight—wasn't that what boyfriends were for? She handed it over.

He picked up his bag, shoving them both over one shoulder and bending slightly from the weight. "I saw a new Thai restaurant I want to try. Come on," he said, and they finally exited the library.

CHAPTER 19
JENNIFER

...I HATED THE FEEL OF HIS HANDS ON MY SKIN—GREEDY, devouring, rough. He rubbed my nipple and kneaded my breast like a baker making bread. It hurt, but I didn't let on. It was my duty as a wife.

After three years of marriage, he no longer tried to kiss me. Instead, he kept his lips pressed against the nape of my neck, his hot breath caressing my skin, stinking of venom and rot.

The moaning with the nudge on my shoulder was his way of letting me know it was time. He shoved me backward, his knee between my legs, hands continuing to massage my delicate flesh.

On the bedstead, I submitted as his wife, spreading my legs without words or movements, pretending to be a tree. I didn't enjoy it. I wouldn't lie about it, but it would end soon with me no more than sore. I bore my duty one more time, as a God-fearing woman and his wife...

Before opening her eyes, Sarah perceived something was off. The sounds of the spring winds blowing through the crevice in the logs, the chatter of the early morning birds, and even the annoying rooster that liked to sit on top of the barn every morning, were missing.

Keeping her lids shut, she used her hands to search the bed for her husband, Isaac. She recognized the faint sound of someone's rhythmic, peaceful breathing somewhere nearby but not beside her and knew the person was not him. Her Isaac sounded like a horse sneezing. Perhaps, so accustomed to him and his constant rattle, she'd woken from the silence?

Curious, she sat straight up in bed and surveyed her surroundings. The ceiling over her head was bright white, and the light in the center was just wrong.

Wait! Electricity hadn't been invented yet! Nor had the word, so how did I know what it is?

Pounding her head to cause blood to flow to her brain, she ordered her mind to think.

Last night, Isaac came in late after sunset. By then, the food had grown cold, but he consumed all of it with a ferocity that only hard labor induced. He even ate the chicken hearts, though he claimed their texture was too tough.

Thirteen years younger than him, she cowered while he dined in silence. A marriage of necessity rather than love, she'd not been his first choice. His first wife, her beloved older cousin, had died in childbirth.

While he gobbled down the greens cooked in lard, he stared ahead toward the bed. Until then, she thought for sure he'd be too tired for the marital duties, but she was wrong. No sooner had he finished than he stood and removed his pants. Knowing what he requested, she undressed and bore her duty. When he completed, she rolled to her side, only to wake here, in this room.

So how did she wind up here in this strange small, apartment?

Searching the area for clues, her hands found an impossibly soft tan covering over her. The material's texture was so complex that only angels could have woven it. It was for her best not to let Isaac see this, or he would expect a miracle, and the end product would be her struggling to create a similar cloth.

She sank into the bedstead. Soft, like being snuggled in a cloud, and not hard like normal, where sleeping reminded her of being suspended on a log. She bounced on the springy platform using her arms, noticing it wasn't a stiff frame. Across from her, on the other wall, she located another bedstead with someone sound asleep, dancing with the prince of dreams.

Located alongside her was a nightstand made of sideways milk cartons turned into a makeshift bookcase. On the other side of the bed, books littered the floor in almost an organized pattern. Further toward the window was a small sitting area. Two closets and a nightstand flanked the bed across from her.

The items in the room should've seemed foreign, yet she sensed their names. A television on a coffee table in front of a small couch had a green blinking light in the lower right corner. A small refrigerator in the furthest crook from the door, she knew, held drinks. On the milk carton nightstand beside her sat a cell phone.

I know all the names. I know all their uses. But they aren't right for my time.

Picking up the electronic device, she pushed the side button. The screen unlocked, revealing a forest background, the time, and the name Jennifer Wright.

Awareness of the passcode, 0705, a reference to this Jennifer Wright person's birthday, arrived without being requested, and she pressed the numbers, feeling the surface's cool, smooth texture.

A message from a Matt surfaced, and with it, more knowledge that told her to pull down the screen and click. Sarah opened the text. She read what appeared to be him telling her he missed her. She pushed the button, closing the device.

How do I know how to read? I've never been taught.

She knew she'd find clothes and stuff needed for a shower in the closet. Floors should be cold, so she ran, expecting the chill to seep up. It wasn't there. She stopped halfway—the floor, the room, all warm. The typical drafty air was missing, so she tiptoed to keep from waking the sleeping woman.

How do I know that's a girl?

She grabbed a basket of things that said liquid soap and shampoo, understanding what they were for without knowing why. She left the room with her shiny pink phone watch and an oversized towel and had no issue locating the bathroom.

After placing her things on a ledge, she entered the stall, removing her clothing to use the unique outhouse seat that wasn't a privy at all but a toilet.

When she sat on the cold porcelain, she reflected on her size. How odd it was to feel tall when, only yesterday, she barely came up to anyone's shoulders. The hips people called great for birthing, making her a desirable mate, were now narrow, with defined athletic muscles.

Did any man find this skinny body attractive?

The apple-sized breasts seemed so small, she could cup one of them with one hand. Sarah's ample bosom was her prized possession; the one thing Isaac said was the loveliest he'd ever seen—prettier than his first wife's. Probably the only thing other than her hips that he liked about her. With these tiny things barely fit for grabbing, let alone nursing a child, how would anyone find her fetching now?

Exactly—how would Isaac find me fetching now!

As the thought occurred, she smiled and grabbed a few tissues from the side. Standing, she went to the sink. How would Isaac find her captivating now, indeed? This might mean at night, she could sleep instead of fulfilling her marital duties.

As she washed her hands, she inspected her face in the

mirror. Hair once called mud brown by her brother and fall leaves by a family friend now rolled softly down her shoulder in soft golden waves. Brilliant green replaced her sky-blue eyes.

That was when the knowledge poured into her. Touching the skin, she said, "I'm not Sarah. I'm Jennifer Wright."

The door opened, and Amy, the redheaded freshman from Michigan, entered the room. The girl stopped in the frame, blocking the door from closing, and she took in Jennifer's countenance. Jennifer left her finger on her cheek and could only imagine the crazy impression that she displayed.

Smaller than her with creamy white skin dotted with freckles, Amy tilted her head. She smiled brightly. "Are you okay? You seem lost."

"I'm fine," Jennifer answered. Her arm dropped to her side, and she returned to staring at her image.

Amy walked into the stall Jennifer just used and sighed. "I hate it when people don't flush. I swear, sometimes girls are nastier than boys." She kicked the knob on the side with her foot, and the toilet gurgled before she closed the stall door.

Ignoring the other girl, she focused on recollecting her life. All the important events in Jennifer's life were there on the edge, ready to recall, but last night evaded her. Something urgent would happen soon, and she had to prepare. On instinct, she grabbed the things she needed to shower and went to the small closets with the valves and the shower head.

"The toilet causes the cold water to run for a few short seconds," she said to herself as she turned the knob and waited for the temperature to heat up.

An image of sitting in a room with other students behind a desk in an uncomfortable chair came to mind as she undressed and tossed her pajamas to the side. Jennifer had class soon.

While waiting for the water to adjust, she considered the

difference between Jennifer's and Sarah's views. Their opinions were so individualized she could use the dissimilarities to ground herself back in realness.

Last night, Jennifer understood the logic behind the forced wedding. Sarah traded for a horse to Isaac made perfect sense. Sarah sacrificed her dreams and desires for righteousness, to obtain a more enlightened position in heaven.

How could she, Jennifer, a modern woman, understand the mentality of obtaining one's self-worth and purpose from being a homemaker to a man she disliked? Sarah agreed with society treating her as a breeder, seeing it as a righteous sacrifice, but Jennifer despised it. Chills of disgust, not from standing naked in the cold, ran up Jennifer's arms.

Jennifer's parents told her to learn from every life event. What could this dream teach Jennifer—if her dreams were a product of her mind, meant to guide her on a more enlightened path? Perhaps empathy for people who didn't believe like she did?

The rattle of the pipes announced Amy finishing, and she counted to five before testing the water. The temperature was hot but not scorching. She stepped inside and let her shoulders relax under the pouring stream.

She closed her eyes and remembered her schedule for the day. Classes ran from nine a.m. until five, with only a small break for lunch. Unfortunately, by the time freshmen registered for classes, the upperclassman claimed all the good slots, and she conformed her schedule to accept the unwanted openings. This meant four of her five lectures were on Monday, Wednesday, and Friday.

Grabbing some shampoo, she thought, *I should learn from this dream to bear what I can't control and be thankful for the things in my life.*

As she lathered her hair, she inhaled the fresh scent of vanilla. *I am thankful for good-smelling shampoo.*

When she finished and slid on her watch, she saw the time

was just seven-thirty. She had time to pack, dress, and contemplate. *I am thankful I have time to prepare for the day.*

Wearing only the towel, she returned to the room, using an app on the watch to unlock the door. An ironic thought occurred to her. The school could afford to update the door mechanisms but not the piping system?

A mild scent of rose wafted from her dorm room. Smiling, Jennifer remembered that her roommate, Belinda, loved the perfume. Staring at the other bed, Belinda's blond hair, in a tangled mess, covered her face. Steady, even breathing indicated she slept peacefully. Jennifer did her best to dress quietly.

I am thankful for a roommate I like.

Sitting on her bed, she still had thirty minutes before she needed to leave for class. She picked up her phone and stared at the name Matt. Unlike everything else, his image seemed harder to grasp. Which didn't make sense. She recalled her class schedule, her roommate, her family—but not Matt. The text messages called him her boyfriend.

If he was so important to her, why couldn't she remember him?

"What's wrong?" Belinda asked, throwing off her blankets and sitting up, stretching like a cat. Her long blond hair, close to Jennifer's in color, coated her face, and Belinda moved it behind her ear.

"I'm struggling to remember what I did yesterday," she confessed.

Belinda exhaled sharply. "You did nothing. You never do anything. I went to a party, and you stayed here. Oh, wait." She picked up an orange toothbrush she kept in a cup by her bed and placed it in her mouth. Mumbling, she said, "You met Matt in the library and studied. Did you know there was a release party at the Pi house?"

The words brought up images of a bakery with different cream and fruit-filled desserts.

"What's a pie house? A release party?" she asked.

She took the toothbrush out of her mouth. "Okay, Jennifer, stop messing around. The fraternity house on the corner near the art building? You remember, the blue house you called a Victorian classic, and you were surprised the university let them use it. It just looked creepy to me—like the kind from horror movies."

She vaguely remembered a building resembling the Berryhill House, a Victorian built in 1884. Why she remembered the name of the building, she couldn't recall, but perhaps it was because her father loved to take her on tours of old architecture, and that was one of his favorites.

Belinda grabbed a basket off the floor that held her shower items. "Whenever someone joins the Pi house, they must list their top three favorite bands. Whenever the band comes out with a new song, a concert date, or video, the Pi's celebrate by hosting a lit party."

Belinda opened the door with one hand, balancing her shower supplies in the other. She said, "You remember? We went to one at the beginning of the school year a few months ago."

"Oh," Jennifer answered, sounding doubtful because she didn't remember.

"Matt missed that to be with you. I've never seen him skip out of a party, and he did that to spend time with you at the library."

The door closed behind Belinda, leaving Jennifer staring at her phone again.

On the counter, a white bottle with a blue label caught her attention. Vaguely, she recalled a tall, dark-haired, handsome man handing her a bag with pill bottles inside.

"Oh," she said a little more enthusiastically. "Matt!"

Grabbing the bottle off the nightstand, she read the label and realized why she remembered nothing. "Oh," she said again, sounding downcast. After she placed the pills back down, she smacked her head. "How could I forget to take a sleeping pill!"

Then, recalling the lesson from her dream—*I am thankful for a boyfriend who thinks of my needs.*

CHAPTER 20

MATT

A SMILING MATT PATTED THE BROWN BAG FILLED WITH FRIED chicken and fries Tuesday morning. In the cup holder, a large sweet tea waited as well. Parked in the student lot behind Jennifer's dorm, he pressed send on his phone and casually observed students run in and out of the nearby buildings.

"Hello," Jennifer said, sounding groggy.

"My lovely Jennifer, do you know who you didn't call yesterday?"

"Matt," she said, but like it was a question.

He answered as if it was an acknowledgment. "The one and only. How are you?"

"Sorry for not calling. I had a—"

"Listen, you missed Monster Monday."

"I wasn't planning on being there. You know that," she said defensively.

"Why does it sound like I woke you up?"

"It's the sleeping pills. I'm having a hard time waking up."

"But no dreams of bears?" he wondered.

She laughed like he hoped she would. "No dreams of bears."

"Why don't you make up for yesterday? Listen, we could go out to eat right now, just the two of us."

"Matt, I have class this afternoon."

He knew this. Jennifer's next lecture started at twelve-fifteen. She didn't have time to visit a restaurant. Thus, he purchased food that waited for her in a brown bag that sat on the passenger seat.

"Well, then, how about I meet you at the cafeteria?" For this, he planned to go if she wanted. He'd throw the food away if she said yes.

"What time is it? I refuse to open my eyes," she asked.

"I take it that the current time determines whether we go out to eat?" he asked.

"Yes."

"You know, you should skip class every now and then. It's only healthy."

"I want straight A's, Matt. Lofty goals require work. Plus, my scholarship."

"Well, when you put it that way. It's eleven thirty-five."

"I'm late," she said, which wasn't exactly true. She had a few minutes. Enough time to grab a shower and whatever else girls did. The noise in the background changed, and he recognized her moving around in her apartment. He imagined her grabbing clothes and shower stuff.

"I tell you what, I'll meet you out back with some food, you get ready, and I'll drive you to class. What do you say?" he asked. If she said no, he could eat the chicken himself. It's why he picked something he thought they both would like.

"Thank you! I'll take you up on that offer! How long before you can get here?" she asked.

"Don't worry about that. I'll be here whenever you are ready," he said and leaned back against the seat.

"Thank you again, Matt. Be right down!"

The phone went quiet, and he took to watching the different individuals moving in and out of her dorm through the back basement exit. Across the street, he barely made out the English building. With so many students going back and forth at this hour, the door remained perpetually open. He pondered how much it must cost to heat the structure.

Then, a red Lamborghini Huracán pulled into the parking lot. Like all the other heads outside, his followed the car until it parked.

Should I count myself lucky to have seen so many rare vehicles in less than a month? he wondered.

The car doors were zipper-style, opening upward, and a tall, lanky blond man stepped out. He wore sunglasses, like the kind seen in movies with jets. In his hand, a cigarette burned as smoke poured from the tip.

"No! You've got to be kidding me! Smoking in a car like that?" Matt yelled, hitting the steering wheel, missing the sides, and slamming the horn. The man glanced at him. Finding nothing of interest, the stranger returned his attention to the dorm.

A girl with long brown hair and a barely-there miniskirt moved to stand in front of him. Pressing her body into his, she whispered something in his ear. He wrapped his free arm around her, and, after nibbling on her neck, said something back. She didn't appear to like his comment, and she slapped him before storming off in the opposite direction.

The man, however, ignored the slap and focused once again on the door, edging closer to it while he took drags off the cigarette.

How could one man be so lucky, with cute girls throwing themselves at him, and he drives Italian perfection? His parents must be rich!

As Matt watched, the blond man stopped in his tracks, intently focusing on someone. Matt followed his gaze to find Jennifer.

Did Jennifer know this man?

Sure enough, as she walked, he continued to ogle her.

Opening the car door, Jennifer leaned over and kissed Matt's cheek. "What, no kiss on the lips? You didn't even bother to turn toward me when I got in," she said, throwing her bookbag on the floor, grabbing the food, and buckling up.

"Do you know that guy?" Matt pointed under the car dash, so only Jennifer saw where he indicated. She looked for a second, not seeing anything fascinating, and focused on opening the brown bag—more interested in the food than the guy watching her.

"I don't see anyone I know, Matt. Let's go before I'm late!" Grabbing a chicken leg, she smiled.

He gave one last glance at the man and then drove off.

A fry in her other hand, she flopped it in the air using it as a pointer, and she said, "Do you know where you're going?"

Smiling, he snatched the fry from her fingers and turned left onto the street. "Art building. I know your schedule, Jennifer." He placed the stolen fry in his mouth, delighted to find they were still warm.

"Really? You know my classes?" she asked, her eyes wide in surprise.

"Yes. Your food is going to get cold," he answered, quickly glancing at the brown bag.

"Stalker boyfriend," she said, grabbing a fist full of fries and downing them. "You should have known then why I didn't call on Monday. By the end of the day, I'm tired. Sorry."

"It's fine, Jennifer."

And it was. One of the lessons his parents taught him, made sure he knew, was to accept and expect everyone to have their own mind and goals. Yesterday, he spent time reflecting on Jennifer's ambitions, and he found himself admiring Jennifer's drive and determination. It took him time to devise how to encourage her, but he hoped the ride, fries, and drink helped.

It's the small things that show someone they are important, his gung-gung always said.

He still thought she should take a day off to recharge, but getting her to relax might take more coaxing.

The overcast sky gave way to a deluge. He turned on the blinker and the windshield wipers, causing water droplets to flop off the window. Taking the next right street, he passed the art building. Jennifer said nothing about not stopping at her classroom, so he glanced at her. She had the drumstick in her mouth, gnawing on it.

"Wait to get out. I'm going to pull in front of the sculpture." He performed a U-turn on the road when he knew it was clear. After gliding the car to the fire lane, he turned the emergency blinkers on.

With the drink in her hand, she held it up toward him. "I take it this is for me as well?"

"Sweet tea, just like you like," he said, then smiled.

After she took a sip, she said, "Like I said, stalker boyfriend."

"Stalker boyfriend who brought you food. I call that more of an attentive boyfriend."

"That too, and I was so hungry I would have eaten whatever you brought." She put the trash in the bag and on the floor.

"You don't like fried chicken?" Matt asked.

"I love fried chicken. I was just hungry enough to eat anything." She smiled.

He placed his hand on her leg. "You're early. Wait for a second. Do you remember me mentioning this weekend? Well, it's official. Doug and Lauren are going camping this weekend and have invited us to go. Would you like to join them?"

A grin crossed her lips, and she patted his leg in an almost patronizing way. "No, not really, but if you want to go, that's okay. The way this week is going, I'll have a test in at least two subjects next week." She sighed. "Scholarship, parents, ugh. I could use the time to study. If I finish early, maybe I can go see a movie with Belinda."

Squeezing her leg, he respected her determination but had concern for her constant single focus. She needed to rest and take breaks to refill her mind with things other than classes and books. "I would prefer if you went, but I can understand if you don't want to."

"It's supposed to rain this weekend; wet, camping—not my thing."

Rain, camping in the soaked leaves, to be honest, wasn't what Matt had in mind either. "Put it like that, and I'm not sure if I want to go."

She sighed, placing her hand over his. "I don't want to be one of those couples who have to be together every second of the day."

He laughed. "You proved that last night by not calling." Then, more seriously, he added, "Yeah, I don't, either." But he'd like to spend the weekend with her. He could ask her to go to the movies. They were going out on Thursday, for sure. She'd already said yes.

"Good. You go camping in the cold rain, and I'll stay here and do girly things." She peeked at her nails. "I haven't had a mani-pedi in a few months."

Changing the subject, Matt leaned forward to view the top of the iron sculpture that resembled a teardrop. "What is this supposed to be?" he asked.

"I'm not sure. Victory over life, I believe," she answered.

"Would you consider going to a movie this weekend? Don't answer now. I just, well, I'd like to do something with you. Plus, wet socks are my personal limit. I already told Doug I'd go, but I don't think he'll want to go either if the weather is bad."

"Sure, Matt. I don't need time to think. We can go to a movie. I'm sure I can slide in a few hours for you. Speaking of hours, when do you study? With Monster Monday, camping with Doug, visits to the Pi house, I'm not sure how you have time."

So far, he understood all the concepts and didn't need to spend hours studying other than the day he spent on calculus. Eventually, near the end of his college track, he'd have to press into his schoolwork, but that was another day. And the main reason Matt liked engineering was that he could have a great paying job in four years without a masters. He didn't need above-average grades; a B-average would do.

Gently, he brushed a few strands of hair away from her face, leaned over, and kissed her lips. Backing away, he said, "Some of us study, some of us are born that smart…Go make an A, my go-getter."

"Thank you for lunch." She smiled brightly at Matt as she grabbed her books, and his heart did a little flip.

After she closed the truck door, she avoided the drain, stepped over the curb, and ran until she was under the building's ledge. He rolled down the window. "I'll talk to you later," he yelled over the racket of the droplets pounding the ground.

"Thank you, Matt," she said, blew a kiss, and opened the building's door.

As Jennifer entered the building, he was about to roll up the window, but another girl with Jennifer said, "Who was that?"

"Matt, my boyfriend," Jennifer answered.

Though Matt couldn't make out her face, he saw the other girl had a nice figure dressed in a cute skirt and jacket. She twirled her curly red hair on her finger as she said, "He's dreamy."

When the door shut, Matt rolled up his window, smiling. He planted his little seed of support for Jennifer…and it felt great!

CHAPTER 21
JENNIFER

"Is that a fashion book?" Matt's whisper on her neck caused chills to run down her spine.

Startled, Jennifer glanced over her shoulder at him. His face was close to hers, so she pecked his forehead. Shutting the book, she leaned back on the green couch to face him, smiling.

"It is. It very much is a fashion book," she said. Standing, she moved to the tan table near the couch, where she piled her research high.

Tonight, the library sat close to empty. So, she didn't worry about making noise as she placed the encyclopedia down on the table and yawned. "I know I should be studying. Did you know Queen Elizabeth loved sugar, and her teeth were disgusting?"

Matt offered Jennifer his hand and pulled her into his arms. She latched onto him and sank into the embrace.

Next to her ear, he said, "No, Jen, I didn't know, but I'm glad to see you somewhat taking a break." He squeezed, released, and then sat on the couch.

"'Tis true. It started a black teeth fashion trend. The villagers would dye their teeth black. I wonder if they used coal all over their mouths? Oddly, to dye your teeth black was a trend in Japan, too. I wonder what dentists today would think about it?" Tired, she yawned again and stretched, then plopped down on the couch beside him.

Matt snickered. "Some dentists would like the increased income."

"I think dentists would have been horrified."

"Wasn't Elizabeth single?"

Jennifer thought about what she'd learned in history. "I think so."

"Yes. She was the virgin queen." He smiled smugly.

Normally, she put away any research materials, but not tonight—the library interns could do it. Standing again, she grabbed her books and placed them into her bookbag. "So, where are you taking me tonight?"

"Oh…First, we are going out to eat."

At just the mention of food, Jennifer's stomach growled. "And where are we eating?" The morning started with an excruciating headache. Now that all that had passed, she was famished.

"It's a surprise," he said as she zipped up her bookbag.

"Honestly, it's a surprise you're here alone. Where's Colin or Doug?" she asked, searching the area for a date ambush.

"Just me. It's a special night," he whispered despite it not being crowded as he ran his finger up her arm.

"A special night?" she asked, but she didn't hear his response. Instead, she ignored the feather-light touches and stared beyond him, past the surrounding bookcases, and out the window. It was already dark outside, even though it was only six-thirty. The change in her vision was the oddest of her more recent adaptations to her senses. As she sat inside and glanced out, she could see darkness. It appeared like it did her whole life, a shadow. Yet she knew the exterior would become visible the second she left the building, like she put on night vision goggles. If she stood outside, the area would be as bright as it would be in the day.

That was how Matt found her reading a fashion book. The search started with publications on optometry. Lots of fancy words and confusing documentation forced her to hunt for some simple version of CliffsNotes or SparkNotes. Even a Google pursuit led her nowhere close to an answer. She hoped she could find a keyword to use in a search engine by scouring the library.

Well, she fell down a rabbit hole that ended with her reading about Queen Elizabeth and sugar-blackened teeth.

"Earth to Jennifer," Matt said, waving his hands in front of her face.

Blinking a few times, she said, "Sorry, Matt. I haven't eaten all day."

"Wait, the holder of the ultimate burger challenge, The Barney, hasn't eaten today?" He stood and grabbed her book bag, slinging it over his shoulder. Then he offered her his hand.

"Yeah. I also missed my first college course today. I couldn't even get out of bed long enough to write a text message or email my professor before the lecture started."

He placed his hand on the small of her back and guided her toward the staircase. That was something they had in common. They both preferred the manual option over the elevator.

"You're already feather-light. We better remedy this problem right away, but as far as class, don't worry about it. It's for a gen ed, right?"

"I hate that you know my schedule better than I do." She frowned, then said, "Or maybe I love that you're my stalker boyfriend. You have a way of minimalizing my experience."

"Hmm, I'm not sure that's a good thing."

"It is. A very good thing. I love that you're so chill. It helps me focus on the important things. Yet there is a part of you that just knows me and what I should be doing. Thank you."

"Well, I guess, but I'm not chill at all. For starters, I'm upset that you were sick. Start spilling the story. I need to know what happened."

"Nothing now. I had a headache and felt dizzy and nauseous. Every time I tried to crawl out of bed, the room spun. Luckily, Belinda was still there, and she brought me the trashcan. I've only been well enough to get out of bed for the last few hours."

She was fortunate that Belinda had still been at the dorm. If it wasn't for Belinda, Jennifer would have had to crawl to the common bathroom. Next year, she'd consider getting an apartment, like Matt, and get away from sharing.

The library glass wall exit loomed in front of them. As they left the building, the experience enthralled her as she watched the outdoors go from dark, moonless night to bright, like with a sun, yet no sun.

"Jen?" Matt asked.

"Sorry. What did you ask?"

"Was it a return of the strange sickness?" he asked as he directed them around the corner toward the closest parking lot.

"No. According to Belinda, it was a reaction to the sleeping pills. It seemed reasonable since the world spun for a few hours after I woke up. Suddenly, two hours ago, all the dizziness just disappeared. Belinda said her aunt had trouble sleeping when she went through a divorce and took the same pills. Even though her aunt had a similar reaction, she refused to stop taking them. It ended with her in the hospital. I checked the labels, and the other brand you bought me uses a different active ingredient. I'm going to switch over to those tonight."

"Sounds reasonable. I wonder if you went to a psychologist or a medical doctor if they could help you."

That thought occurred to her earlier tonight. "If the new pills don't work, I can make an appointment over the winter holiday."

Abruptly, he stuck his hand in front of her and shouted, "Stop!"

Frozen in place, she waited while Matt opened the passenger side door. "Please, my beautiful, amazing, nerdy girlfriend, your chariot awaits." He stood there with a big, wonderful, toothy grin. As she placed her foot on the ledge of the truck, he wrapped his arms around her waist and hoisted her into the cab.

"Put your seat belt on," he said seconds before shutting her door.

After he made it to his side, he tossed her bookbag behind their seats. Jennifer followed her stuff as it landed on a bunch of suspicious-looking blankets. "So, Matt, what are our plans tonight?"

"I told you, it's a surprise," he said, then grinned, placing the truck into drive.

"So, is this like one of those official dates? Or are we picking up someone to go with us?"

"Jennifer," he said, mimicking surprise. "Are you saying I like to spend our dates with other people?"

"Matt, we've been dating for a while and have yet to have a date by ourselves."

"Point," Matt agreed as he pulled out of the garage and onto the street. "Though, I must remind you, you've slept in my bed with me. We were mainly alone then."

"Now you're making me sound cheap. Like I'm easy," Jennifer joked.

"I wish." Matt squeezed her leg. "On both accounts. Cheap and easy would be my kind of date."

"Ha-ha." Changing the subject, she said, "So now Colin is showing up?"

"Nope, just us."

Matt removed his hand, placing it on the steering wheel as he pulled into a Japanese steakhouse parking lot.

The last time she ate at this restaurant, her meal cost as much as three at any other eatery. She said, "Oh, wow. I can't eat here on my student budget. Are you paying?"

"Well, it's a special day, so yes, I'm paying," Matt said.

Special day? Searching her memories, she couldn't think of anything to celebrate. Glancing at him for a clue to what was so special about today, she asked, "What day is it?" Was she expected to buy him a gift?

"Our first official date was a month ago today." Matt seemed to sit up taller. "It's our monthiversary."

"Um, our first date was when we went to the track with a group so they could drink every time they made a loop until they passed out. Whose idea was that anyway, drunk track running? I thought our first date was at the coffee shop."

Matt huffed as he parked the vehicle. "No, that wasn't what I was referring to. After Thanksgiving, I got to thinking about when we did have our first date. The coffee shop doesn't count. It was special, for sure, but every day I'm with you is special."

As he exited the truck, Jennifer felt her cheeks warm at his words and waited for him. When he opened her door, he continued, "It was the week before the coffee shop and right after the drunk running. Remember, we stayed up talking after we grabbed ice cream. We used your—"

"My honors key and went to the walking track in the basement. I felt guilty for eating so many sweets and wanted to run it off. We stayed up all night at the track, just talking. The next day, we took quick showers and met up outside. We nap-studied until the football game. That was our first date?"

"Yes, just you and me, alone," he said.

"Colin was there," she reminded him.

"He was asleep…I held your hand the first time the next night at the—"

"Yeah, the football game. We lost horribly."

"I didn't. I found you. Well over twenty-four hours together, mainly alone…at least, our friends came and went. That's the night we started planning all our free time together," he said.

Technically, she'd been planning her free time around Matt for longer than that. "Alright, I accept that as our first date. We were alone, we were talking. Agreed. But whose idea was the drunk running? You guys looked like absolute idiots."

"It was Colin's."

"Colin has some of the dumbest ideas," Jennifer mentioned. "I believe he was with us when we got that ice cream." She took Matt's hand as he led her into the restaurant.

"Need I remind you, so was Belinda," Matt answered. "Hey, are they still dating? I forgot to ask Colin."

At this, she laughed, walking under Matt's arm as he held open the door. The weird sight thing happened when she entered, except it wasn't dramatic because of the restaurant's low illumination. She recognized the attempt to create a romantic atmosphere with soft lighting levels, but it was lost on her. The room appeared as clear as a school cafeteria with fluorescent lights. Turning, she stared out a nearby window. The luminescence almost balanced with the outside, making it seem like the dawn, without the oranges and pinks.

Continuing the conversation, she said, "Belinda and Colin are both like candles. Passion lights easy, but they die out when a lid is placed on top. They don't do well in long term relationships. Not soon after they start a relationship with one person, they burn out and go on to the next. I believe she's dating someone at the Pi house, and Colin is dating a waitress or something like that. I can't keep track with how fast they move onto someone else."

He wrapped his arm around her shoulders as he sighed.

"And that is why we are celebrating tonight. Our friend group seems to not make it a full month with just one person. After we finish dinner, I have another surprise, all to celebrate our relationship. Maybe we can be an example for Colin and Belinda?"

"Maybe, Matt Davis, maybe, but I have to ask, was I expected to get you a gift?"

"No, of course not."

A cute auburn-haired girl waited behind a pedestal. "How many?" she asked.

"Just two," Matt answered.

"Follow me," the hostess said and sat them facing the back wall, close to the entrance.

When she left, Jennifer leaned over. "I think we need to establish rules. I don't want to wake up and discover I've missed a monthiversary."

"I tell you what, Jen..." He breathed on her fine hair and nibbled on her ear but didn't immediately finish what he was saying. Too embarrassed to even glance around the room to see who might have viewed such a public display of affection, she glanced at the table.

When he finished kissing her neck, he said, "Next month is yours. You can have the even, and I'll take the odd. Let's just start there. We can make it a game and try to outdo one another. What do you say?"

She scooted in her chair to face Matt. "You are on, and I will win next month, no matter what you have planned tonight."

CHAPTER 22

PETR

STEPPING INTO THE CLOSEST RESTAURANT NEAR CAMPUS, PETR shivered. Though the temperature in the area had dropped a few degrees, it wasn't the cold weather he was reacting to. All day long, no matter where he went, he felt eyes on his back. Glancing behind him, he hunted for someone following him.

Nothing.

At this late hour, he expected the dim lighting to encourage a romantic atmosphere for the guests, so he requested to be moved to the sushi bar area to the right. Not only to allow him an advantage should someone decide spying on him wasn't enough, but the quiet room also allowed him to focus on grading. Though he wished it were brighter. It would still be better than the stove islands where they made the food in front of you.

The hostess sat him near the bar at a four-chair table. Before moving the plate out of the way, he checked the cleanliness of the surface, ensuring he didn't ruin the papers when he placed them on top. The wood counter, protected by a thick plastic, had a dragon pattern prancing around the outside. He laughed at the humor of it—he a guardian of dragons, eating at a table with their likeness painted for decoration.

Clean enough, he cleared a spot to make room for the papers.

When a new server returned with water, he barely glanced at them before ordering number three—the grilled chicken hibachi—and a sweet tea.

The first paper on his stack discussed the linguistics of subcultures in the South. He raised his eyebrow, wondering how on earth a student in a general education course decided this would be a good topic. Interesting, yes, but the level of effort, in his opinion, was torturous. All he wanted was something the students found fascinating, not a dissertation.

Personally, he found linguistics engaging and sometimes challenging to mimic. It took him years to sound like he came from the United States. Yet occasionally, he met someone who heard his accent, including the sharp-witted Jennifer.

A shadow crossed in front of his notes. As Petr glanced up, the person sat at his table in the chair across from him.

Petr recognized the man from the diner in Cherryville. Like before, he wore a thick bike-riding jacket, T-shirt, and jeans. On his face, he had pale blond stubble, blue eyes, wrinkles on his forehead, and his skin appeared chapped. The man reminded him of an irate lumberjack.

"Dr. Smith," the man said, bringing his hands up to rest on the table. His knuckles stood out as dry and cracked from the winter winds or from fighting—Petr couldn't tell.

"You know my name. What can I call you?" Petr asked, hoping the man said the White Jaguar, but not wanting to give anything away if this was an Immortal.

"You can call me Thjasse," he said, lowering his voice and glancing around the area.

The reference to an old Norse myth surprised Petr, who fought the urge to huff. *Like anyone would know the story of the eagle that tried to steal Asgard's youth and beauty.* Then, another thought occurred to Petr. *In a way, I have eaten the apples of eternal youth when I ate a dragon's heart; and apparently, so has the one calling himself Thjasse.*

"How can I help you, Thjasse?" Petr asked, drawing Thjasse's attention back to him.

"Mm," Thjasse said, pulling the fork out of the rolled-up napkin and stabbing the dragon design on the table mat. "Who do you answer to?"

Shaking his head, Petr responded, "I don't understand. Do you mean my religion?"

Thjasse jabbed the dragon once more, his fork screeching across the table's surface. "That answers my question. You're too scrawny to know how to fight, so I will give you a few days to leave. The dragon at South Holt University belongs to us. I don't care if you must quit your job and lose money. If you don't leave, I will kill you." Standing, he laid the fork back on the table.

"Good day, Dr. Smith." As he left, he walked with the dexterity of someone ready to brawl. The front door banged shut when he exited the building.

Petr breathed out. Somewhere on campus, a young dragon shifter needed help. But at this time, without knowing who the person might be, Petr couldn't offer safety. Perhaps tomorrow, he could get someone in the security department to help him search the cameras for the person Thjasse was stalking.

What I wouldn't give for a Nose right now!

With nothing more he could do, he pushed the encounter out of his mind. This wasn't the first person who thought they could take Petr in an unfair fight; it wouldn't be the last. He returned to grading papers.

Behind the sushi bar, a faux wall of hanging dividers separated the lit area from one of the grills. He wasn't sure what caused him to look up. Perhaps his brain registered Matt's or

Jennifer's voice. There they were, backs to him, watching the chef's display of culinary theatrics.

Unabashed, Petr stared. Never had he seen them this lovey-dovey. Their chairs pushed close together. Jennifer leaned over and whispered something in Matt's ear. Despite dragon hearing, he couldn't make out her words over the background of the fire volcano as the chef scooted it along the metal, choo-chooing as the onion pile moved.

Thjasse's presence at two of the places he found Matt and Jennifer could mean Jennifer was the dragon shifter.

There was just enough gap between the two of them that he watched as whatever she said inspired Matt to place his hand on her thigh before he nipped her neck. Matt's shoulder touching hers moved, and Petr imagined Matt rubbing his fingers up and down her leg. Matt said something. Over the background noise, Petr distinguished the distinct chorus of her joyous laughter.

Unprovoked, several conflicting emotions joined. Petr wanted to protect, throw up, leave, or rip Matt's head off.

He recognized the cause of the emotion. *Why am I jealous of Matt?*

The person bringing out his meal raised their eyebrows in surprise and hastily sat the food and drink in one of the empty spots before abruptly departing. Apparently, the overpowering emotion emanated from Petr in waves.

Come on, Petr, you glared at the poor boy! He predicted you wanted to pull off his head.

Sighing, Petr exhaled all the tension and squeezed the jealousy back inside.

Why does this mortal girl bring out such a strong passion?

He breathed out again, releasing more of the anxiety. Perhaps she reminded him of something missing, something he never honestly had, or maybe sitting alone at a restaurant inspired his strange behavior.

The hand on her leg moved away, and Matt picked up his

fork. A vice grip Petr didn't realize had been there lifted off his chest, making breathing easier.

Returning his attention to the table, Petr placed all the school papers back in his briefcase and took a sip of tea.

Excitement built in his chest. *Did this mean that Jennifer was the dragon? Think, Petr, is there a clue?*

First, he surveyed what Matt wore. A simple black golf shirt, jeans, and running shoes. The chair's legs had a midway support, and Matt rested his heels on the ledges. His right leg bounced as if from nerves. From the angle, he couldn't make out facial features, but from the back, his hair appeared combed—nothing to suggest poor sleeping habits.

Unfortunately, staring at Jennifer's posture became more sensual, like he undressed her with his eyes. No one saw him; it was only her back, so he continued his observation. Her golden blond hair reflected the dim lighting like spun gold. Typically, she wore it naturally, with a slight wave. Tonight, it hung straight. So, she took time to fix her locks before arriving. That, combined with the green sweater and knee-high boots over her jeans, made him suspicious this outing meant more than the other two times he accidentally bumped into them.

She placed her hand on Matt's wrist. It dawned on Petr—they were on a date, a proper date.

That thought forced the breath out of his lungs, and he drank in the air to recover.

Great, more illogical, destructive emotions to suppress, he thought to himself.

Right then, he didn't notice any indication of a mental breakdown in either of them.

A waitress came over to him, disrupting his thoughts. Not wanting a repeat of the earlier server, he forced himself to smile.

"Sir, it doesn't look like you've eaten any of your meal. Is everything all right?" she asked.

Steam rose from the fried rice. He didn't perceive when they brought the untouched salad with ginger dressing and the soup. Despite how ravenous he was when he entered the building, he'd lost his appetite.

The woman stared at him, waiting for an answer.

He grabbed his fork, acting like he was ready to consume his meal. He said, "Everything is fine, thank you."

An idea struck him as she walked away. "Ma'am," he said, then searched past the divider to see if Jennifer or Matt had turned around. Neither seemed to notice him.

The waitress returned. "How may I help you?" she asked.

"Would you please bring me some containers, chopsticks, and a drink cup? Oh, and the bill, please. I'm going to take this home to eat."

"Yes, sir. I'll be right back." She left the area, and Petr resumed observing the couple. The chef had cleaned the space and exited. The restaurant noise settled to a low roar. Matt said something. He made out the word 'surprise' and caught the way Jennifer latched onto his hand. It appeared to Petr there was a race as to who would depart first.

The waitress returned with his to-go boxes, a bag, and the receipt. Before she had time to leave the table, he handed her his credit card. While keeping one eye on Matt and Jennifer, he loaded up his food.

When the slip of paper he needed to sign arrived, he had his meal packed and ready to go. His heart raced in his chest, and he glanced up. Matt had a credit card in hand, handing it to the poor boy Petr had scared earlier.

Quickly, Petr signed his name for this century and left a generous tip. Grabbing his to-go bag, he headed toward the door.

"Sir," the hostess said as he had his hand on the doorknob.

Before answering, he turned and surveyed the room but didn't see Jennifer or Matt.

"Yes," he replied, trying to sound calm.

She handed him his briefcase. He'd forgotten something again! "Thank you," he said, leaving the building.

Enough time hadn't passed for the food's odor to permeate the car's interior when the two came out hand-in-hand. Petr shot daggers at Matt. Like a gentleman, Matt opened the door for Jennifer and offered his hand so she could step into his vehicle.

A motorcycle lined up behind them as Matt pulled out of the parking lot. It didn't take Sherlock Holmes to recognize it was Thjasse.

"Not going to let you hurt them," Petr said as he followed. Taking the highway toward the coast, Matt left the city and headed for the country. Eventually, he got off the interstate and took a dirt road to an area with more cows than people.

As Matt pulled off the road, Thjasse continued straight. The fact he followed Matt could be a coincidence, but Petr doubted it. Parking a reasonable distance away but close enough to make out their heads and the truck bed, Petr realized his appetite had returned. As Petr pulled out the food and took a few bites of his dinner, Matt prepared the truck bed with sleeping bags and blankets. He helped Jennifer onto the bed, and they both lay under the covers, glancing up at the sky.

As he sat there, Petr felt the sting of jealousy again. Matt would point, and Jennifer would laugh. Or sometimes Jennifer would nuzzle against Matt.

The stakeout was lonely. Petr was lonely.

After finishing his food, Petr felt the cold seep into the vehicle, yet Matt and Jennifer stayed under the blankets.

Thjasse never returned.

"What are you doing, Petr?" he whispered to himself.

Turning on the car, Petr kept the headlights off. He thought he saw Jennifer's head pop up to glance at him, but Matt distracted her by saying something, and she returned to snuggling him.

Backing off the shoulder, he did a U-turn and faced civilization, leaving Jennifer and Matt alone. If Jennifer was the dragon, he couldn't tell by how she behaved. Neither one of them seemed to go through any kind of massive metamorphosis. Yet the presence of Thjasse added an extra layer of possibilities.

CHAPTER 23

JENNIFER

CLOSE TO THE EDGE OF CAMPUS, A BRIDGE OVER A ROARING creek held a secret. If someone followed the trail after the last guard rail, the path looped to an amphitheater built into the support structure and above the waterlines.

Around Holt University grounds, the concerts given at the theatre once a year were legendary. The upperclassman still talked about the violinist who performed last June.

Of course, the outdoor stage held music bands and other shows at other times, and artistic students often displayed their talents by practicing there.

As Jennifer stood on the bridge, staring over the water toward the architecture and engineering building, she heard a saxophone playing a sad blues tune. She thought about trekking down to the arena and studying on the built-in stairs but opted to leave the musician to practice alone. Occasionally, the person stopped and started over. Regardless, most of the time, the smooth sounds of an accomplished saxist calmed her nerves.

Sighing, she set her bookbag on the ground and pulled out a notebook she purchased a few minutes ago at the campus store. Last night, she didn't take a pill, hoping the medication would clear out of her system. This morning, she searched for a horse called Meadow she knew she had tied up nearby. Fortunately, she woke up early, around four a.m., allowing her time to walk around in her pajamas without everyone noticing.

Clutching her new pen in one hand and the spiral notebook in the other, she held up her new tool toward the setting sun like a magic sword to ward off evil. If the new medicine didn't work tonight, she had a backup approach. She had already programmed the alarm in her phone for seven in the morning. The plan was simple. She would stash the new journal with all the details about her day close to her cell. With any luck, she'd find the notebook and have enough time to reclaim Jennifer, her life, before anyone noticed.

She'd like to say the idea was original, but it wasn't. It came from a movie her mom watched. In it, the main characters left creative messages for the woman with amnesia every morning.

She hoped it worked.

But what do you say to yourself, when you're not yourself, to convince yourself that you are you? That contemplation alone was confusing, to say nothing of defining the essence that makes you, you.

That's it. The book should be called Jennifer Wright. Writing her name on the top of the first page, she thought about what she might want to know.

Your name is Jennifer Wright. You are a college student at South Holt University in the United States North Carolina. I know this is hard to believe, but find a mirror. Please be quiet. Belinda, your roommate, is asleep. It is Saturday. I'll leave some clothes out. Get dressed in the bathroom down the hall and go for a walk. It seems to come back to you best when you exercise and get the blood flowing to your brain.

Taking the pen, she pushed the button several times, trying to think if there was anything else she should say. Then she remembered bathrooms and dental hygiene; if her dreams kept going backward, she wouldn't remember how to do either for a few hours and most mornings, it was the first thing she did. She couldn't help but smirk as she imagined using the small waste basket in her room and Belinda catching her.

That would be so embarrassing.

Pressing the pen on the paper, a cool breeze from her right brought the distinct odor of mold, combined with sweat, cigarette smoke, and strong aftershave. Until that moment, she loved that scent and was pretty sure Matt wore the same cologne. Now, though, the foul stench of wrongness overpowered anything good about the manly fragrance.

Glancing quickly, the person appeared to be approaching her. Tall, blond, and fair, he wore a black leather jacket over jeans. Most girls would consider him attractive, not too bulky or thin. He had a natural smirk in his eyes that marked him as dangerous—a bad boy.

Personally, she didn't like the troublemaker type and had no desire to fix them. She'd like him to stay away, but no one else was on the bridge, and he focused on her, getting closer, like he was on a mission.

Stand! Don't let the predator get close to you. It's easier to run that way.

When she leaned over, she dropped everything in her hands, the momentum rolling the pen until it stopped, dangling partially over the stream.

"Drats," she said, but he was on her, close, and she left her stuff sitting on the ground.

In one of those moments when you knew you should look away but couldn't, Jennifer's eyes kept darting over to the approaching man. She watched in horror as he bent down and seemingly shoved the pen over the side.

The pen clicked and clopped between the beats of the sax as it hit the rocks below and then splashed into the water.

The cocky expression on his face reminded her of when a bully took a baby's sucker. *The jerk did it on purpose!*

He lowered his arms, palms up, and extended them in humility or a peace offering, and said, "I am so sorry. Let me make it up to you."

Did that really work on girls? She'd read the bully books. There were enough for her to think some girls did. She wasn't one of them.

Long, thick, manicured fingers brushed inside his dark jacket to produce a pen. Two steps, and he was in front of her. Her feet stuck to the ground like a deer caught in the headlights, and she couldn't move as dread made her sick.

There was something familiar about the stranger. Something in his ice-blue eyes, aristocratic sharp-pointed nose, high cheekbones, and cool-toned blond hair that she recognized but couldn't name.

Right then, her heart outraced the fast-paced song.

She wanted to run.

The guy's odor spoke of danger, but she didn't understand why. Yes, moldy and sweaty, like used gym socks, but her body reacted as if he was a predator and she, his prey. Even stranger, she recognized Dr. Smith held that same unique weariness, but she craved him.

When he came within her personal bubble, his pen sticking out, she stuck her arms in a defensive posture, hands out to keep him from her space, and shook her head, refusing the offering. "I don't want it, thank you. I have more pens in my bag." She turned her head away from him toward her books, then remembered she needed to face the predator.

"Listen," he said, placing the pen back into his jacket. "I'm new to this town and could use a friend." The way the first syllable on some of his words lengthened, she thought she detected an accent, perhaps Nordic.

He reached his hand out in a friendly gesture, and she took it despite the foreboding.

Run! her mind screamed.

"I'm Johan. What is your name?" He tilted his head to the side, nose down, and she got the distinct feeling he believed her to be property, in that creepy guy kind of way.

After the third shake, she tugged on her arm to unlatch him, but he held on tight and brought her hand up for a kiss.

She ripped her hand free and broke the rule about facing away from her enemy and hurriedly placed the notebook in her bag and zipped it.

Run, flee, live to fight another day.

As she swung her stuff over her shoulder, she said to him, "I'm Jennifer. Nice to meet you, but I just remembered, I have to go meet my friends."

That's it, hide in a crowd.

She didn't wait to hear if he said anything else. Moving like a speed walker, she fled in the direction of the cafeteria, where there were other people.

He followed, matched her pace, and kept in step beside her. "That's perfect! I will walk with you, make sure you are safe, and you can introduce me to your friends. You see, I'm starting college here next semester, and it would be nice to know at least one person on this" —he paused for a second as if he searched for the word, then added— "campus."

She wasn't sure why, but right then, he reminded her of a vampire, trying to lure her to a dark alley and drink her blood.

"Thank you, but I know my way. I don't need help." She quickened her pace to get away from the man.

He sped up, maintaining her stride. "I know this is forward of me, and I rarely do this, but would you like to have dinner one night this week?"

Glancing over at him, he had a smirk on his extremely handsome face. She doubted his words. Her initial opinion was he dated a lot and preyed on women, taking advantage everywhere he could. Experience told her he lied now.

Breathing out, she realized this was the first time in her life that she wouldn't have to lie about being in a relationship to escape from an overly ambitious reprobate who wanted to mark her off as a notch on his belt. "I'm sorry, Johan. I have a boyfriend."

Without missing a beat, he said, "Oh, Jennifer, my sweet girl, I didn't mean it that way. I meant as friends. Would you like to grab a meal as friends?"

That was such a typical thing for a caught rat to say. Of course, Johan wanted to be friends—with benefits. What the man wanted didn't count as dating; he wanted sex. At least, in that, he was honest.

"It's a big campus, but if we see each other again, sure, sometime," she said as noncommittally as she could.

That seemed to appease him, and he stopped walking. "Catch you later, Jennifer," he yelled as she hurried away.

Despite the distance that grew between them, the tiny hairs on her arms crawled in disgust. The odor of mold, sweat, cigarettes, and body wash clung to her skin. Instead of heading to the cafeteria, as madly as her legs would move, she changed direction for her dorm and a shower.

Somewhere behind her, Johan disappeared, and she hoped he was now off campus. However, the odd sensation of being watched continued to tickle her nerves and made her uncomfortable.

CHAPTER 24

MATT

THE PARKING LOT CLOSEST TO THE LIBRARY SAT FULL, FORCING Matt to park two lots away. Exams started soon, with only a few more days left of class. As he approached the library doors, he recognized a few of the people entering the building.

Did they really think they could cram a semester's worth of knowledge into a few days? Or that the professors monitored the library, and they would instantly get a boost to their grades? Even though others might think he procrastinated, he knew the true secret to life was balance—play, work hard, and enjoy.

Besides, now there were too many people and too many distractions at this location to really focus, but Jennifer liked this place. He'd endure the crowds for her.

As he entered through the glass door, he noted not a single unoccupied chair. A few people gathered along the wall, earbuds in, with their heads close to the books, without a place to sit. Some people moved around, but other than that, the extremely packed room remained eerily quiet.

When he climbed the stairs to the second floor, true to Jennifer's words, he recognized the faces here. Level two, she had said, was for the serious students. The only surprise was finding Jennifer's green couch without her. Her bookbag rested on the table she used, but she was missing. He flung his down beside hers and searched the area.

Near the windows, a row of PCs that typically sat empty had a single creature with strands of hair sticking in odd directions, like they rolled around in a hayloft or a bird made a nest at her roots. The color of the locks and the length sort of reminded him of Jennifer.

Hesitantly, he approached the oddity. The person intently focused on the computer in front of them and ignored his approach. He leaned over the shoulder of the wild-haired individual and found the screen displayed a medical article on brain tumors.

The creature mumbled, and there could be no mistake. Jennifer, with wild hair, researching head diseases!

"Jennifer?" Matt asked.

Her shoulders tensed, and she stopped typing.

"Jennifer?" he asked again.

Like in a horror movie, each part of her body moved one at a time, starting with her head and ending with her legs. At first, the person appeared puzzled, fully opened eyes focusing beyond him, but then he saw the recognition, and she smiled.

"Matt." She seemed pleased with herself. Or maybe the joy was at seeing him.

Before he said anything, he surveyed her appearance. From this angle, her clothes seemed normal for a college student: jeans, a red T-shirt, running shoes—her norm. Then he regarded her face. Bags sat under her eyes like she hadn't slept in a while. She sported a purple and blue bruise on the corner of her chin.

"Rough day of studying? Do you have a paper due on medical stuff?" he asked.

Instead of responding right away, only her head moved as

she gradually surveyed the room. He followed her eyes' path but noticed nothing out of the ordinary.

She held her finger in front of her mouth to indicate quiet, then walked over to the green couch. When she sat down, she gestured him to move beside her by waving her arms and patting the faux leather.

When he joined her, she whispered, "No, I don't have a paper due in anything right now. The sleeping pills started making me sick." He knew this. She had told him on their date Thursday.

Tilting her head like she waited for him to say something, she waved him to lean in close. "I had to stop taking all the pills. I fell out of bed." She pointed to the bruise on her face.

"Ouch, Jennifer. That bruise has some yellow in it, like you did it a while back, but you didn't have it Thursday. It's Sunday, so that's just weird," Matt observed, gently stroking the fading edges.

"I know, Matt. It's almost healed. Yet yesterday, when it happened, I thought I broke my jaw. So, last night, I didn't take any pills, and the vivid dreams started again."

"You don't have a tumor if that was what you were wondering. But don't take my word for it. Are you making a doctor's appointment?" he asked.

Putting her hand in front of her face, she shh'd again. Then she slowly glanced around the room. "Someone has been following me. I see them for a second, but they're gone when I try to find them."

"What do they look like?" he asked, though, to be honest, she seemed off her rocker. More evidence that the key to life was balance. Now, he had more proof of the advantages of skipping class once in a while. Not that he required more results on the sanity and benefits of relaxing and taking scheduled breaks.

"I'm not sure, Matt, but I just feel like he's always staring at me."

"Sweety," he said, placing his hands under her elbows and bringing her in for a hug. "No one is going to touch you. Everyone knows you are my girlfriend, and they'll stay away."

Pushing away, she said, "I'm dreaming in Gaelic now. Last night, I was Aine Dalzie Agan in the early eighteen hundreds. The man she married reminded me of Randy. Talk about being grossed out." As she talked, she got louder, and the students at the table across from them gave them the evil eye.

When she first experienced the dreams, he read that some people dreamed in languages they didn't know. Her confession still surprised him, and he had to blink several times to hide that he thought that was crazy.

Jennifer seriously needed to learn to chill and not work so hard without a break. How had she not had a psychotic breakdown before now?

"I think there's something wrong," she whispered.

"Jennifer, many people have realistic dreams. If it's bothering you, make a doctor's appointment." He ran his fingers through her hair until it caught on a knot.

Yesterday, he found an ad for feeding sharks off the island of Hatteras. Something with a dangerous element might clear up the stress dreams.

"No, Matt, these seem real. I've dreamed I was a man. I know what it's like to pee standing."

Puzzled, Matt stared at her for a second. "Don't you stand up when we go camping? You don't sit on the ground, do you?" he asked.

"Well, no. I stand." Jennifer sounded surprised.

"Jennifer, you are fine. The problem isn't a tumor. You need to relax. All this pressure to make straight A's has gone to your head." He pecked her lips with his. "You are adorable, smart, and funny but way too intense. It's time I teach you, my pupil."

Smiling, she leaned back and put her hands on her elbows. "You, teach me?"

"Absolutely. I excel at the art of mental health breaks. Perhaps I should become a psychologist instead of an engineer. Of course, every person should take pride in their mental health, and you, my dear, lovely girlfriend, are in need of a break. Please pack your stuff up. First, we are headed to your dorm so you can brush your hair."

"Matt, I never unpacked. I haven't even cracked a schoolbook today."

Intentionally, he widened his eyes and put on an expression of shock. "It's worse than I thought. Well then," he said, standing. Moving over to the table, he grabbed their bags. He held his hand out and waited for her to hold it.

Once they left the library, they climbed a small hill. He followed her to the dorm's front desk, where Jennifer signed him in as a visitor. She took him up to the second floor and unlocked her dorm room. He'd only been up there once but remembered that the room smelled of roses.

The beds were made, with Belinda's piled high with stuffed animals. Jennifer's pillow plopped up against the wall as a headboard, a multi-colored quilt tucked around the mattress. "I thought you had a tan comforter."

"I do. I change them out and wash them about once a week. Belinda says I'm crazy, that it fades the fabric, but if I don't, my skin crawls from the thought of dirt," she said.

He sat on her twin bed, dropping both bookbags to the ground and leaning backward. Surprised to find the twin so comfortably squishy, he wondered if she bought a foam cover.

Yawning, he closed his eyes. "Let me know when you're ready. I'm going to catch a nap," he said.

"Silly," Jennifer said.

A new weight pressed against him, and he opened his eyes to find she'd placed a blue denim blanket over him. He glanced up at her, a purple hairbrush gliding through her hair.

"Thank you for the blanket," he said.

The door unlatched, and Belinda, wearing a bright pink shirt with matching lipstick, walked into the room.

"Brushing your hair? Are you going out tonight?" Belinda asked. She swayed a little, and Matt guessed she'd had something to drink.

Jennifer sighed. "Not without duress. Matt accused me of over-studying and says the only cure is for me to go out and have a good time. Before you change clothes—" Jennifer pointed at him, but Belinda had walked over to her side of the room, closer to the window and further from the entrance.

"You know, you've been seeing Matt a lot lately. So, what's new? You milked that cow yet?"

A cow, milking—both disturbing and oddly arousing. He tilted his head to watch as Belinda removed her heels, using the wall for support, facing away from him.

Jennifer blushed, staring down at him. "I'm still a virgin," she replied after a delay. Matt knew Jennifer was innocent. They'd talked about her lack of dating. Still, it made her uncomfortable, and he hoped Belinda caught the hint.

"Well, I envy your fortitude. However, I can tell you, you are missing out. I met this guy last night at the Pi fraternity party—oh my gosh, was he incredible in the sack!" She looked around her side of the room. "There it is," she said as she picked up a business card.

"What are you doing?" Jennifer asked.

"Seeing if I still have his number or name. Man, it's his friend's card. His name isn't on here." While one hand slapped the stiff paper against her palm in frustration, she said, "I think I will call him Dick. He'll answer to it."

"Dick?" Jennifer asked.

"Oh, my, his was nice, so yes, Dick," Belinda confirmed.

Frantically, Jennifer brushed her hair like she was embarrassed and needed something to do with her hands. Yet Belinda didn't recognize it and said, "I'm about to head over there. Want to go? I'm telling you, Jennifer, Dick was good. He had me screaming and clawing the air."

Sitting the brush down, Jennifer asked, "Aren't you concerned about what other people are going to think of you? This is the South, after all."

"Nah, everyone is doing it," Belinda answered. "You should try it. With Matt. I bet he has a nice dick as well."

At this, Jennifer pointed toward him, so he sat up.

"Hi, Belinda. Interesting conversation," he said, aiming for confidence.

Blinking deliberately, like her eyelids were heavy, she smiled first at him, then at Jennifer. Belinda said, "I'd be embarrassed at everything I confessed, but I have it on good authority that you want Jennifer to pop your cherry."

Laughing, Matt glanced at Jennifer's red face. For her benefit, he admitted the truth. "I wouldn't be dating her if I didn't want to eventually explore more than kissing, but you are right. I'm innocent as fresh snow before anyone walks on it. Do you mind if Jen and I tag along with you back to the Pi party? Jen needs to unwind. Not drink, mind you, just have a good time. An innocent, clean, good time," he added to encourage Belinda not to bring up sex again.

Belinda placed a pair of jogging shoes on but left the skirt. Swaying over, she draped her arm over Jennifer's shoulder and kissed her cheek. "Come, my virgin friends. We have a Pi house to play in, and I have a Dick to conquer!"

CHAPTER 25
JENNIFER

THE GRAY SPIRAL NOTEBOOK AND THE CELL PHONE LAY IN A puddle of water while the rain poured. The shift from the dream last night to Jennifer hadn't happened. Seamus understood this wasn't his life. He understood he was Jennifer, but Jennifer's memories hadn't awakened yet. Instead, now and then, he comprehended an item that didn't exist in his time, such as cars, electricity, and indoor plumbing.

Earlier, he'd used the papers to fake his way through her day. After confirming in a mirror that what the notebook said was true, he followed the directions. Visually displayed and taped onto pages were small images of the campus from online mapping software. The words he shouldn't be able to read even told him what name to answer to...Jennifer Wright.

That alone wouldn't have helped in his first class; a paper was due. Had the instructor not asked for the homework to be turned in at the end of the lecture, and he not frantically hunted for the correct document, finding it buried in her supplies, her work would have been missing.

Before talking to himself, strike that, herself, she scanned the area for eavesdroppers. Coast clear, he said, "Well, you've messed that up, Seamus. Those directions were the only thing getting you around this overly crowded and extremely gray place."

Placing the hands on the hips, he searched around again. "You need to dry off. Let's find a bathroom," he said, hoping the very feminine voice would trigger a memory. It didn't.

Reaching down, he retrieved the drenched phone and notebook. Shaking them, frowning, he found the closest building with coffee shop called Cat's Cradle. The cafe sat flush in a row of buildings. The only thing distinguishing it from the other stores was a red, blue, and white striped awning in front of the window and door.

The fact that he knew the difference between an awning, a sunshade, and a canopy did not pass by him. More knowledge he understood because he was indeed Jennifer and not Seamus.

As he approached the door and stood under the covering, the smell of coffee and baking treats caused his stomach to grumble.

Sitting inside at a dry table and deciding what should happen next sounded great.

Instead of a purse, Jennifer used her bookbag to hold everything, including her wallet. Utilizing a knee to prop up the satchel, he searched the side pocket until, eureka, he found the emergency credit card. With it was an image of her father handing it to her with stipulations. He located enough cash for a cup of warm liquid and something sweet.

Seamus stared at the menu, trying to remember what Jennifer liked. None of the drinks sounded familiar. His only conclusion was that Jennifer didn't drink coffee or tea.

Then his eyes caught a word that made him feel toasty and happy. Moving up to the front counter, he waited for the barista to face him. In Jennifer's voice, he said, "I would like the hot chocolate, please. Oh, and the chocolate pie as well."

After he paid and left a tip, he said, "I'll be right back for the drink and pie."

With a nod, the cashier pointed toward the other side's surface, where a few customers waited for their orders. "They will be right there."

He discovered a small hall opposite the entrance. The first door on the left had a sign for either sexes or families on the outside. He knocked and waited for a reply. When no one answered, he went in and stared at Jennifer's face again.

Earlier today, when he found the notebook, he didn't believe it. But, after glancing in the mirror, he saw the pretty blond staring back at him, and he understood it was true. Seamus existed in her dreams, and for some strange reason, his personality and memories implanted over hers.

Dripping wet, her golden waves appeared brown and straight. Moving over to the sink, he drained as much water as possible and watched the normal wave bounce back like a spring.

"Come on, Jennifer. Come back. I know you like Seamus, but he's lived his life," he said, speculating that was the reason for such a slow return, that Jennifer liked Seamus's easy-going personality.

Sighing, he grabbed the notepad and phone. With the brown paper napkins, he did his best to dry both of them off. Unfortunately, the screen cracked on the cell when it fell and shattered beyond repair. With the phone no longer working, he doubted the wristwatch would open the dorm room or anything else.

"Bother," Jennifer's voice said.

Drying out the notebook didn't work, and the pages stuck together.

Glancing at the reflection again, trying to connect with Jennifer, he said, "Well, at least I completed everything on the list before it became drenched."

Images of other events during the week passed before his eyes, such as missing classes, using the restroom outside without getting caught, thankfully, and not answering professors when they called her name—just to name a few.

"It's Friday. You made it through a crazy school day, but I need you back to make all the hard decisions. Plus, exams start next week. Come on, remember," Jennifer's voice said.

He tapped the mirror where the wrinkles gathered on her forehead. "Come on, Jennifer, come back."

When nothing happened, he frowned but returned to the coffee shop counter and retrieved his order.

Several tables sat in front of a long window that faced the campus. Seamus took the treats and moved to a seat, staring outside, watching the students as he swallowed the pie. Not sure what to expect, only that the sweet treat reminded him of pudding, he took a bite. His mouth exploded with buttery flakes of chocolate layers, thick like a chunky brownie, with the crust of a giant chocolate chip cookie. The flavor was so rich that the back of his neck hurt. Jennifer's taste buds enjoyed the food, so he ate some more.

With a dessert so chocolaty, he worried the hot chocolate would taste like dirt, but he was wrong. Somehow, the two flavors worked.

Satisfied and slowly drying, he watched as students and shoppers with colorful umbrellas and rain jackets bustled around the sidewalk, making a scene of beauty all on their own.

Off in the distance and coming closer, a redheaded woman casually walked beside a tall man without any protection from the storm. The man wore a black jacket, possibly leather, with black combat boots. The girl dressed in a green miniskirt and tight beige sweater that emphasized her ample chest. To his surprise, the strange couple that strolled without a care in the world seemed familiar.

They stopped in front of the window under the awning. The man pulled out a cigarette and lit it. The petite girl grabbed the smoke from his hand and inhaled. As she breathed out, she bounced and twirled, giving the tall guy googly eyes.

Seamus couldn't take his eyes off them, like a train wreck or a car accident. They stood only a windowpane away, yet neither noticed Jennifer. Two things bothered him, one about the girl, the other about the man. At that second, he couldn't remember what, so he stared, hoping for clarity.

Amy cheered in high school. She's athletic. I expected her to be more into her health. Someone into their health wouldn't smoke, Jennifer thought.

Amy inhaled, held it without coughing, then breathed out a cloud of tar, like she smoked every day of her life.

Seamus, however, raised Jennifer's eyebrows. Did this strong distinction in Jennifer's voice mean she was coming back?

Now, more than before, he scrutinized their actions. The way the taller man surveyed and studied everyone that walked by made him uncomfortable. His eyes lingered on young ladies more than the males, like he sized them up as a game hunter would his prey.

The girl, Amy, kept her eyes focused on Johan. Jennifer remembered his name as well. When Johan glanced in a direction away from Amy, a minute change happened. Her face went from desire to contemplation, though Jennifer couldn't decide how she knew that.

Finished with the cigarette, Johan stomped on it. Amy, however, bent down and carefully picked up the bud. As Johan held open the coffee shop door for Amy, she disposed of the filter into the garbage can. Johan's eyes focused directly on the smaller girl, a look of surprise on his face.

Did Johan not want Amy to be environmentally conscious?

Wrongness, powerful and overwhelming, blended in with the scent of ground espresso filling the air she breathed. Until that instant, Jennifer couldn't think of another odor stronger than the black bean brew.

Then Amy entered, and all Jennifer could smell was something spicy with cinnamon and nutmeg.

Once the couple reached the counter, Johan glanced at Jennifer. He paused for a moment before hunger and desire clung to his eyes. His stare at her was so intense that Amy turned her head toward her, and they locked eyes. For a heartbeat, Jennifer saw hate.

The barista saved her by asking for their orders. When their eyes were off her, she breathed easier.

At least seeing Johan woke Jennifer, though the memory of Seamus was still fresh and raw.

Staring down at the broken phone, she thought about how easy it would have been to call Matt and ask for a ride, but she remembered that he had left a message. He was chasing the sun before exams, which translated to he and his friends were headed to the beach for the rest of the week—the ocean was only a two-to-three-hour drive from their university.

Right then, Jennifer would love to be sitting in the sand, being a normal college kid and enjoying the fellowship of friendly faces. If he'd asked her to go early this week, she couldn't remember. Though, if it was yesterday, she would have said no because she had to study.

But today, her answer would be yes. Yes to the beach, yes to friends, and yes to enjoying life a little more.

Without another option, she was at least thankful the phone company she utilized had a store right off campus. If there was ever a reason to exercise the emergency credit card, a destroyed cell phone and the inability to use the app to unlock her dorm room seemed like a reasonable excuse. With a plan in place, Jennifer gathered her waste and headed out the door without glancing at Johan or Amy, though she felt their eyes bore into her skin.

After placing the tray on top of the trash can, and before

she reached the door, with her hand propped on the handle, Amy called, "Hi, Jennifer."

Regretfully, Jennifer faced the food display counter as she tucked a curl behind her ear. She glanced up, finding condemnation resting on both their faces.

What have I done that I'm being judged for? she wondered.

Assuming she misread their facial expressions, she said, "Hi, Amy. Hi, Johan. I'll see you both later." She tried for confidence and friendly and failed at both.

Without giving them time to respond, she exited the cafe. Her heart beat ten times for every step as it tried to climb up her throat and out of her body. The rain formed a coat of water over her skin, and steam rose from her arms. She walked in a fog until she safely reached the phone store.

CHAPTER 26

MATT

The Pi House, one of the more popular fraternities on campus, though Matt couldn't confirm they were a university approved fraternity or just a group of guys that organized events regularly, often threw killer parties. So, if they weren't a legit organization, he didn't care.

On his way back from the beach trip, a Pi member named Olan texted him about a party Sunday night that he must attend. He agreed. After all, Matt had a reputation as the best poker player on campus to uphold.

The event would kick off at seven, with a light game of twenty-one, breaking into Texas Hold'em soon after. Twenty-one wasn't interesting to him, so when he arrived, he and his roommates, along with his friend Colin, quietly strolled to one of the small upstairs bedrooms and warmed up with a game of spades.

Surprisingly, the odor in the room reminded him of the outdoors. He assumed they opened the windows earlier that day to air out stale scents. The small single bed, decorated in a plain blue comforter, sat in the center, forcing the small four-person card table to be scrunched close to the wall. Someone piled gaming gear in a corner. Anime posters plastered the sheetrock. Other than a few stains on the carpet, the area seemed cluttered but clean.

The cleaned house wasn't a surprise. The fraternity typically collected money for drinks and a cleaning crew pre- and post-gatherings.

During Spades, they broke into two groups. For this game, Colin was his partner, and the other team, Doug and Lauren, sat on either side of him.

As Doug shuffled the deck, he winked at Lauren. They wore their cards on their face. Under normal circumstances, Matt would focus more on the two of them, trying to read the clues they gave as to what their hand held.

But not tonight. He pulled his phone out of his pocket, checking one more time that he left the phone on vibrate in case Jennifer called or texted.

"I think we should go camping this weekend," Colin said to Lauren.

"I'm willing if you are, Doug. What do you say? Two more votes, yes?" Lauren asked, giving him a return wink.

"Sure," Doug answered without bothering to glance up from shuffling.

"I'll ask Jennifer if she wants to join us," Matt said, turning over his card and finding an ace of clubs.

Across from him, Colin leaned in and emitted a loud noise followed by an overpowering stench. Proud of himself, he giggled.

In disgust, Lauren laid her cards down and gave Colin the look, her personal death stare.

Most of the time, Matt said something in defense of Colin, something that lightened the mood. But tonight, Colin could defend himself, and Matt suppressed his response and ignored Colin's antics.

When Doug finished dealing the cards, he leaned back and pointed to Colin. "Go, open the window." It was a command.

Scooting his chair back, standing, and moving the blinds out of the way, Colin snickered. He grunted as he struggled with the single window latch. After the popping snap of success, cool fresh air flowed into the room.

"I thought that you broke up with Jennifer," Colin said, sitting across from Matt.

"Why would you think that?" Matt surveyed his hand again. With the ace, three spades, and the rest of his deck useless, he knew his max bid was three.

"Just what Lauren said," Colin answered, grabbing his cards off the table.

Quickly, Matt glanced at Lauren but waited for Colin to start the bid. Lauren shrugged. "Matt, it's just, well, Jennifer didn't go with us to the beach."

"Oh, you know how she is, focused on school and all. If she went with us and made less than an A, she might blame me. If I asked and she said no, she might wish she went and blame me. It was a no-win scenario, so I didn't invite her."

In truth, Matt worried not asking her to join was a mistake. Since he left for the ocean, their relationship had been one-sided. On their way to the ocean, he sent her a message. He called and texted when they were there and when they drove back. She never responded.

Doug put his cards on the table face down. "When was the last time you talked to her? Because I don't see her sitting across the table from you."

"Yeah, it's strange," Colin agreed. "Not that I'm complaining. I think we make a cute couple." He winked at Matt.

Matt rolled his eyes. "I'll call her and see her after final exams."

"That wasn't what I asked," Doug responded matter-of-factly and stared, waiting for an answer.

"Look, Matt," Lauren interrupted. "There is something wrong with Jennifer." She held her hand up to her ear, circling, using sign to indicate crazy.

"You mean the camping trip over Thanksgiving break?" Matt asked.

"That and, well, other things," Lauren said.

Glancing down at his cards with a single wink, Colin said, "I say we'll take five points."

The card game lost importance. Not that he cared tonight, anyway. "What other things?" Matt asked, concerned.

Lauren studied her cards. When she finished, she placed them face down on the table and said, "I call five."

"What other things?" Matt repeated. "Pass."

"Man." Doug put his cards down. "I pass, as well. Oh, Lauren saw Jennifer at school, and Jennifer was all over the place weird."

"How so?" Matt asked.

Taking the direct approach, Lauren sat straight in the fold-up chair, facing Matt. "Well, for starters, when you introduced us to Jennifer, she cared about her appearance—her shirts were tucked into her jeans, her clothing matched. When I went to meet with my professor, before we left for the ocean, I ran into her coming out of the cafeteria. She ignored me, stared straight through me, like I wasn't there. Her hair stuck out at odd angles, like she hadn't brushed it in days. This time, she wore a button-down shirt, inside out, with the buttons misaligned, one side tucked into her jeans, the other flopping in the wind. It just didn't look like the girl you brought home a few weeks ago. I'm not sure she's sane."

"Are you sure it was her?" Matt asked.

"Absolutely," Lauren confirmed.

Instead of alleviating the guilt for not asking her to go, he felt more condemned. He saw the impact the dreams had on her. An outing with friends might have distressed her some, even though last weekend did very little to help.

Colin stacked his cards on the table's surface. "If you up to six, you can take the pot. Do you call six?"

Instead of answering, she reached forward and acquired

the cards left in the middle of the table. Doug and Lauren thought they could win six rounds. If Colin had the hand he bid, she would lose.

After sizing up her hand, she discarded three cards, lying them down so no one could see what she rejected.

"My favorite part was the socks." Colin snickered.

"What about the socks?" Matt inquired.

"Just one of her jean legs was tucked into a sock, right, Lauren?" Colin laughed like they were sharing a private joke.

"Yes," Lauren agreed but didn't glance away from her hand.

The rest of the game flew by because Matt didn't pay attention. His thoughts drifted to the night he saw her in the library, her hair in a tangled mess.

The next day, he called. She texted back that she was at the library studying, and he didn't think about it again. Not because he didn't care, but because she joked and laughed with him. He'd thought she was better.

He didn't know there was an issue until she didn't text him back on the way to the beach.

They'd talked about going to the movies before he left, but in the end, she said she had this or that due. So, when the opportunity to go relax and hang out before exams came up, he didn't invite her.

Sure, he'd called and texted, and she didn't respond.

Would he want to continue their relationship if she was the grudge-holding type?

Outside the room, the first-floor volume picked up. Twisted in indecision, when the game ended, Matt left the table and headed downstairs. The dining room table held different drinks, including alcohol. College students of varying ages gathered around, cups in hand, and he shoved himself through with excuse-me's and hi's. Grabbing a beer, he moved toward the kitchen. He watched a group of giggling girls heading to the bathroom. When they opened the door, a cloud of smoke and skunk scent let him know more than he wanted. He rounded the corner to the living room and sat on the bright red couch with dark stains, a souvenir from another past Pi gathering.

The roaring party reminded Matt of every clichéd movie scene ever made. He sipped the beer and glanced around for his friend Paul, who texted that he planned to attend.

Usually, Matt enjoyed nights spent at the Pi fraternity house, but not tonight. He peeked at his watch and wondered when it would be polite to leave and let someone else hold the poker king hat for a while—he could win it back later.

Somewhere behind him, Matt heard his name. Turning in the seat, he found Belinda staggering toward him. One of the Pi members followed close behind her.

"Matt." Belinda let go of the other man and bent down to hug him. "Did you see the full bar?" she asked, peering down at his beer. "The good stuff is at the bar in the basement." She grabbed his can and replaced it with her cup. "This is a strawberry margarita. No one has drunk out of it. I'll get another drink."

The man behind her leaned forward to whisper into her ear. He turned to leave, taking Matt's old drink with him.

"Drink up," Belinda encouraged Matt, waiting for him to take a sip.

Succumbing to peer pressure, Matt tasted the margarita and choked on pure tequila. "Holy crap," he said.

"I know, right? No scrimping there. It takes a few sips to get the strawberry flavor. Trust me, I've had a few. They don't need salt, so I've started leaving it off."

The man returned and handed her another drink.

"Matt, this is Rick. Rick, this is Matt," Belinda said in introduction.

The tall lanky guy had mouse brown hair and a big nose—not typically handsome. If Belinda hadn't said he was packing, Matt would wonder why she dated him.

She turned toward the guy. "Rick, Matt is Jen's boyfriend. He's the one I told you about. The one that overheard my nickname for you." Belinda turned back to Matt. "See, he is a Dick, after all. Where is Jen? I didn't think she enjoyed last weekend's party, so I'm surprised to see you here."

"I was hoping you would know. I haven't talked to her in a few days."

Belinda leaned back into Rick, and he put his arms around her waist, but otherwise, Rick ignored Matt and talked to another guy on his left. Belinda disregarded the other conversation and said, "I've been staying here with my dick." She turned around and pecked her new guy on the cheek.

"Do you mind checking on her? Do you have your phone?" Matt asked.

Reaching in her pocket, she pulled out her cell, wrapped in a pink glitter case. "Jen is a big girl. Why don't you call her yourself?"

Matt held his head down so she wouldn't see his shame. "I went out of town without telling her. I've called and left messages, but she's not responding. I'm not sure if she's angry, studying too hard, or if something's wrong."

"Scandalous, Matt! I guess I need to go back to the dorm tomorrow, anyhow. I'm out of clothes." After unlocking the screen, she held out the phone and said, "Sure, Matt. I'll check on Jennifer and ask her to call you."

Taking her cell, he noticed the background screen was of her holding an oversized white poodle. He opened a text string and sent himself a message that simply said, *this is Matt.*

"Matt Davis!" a larger-than-life voice boomed off the wall and over the music. He turned and peered over the back of the sofa to find Paul standing at the exit to the living room. In his hands was a bag of gambling chips.

Feeling slightly better knowing Belinda would talk with

Jennifer and holding the tequila level so as not to spill it, Matt stood.

"It's time you lost to the better man," Paul shouted, motioning at him with his head to join him.

Someone turned off the music, the chatter stopped, and the room focused on the ruling champion, Matt.

"Oh, that's right, Texas Hold'em time! Paul, you will never beat me," Matt enthusiastically said.

At his words, they cheered, cleared a path, and followed him to the basement.

CHAPTER 27

JENNIFER

UNLIKE THE OTHER NIGHTS, JENNIFER KNEW SHE WAS ASLEEP. This dream she started as an adult instead of a child. She tried to stand, but her body didn't react.

Mentally, she sighed and reached for anything to tell her whose memories and emotions she would experience.

She got more than a name. *This day is from River's life. He is one of your dragon ancestors,* a British-accented male said.

Another dream, another person, and back to the idea that she was a dragon…

As River waited for Petr at the edge of a lake called Sleeper, the wind blew across River's face, forcing his thin sandy hair into his eyes, and he squinted to make out the details. A vibrant blue sky with white puffy clouds watched over a hill of tall grass. The stalks parted, revealing patches of smaller plants with dark, almost violet flowers.

Reaching over, River grabbed a blade of grass and chewed on the end. Peace swelled in his heart as he enjoyed his paradise with the cool gray rock underneath and the harmony of nature surrounding him.

Soon, he'd declare his love for the human girl, his mate.

He heard the footsteps of someone approaching, so he

swiveled his head to find his friend, Petr. Today, he'd find enough courage to tell Petr about his human mate and ask for advice on how to break the news to his parents.

With an extra bounce to his steps, he appeared youthful, unlike his normal have-to-fix-the-world self.

"What took so long, Petr? I almost went to the village without you," River said in a rich baritone voice that poured out almost like a melody—like King Author in the old movie musicals.

"No shopping today. I have another idea." Petr proudly held up two long sticks with one end sharpened.

"You were sharpening sticks? I sat on this cold rock waiting for you to sharpen sticks?" Standing, River dusted his pants and took the grass stem out of his mouth.

Raising his eyebrows, Petr answered, "Not just any sticks, my friend. Sharpened sticks for spearfishing. I've neglected your lessons. It's time you learned the art of hunting your prey with a spear. Water slows down your weapon, making this an excellent opportunity to hone your aim." When he finished talking, excitement and a giant grin lit up his face.

Searching around, River allowed his eyes to focus on the body of water. The poor lake sat atop a mountain, with no water sources other than rain feeding its banks. There was no way Sleeper held fish. "And where would we go fishing?"

Petr pointed with the fishing pole toward Sleeper. "There," he said.

"Petr, there are no fish in that lake."

"There are fish. I put them there myself, long before you were born."

"Before my sister?" River asked.

Petr's smile dropped, and the atmosphere changed. He searched River's face, perhaps for his maturity, before answering. "No. Your sister liked mud and bugs when she was a little girl. She and I brought them up here in a basket lined with goats' stomachs. I'd say she was ten."

As Petr approached, he held out one of the two spears, and River grabbed it, turning and tossing the weapon to gauge the weight. Checking on Petr, he found him surveying the water. He needed Petr to listen and advise him for his mate's sake. River said, "I remember her, you know."

"Remember her?" Petr asked. "You weren't born for another four hundred years."

"I remember her through both my parents."

He only nodded, watching the water lap the shore.

Think, River, what can you say to get Petr back on the subject? But nothing came to mind.

Finally, Petr glanced upward and said, "It's a perfect day for fishing."

River followed Petr's eyes and spied a bird flying overhead between the white and puffy clouds. "Very nice," River agreed.

Swallowing, River studied Petr, who continued to squint at something in the distance. Drawing Petr back into the conversation because this was important, River said, "I'm serious." For emphasis, he stuck the fishing stick in the mud.

"What are you serious about?" Petr asked but sustained his focus far from them.

"I remember everyone and everything my parents remember, even down to the smallest detail. It's called a legacy. Every dragon, no matter what race, has the gift of legacy. It involves searching for details and can give me headaches, but they are there. We dragons, whether human-born or not, have a legacy."

"Why are you telling me this? Even your parents, whom I think by now trust me, keep the secrets about dragons close to them. My sister's husband, a dragon from the mother of dragons, who loved me as a brother, neglected to tell me about human-born dragons. I learned of eating a heart, dragon senses, and even human-born dragons from my sister on her deathbed."

"Ah, but you knew there was more." It was a statement, not a question, so River continued, saying, "Well." River grabbed the stick and started slinging water across Sleeper. Now, to prime Petr for his advice, he said, "There is more than one reason."

In River's thoughts, he showed Jennifer the image of his mate. She had long, thick black hair, a braided section tied with a red ribbon to signify a master hunter. In her hands, she held a bow and smiled when she knocked the target from its foundation.

"And what are the reasons?" Petr asked, sitting on the bank, pulling off his foot coverings.

"Well, you have to know what it's like to be one of us if you are going to protect us. Any descendant of mine or your sister's that is a dragon will know who you are, Petr. And from my understanding, you've pledged to protect those of us born to humans. The human-born dragons from your friends will know who you are; they will have our memories." River put his stick on the ground and sat down. "My parents say if a child is born to humans and becomes a dragon, that person will go through massive changes during the awakening. The few humans who have changed have struggled with understanding these ancestral memories in the first few months."

At this, he expected Petr to ask why he would have a human child, which would be his opening into discussing Chulin. River placed his shoes behind him and waited for Petr to say something.

When he didn't, River surveyed Petr's blue eyes. Petr stared intently at River, and River couldn't tell if this meant he wondered why River asked or found a different direction for the questioning. He could never tell with Petr.

Shaking his head, he wondered if the dragon term possibly confused him. River said, "I guess we dragons don't trust human friends enough with our hard-earned secrets.

The awakening is that noise you hear when humans become dragons. You have to understand, Petr, and I think you do. It's true that some of us lay eggs, and some prefer never to become human. That noise you hear occasionally, the noise that sounds like someone blowing a loud horn?"

"Yes," Petr said, but he scrunched his face like when they played games, anticipating River's next words, like he expected his next moves.

"I see. You figured out the connection already. You know when you hear that sound, somewhere, someone became a dragon."

He nodded, then said, "If you want to explain something to me, what's so different about the awakening in a dragon than in one born human?" Petr asked.

"The difference. I knew the first time I took dragon form what happened. I never had an awakening. For a human, the first time is a surprise, and changes occur to their mind and body to accept the differences."

"So, you're saying that the humans who awaken have no idea they might turn into a dragon?"

"Unlike you, who stayed in your sister's descendant's lives, most humans do not know they descended from a dragon."

Petr pulled his legs up and wrapped his arms around his knees. He was so deep in concentration that his furrowed eyebrows nearly touched. Petr asked, "So dragons don't watch over their young?"

This conversation was spiraling out of control. All River wanted was Petr's blessing and advice on how to tell his parents he had mated without their consent.

He said, "Now, wait, Petr. You, for one, should know that humans marry, move away from their families, and have their own lives separate from their parents. Children of dragons do the same thing, and there might be a rumor or two in a family line, but they don't know they could mysteriously turn into a dragon one day."

"So, all these awakenings I hear, no one is finding them and helping them through this awakening process?"

"I'm not sure it's necessary. First, we are the apex predators, and who would challenge and kill a dragon—"

"The same people who killed my sister's husband, Perun. The same people who killed your sister, Spring." He ran his hand through his hair.

"Well, that was an exception. It won't happen again. If it does, you can form a group and find all the awakened children. I mean, you hear the awakenings yourself. But, before you do that, they have an advantage, I don't. Where I can recall, with effort, my ancestor's memories, an awakened dragon knows their ancestor's information like it was their own. They dream of them. This gives them an advantage. Thus, another reason not to defend a dragon child. They will be all right."

Petr, absorbed in his thoughts, moved without explaining his actions. Mimicking Petr, River rolled up his pant legs.

Perhaps River could use the human-born dragon to bring up Chulin. "Imagine seeing your parents' life until the moment they conceived you. If it has been centuries, like I believe it will take, the poor person will have to dream of so many lives before the legacy takes hold."

Out of the corner of River's eye, he watched a bird swoop down and grab a fish out of Sleeper. "Okay, there are fish in the water." He smiled at Petr.

A familiar tingling started at the soles of his feet, where they dug into the dark soil. He recognized the sensation immediately as the gift of earth.

Some dragons, and River suspected all dragons, carried innate abilities that matched the distinct elements: fire, water, air, and earth. Dernogard, the city of the dragons, tested young ones for such strengths. Earth was the only exception because he knew only one other dragon with this gift: his brother, Yangdi.

The fact that Yangdi, the mystic, scared everyone with prophecies of doom and hurt their parents by disappearing forced River to keep the gift a secret. He didn't want to hurt his parents with a reminder of Yangdi or the fear he, too, would abandon them.

He never met his crazy, fortune-predicting brother. Years before his birth, Yangdi ran off to be one with nature, but the pain lived in his parents' memories.

At that second, earth told him inevitable things.

This time, he scrutinized his friend for what he understood would occur. To him, Petr was an old man, though he didn't appear a day over twenty-five. Brown wavy hair, his eyes held all the colors, though blue stuck out. He guessed Petr could be handsome. More importantly, River described him as faithful, dedicated, loyal, and a friend.

Thinking hard to leave a message for Jennifer specifically, River thought, *If you haven't already been conceived, I guess he is attractive, and I love my friend. You have my blessing, young dragon.*

Holding the pole, River sighed. "Do you know what a claiming is?"

The change of direction caused Petr to stop, turn toward him, and scrunch his face again. Maybe it was the thick eyebrows, Petr showed his thoughts too easily—not that River could distinguish between the meaning, just that he thought a lot.

"Yes, River. I was there when your sister claimed Chenon."

"Did you know they were rare?" he asked.

"No, I hadn't thought about how common it might be."

"I've heard the rumors about my parents having a claiming, but that's not true. My mother never claimed my father. Theirs was strong attraction and mutual desire."

"I understand, but you've been all over the place today."

This was his opportunity! His chance to tell Petr about Chulin! Yet he knew, beyond any doubt, there was something else he needed to say.

"You know, one day, I could have a descendant, human at birth, a dragon at adulthood. It might even be a girl who would be your heart, your claiming."

An odd sensation came over Jennifer as River had a vision of her standing transfixed in the woods, facing a bear. As the bear clawed, she exploded into a red, elephant-sized, long-necked, like a plesiosaur on land, complete with wings, dragon.

Petr laughed. "You would wish me to be your son-in-law?" He broke into hysterics. When he caught his breath, he said, "I'm old enough to be your father, over and over."

"But you're not my father or even related to me." Though now that River stopped and thought of the possibility of what his hidden gift told him, he said thoughtfully, "And it would be an honor and a blessing to have you officially be part of my family."

"Come," Petr said, motioning for River to join him at the ledge. Petr placed a foot on a rock and started wading into the water. "It's a little cold," he said. A few more steps, and he disappeared beneath the liquid as the edge dropped off. When his head popped up, hair pressed long against his face, fishing spear in hand, River laughed.

"All right," Petr said. "If you have all your parents' memories, prove it to me. What is God like? Your father was the first dragon; surely, he remembers that."

Instantly, Jennifer became consumed by darkness all around her and in her. She floated aimlessly on a breeze that would challenge a tornado, though it made no sound. For who knew how long, she bobbed in what she could only describe as energy, like the hair-raising sensation of a lightning storm rattling nearby.

A random musical note turned into the high-pitched plucking of many harps, not playing a song or even a tune, but arbitrary notes that vibrated through her being, soft at first, then louder. She missed the moment when the disorderly chords became a rhythm, like when an orchestra practices and it slowly formed into a collective artistic melody. As the hidden band built up speed, an overwhelming sense of love and peace ran through her body as if the music lived.

Gasping from the intensity, Jennifer, in her body, sat on a bench outside in the dark. This time, Jennifer realized she controlled her limbs as she wiggled her fingers. This was the first time controlling her body in a dream since the night she ran into the bear.

As her blond hair fell across one eye, she used her fingers to brush the strand behind an ear and sighed, surveying the surrounding area. Beside her, a streetlight gave off a yellow glow that blocked the darkness around her. She raised an eyebrow.

In the real world, at night, the streetlight would do nothing other than be irritatingly bright. She would be able to see past the light's path.

The scene reminded her of a *Dick Tracy* comic or an old black-and-white detective movie.

A voice interrupted her contemplation. "I know you're lost. It's all a little confusing." The spokesperson reminded her of the main character of a vampire show set in the South she liked to watch sometimes.

From the corner of her eye, Jennifer caught a flicker of movement just past the orb of yellow illumination. A man's silhouette, outlined in a faint electric purple, traveled along the edge of the beam's circle. He skipped a little. "But it will be okay."

As he walked, he said, "I'm surprised at your ability to adapt. You've been doing well for a human, dragon girl."

"Dragon girl," Jennifer scoffed. "More like a crazy girl.

However, I am delighted to be having a different dream. I'm also glad to be myself for a little while." She held up her hand, amazed it obeyed.

"Just a few more nights, dragon girl, and the transformation will be complete. Then it will all be easier."

"Who are you?" Jennifer asked.

His pace increased around the outer circle of light. The outline of his head showed he was staring at the ground.

"I am your guide, in a way. How do I say this without it being too soon? I do so like surprises."

He had walked behind the bench again. "I am you, and I am someone else altogether." He started laughing. "Soon, dragon girl, I will be able to explain who I am. Hopefully, in the meantime, you can stay alive."

"Alive? Am I dying? Will someone kill me?"

"You can see in the dark as if it was day. You notice odors in the room no one else does. Not to mention, you can eat a cow by yourself and not gain weight. If you haven't noticed, you're not human anymore, and, since you seem to be pretending to be human..." The shadow stopped, and Jennifer could feel the pinpricks of someone watching her. "I will tell you that all the folklore and stories about humans killing dragons are very true. I know you have been doing a good job shoving off the dreams, going to class, pretending to be someone you are not, but you must be careful. A slip-up and —" The shadow stopped speaking abruptly. The outline of his hand slid across his neck while he made a guttural rasp. She knew what he meant; she would be murdered.

"You feel Johan staring at you, though you try not to accuse him outright. He stinks of danger. Is he friend or foe? He reminds you of someone locked in your brain, but you don't remember who, only that this person scares you. It's his eyes that remind you of someone. Someone I'm sure you long to forget. Right now, you cannot recall the memory. It's suppressed. Your mind is changing more slowly than your body will. It's hard for humans to comprehend these memories of generations past." The man's outline made a gun with his fingers and pretended to shoot himself.

He stepped into the light but remained a shadow, edged with purple. He said, "How does Matt play into this game of yours?"

He halved the distance and continued, "Dr. Smith, you like him, not Matt. Petr, Professor Smith, whoever he wants to pretend he is this decade. You have chosen him. Or maybe River hand-picked him for you. You are putting out enough pheromones to create a herd of horny single dragons when he is around." The name Petr came out sassy. It reminded Jennifer of kids who would tease her when she had a crush on a boy and then said the boy's name mockingly.

She blushed. "I don't really know Dr. Smith. I haven't chosen him."

The shadow man halved the distance again. This time, she scented the fall forest, with leaves decaying on the ground, and smoke. He said, "Yes, you do know Petr. Or your ancestor did."

The shadow creature smiled, showing bright white, sharpened to a point, teeth. She glanced away, anywhere but at the talking monster.

Nothing happened.

Curious why he stopped talking, she focused on him. A mythological dragon, slightly taller than her, with a dark blue underbelly and a bright purple-blue back, stood in front of her. Instead of scales, its skin resembled a lizard's, complete with a slimy-oily or wet shimmer. It had thin wings with talons on the ends, like a pterodactyl. Itty-bitty eyes filled the oversized head, dominated by a long mouth full of rows of pointed teeth.

Like a scene from a horror movie, the dragon-like creature

sniffed her. Warm, humid air filled with the stench of rotting meat and caused her hair to whip around her face.

In terror, all Jennifer could do was stare.

"I know all these things," the dragon said in the same voice as the shadow man. He licked her face with a slimy sandpaper tongue like a cat's. "Because I am part of you."

CHAPTER 28

JENNIFER

...After working all day in the scorching summer sun, I desperately wanted a dip in the nearby stream to clean off the salty sweat. Close to the banks, the rippling current became almost calm.

In the distance, I heard the distinct sounds of someone walking through the reeds near the water's edge.

I froze in anticipation, parts of my body hardening, expecting to find Ava, the vicar's wife. Almost every day this summer, she left her children at home to bathe in the waterhole.

In the spring, Ava gave birth to her fifth brood, causing her lovely breasts to swell with milk. Unlike most girls with wide hips, she was built for pleasure.

I licked my lips. After the last church service, she shyly smiled while making eye contact from hooded eyes on my way out. She whispered my name as I passed. That alone fueled fantasies of hearing her lyrical voice beg while I mounted her.

I traveled a short distance and found my desire standing in the tall grass. "Niall, is that you?" she asked. She blocked the sun that touched her face with her arm. Her long brown hair shimmered in the light, her chest bare, the dress hanging loose around her hips.

When she saw me, she didn't try to cover her nudity, instead flaunting it proudly before me. I licked my lips, thirsty for something more than water.

But I remembered my manners and removed my hat, holding it in front of me. "Yes, ma'am," I said, lowering my head.

"Well, come over here." She waved, encouraging me to come closer. Who was I to deny her? As I approached, she continued, "I'm washing off and cleaning my dress, but there is more than enough water for both of us. Come and keep me company."

Now that I moved out of the brush, I was able to view her full form. Her brown dress gathered at her waist as she stood ankle deep, the bottom collecting water. Her nipples were erect, swollen, and uncovered.

With eagle eyes, she surveyed me. Like in all my hopes and wild fantasies, she kicked her dress away, allowing it to float in the pool's shallows. "You are a strong man with broad shoulders, unlike my husband. Will you help me?"

I had been told there were creatures that could imitate my evil fantasies and take me to hell. She wasn't a banshee; they screamed. Whatever stood in front of me wasn't one of them. The Fairy Queen, maybe, but what she planned to do with me, I didn't know.

Nervous and excited, my voice sounded weak and guttural, but I said, "How may I help you?"

Instead of answering, she bellowed tears of regret and sorrow, her chest heaving.

Her pleading was so loud that I searched the area for anyone close enough to eavesdrop. If someone came upon us, they might think her crying had something to do with her state of undress. As I surveyed the region anxiously, I asked, "Please, Ava, keep it down. Is this like that story of Joseph? Are you Potiphar's wife and trapping me into things I have not done?"

At this, her weeping turned to hilarity. When she stopped laughing and took two gigantic breaths, she said, "I'm fairly certain, Niall, that I am more like Delilah. My husband has had his fill of me. He says I am a temptation too strong. In order to maintain his relationship with God, he has shoved me aside. No, worse than shoving me to the side. I am a sinner. A vessel made for evil and to be used by the devil. My husband has abandoned me to hell and only keeps me because of our children."

She swallowed loudly, and I moved closer. Her forehead creased in concentration, and she sniffed. "Maybe he is right, and I am of the devil. I have so many carnal needs. I need to be touched and to feel a man in me. I've seen the way you watch me at church." She flung her arm out and continued, "Here. You watch me while I bathe.

"I can't take it anymore. I'm asking you to go to hell for me. I want you to take me, Niall, to risk your soul for me."

Before anyone recognized us, I led her to an abandoned building deep in the woods. Most people considered the area haunted, but the only tormented souls around were me and the bewitching woman I'd risk damnation to please.

When I finished and my seed covered her legs, I needed more. My soul was already damned, and I would drink of her as often and as much as she would let me. Staring at her nipples and preparing for another round, something hit me in the face…

The soft object forced Jennifer awake from the intense dream about Niall. It didn't stop a moan of need that escaped Jennifer's mouth—guttural, raw, real. The need made her skin feel like a feather tickled every inch. Every move brought both the need for completion and the need for more. She moaned again.

"Jennifer!" Belinda threw a small stuffed animal directly at Jennifer's head. "I don't care what crazy dream you're having; stop moaning. You sound like a porn star."

Ava had to be in the area somewhere. "Where is Ava?" she asked.

This time, instead of two distinct personalities and struggling to remember her thoughts, Jennifer knew her name. However, her body prickled with Niall's desire as lust licked her from head to toe. Instead of capturing her mind, Niall's wickedness entangled her body.

Sitting on the bed with her phone to one side and a book in her lap, Belinda said, "A girl! Oh, Jennifer, I'm sure Matt is like every normal guy, but you surprise me. I thought you were straight and a virgin. So, are you experimenting now?"

"No," she answered. Despite her words, the images of Ava's glowing body under Niall's ministrations sent waves of tingles through her nerve endings. She breathed to release the tension.

Porn, in 4-D, combined with committing adultery, and knowing that what you did was condemnable, was overwhelmingly sexy.

"I'm fighting the urge to moan again. What a dream," Jennifer admitted. Perhaps if she jogged around campus, she would expend the energy.

"That's funny. They make toys that could help, you know. Plus, I'm not willing to be your experimental partner. I'm not going to play Ava for you. Anyway, maybe if you saw some pimply college boys again, you'll calm down. Do you have time to go to the cafeteria? You look hungry. I mean, for food, not munching on someone's rug. You can give me a break from studying. I really hate math," Belinda said.

Ignoring the notepad, she grabbed the watch off the charger. "My skin is crawling. Yeah, that sounds like a good idea."

"Perfect." Belinda shut the book and placed it in front of her on the bed. "Would you please throw Maddie back to me?"

Glancing around the room, a blue and white plush dog lay between Jennifer's bed and the small sofa. Leaning over and grabbing it off the floor, Jennifer asked, "That's what hit me?"

Belinda lovingly caught the stuffed animal and hugged it before placing it on the calculus book. "Yes."

Pointing at the book, Jennifer asked, "You're an economics major, and you hate math?"

"I'm accounting, and yes, I hate math." At the counter, Belinda sprayed a healthy dose of the rose perfume around her neck, the scent both overwhelming and romantic.

She wasn't sure how she knew, but where the tiny droplets touched her skin, a warm spot developed and prickled with desire. Wanting to calm her uncontrolled passion, Jennifer breathed slowly.

Belinda opened the door and waved for Jennifer to pass in front of her. "Jen, I'm telling you, even your cheeks are flushed, and you're glowing. If that's the response to whatever you dreamed, I'd like to hear about it." She laughed. "How hot is Jennifer's dream fet—"

"No, let's not talk about it. I want this..." —Jennifer waved her arms in the air, like she could make the sensations leave — "I want it gone. This icky craving has to go away."

They made a quick stop at the bathroom.

"Well, I'll tell you about Rick, who is better known as Dick. Can you believe that name stuck? The guys in the fraternity house are calling him that. He likes it, and I like it... like all nine—"

"Please don't. I need to think of something non-sexy. Something different, please. Tell me about your classes?"

"Better yet, why don't you tell me about Matt?" Belinda asked.

That calmed her some, her skin less electric. "What about Matt?" she asked.

"He said you hadn't called or texted since a week or so ago."

"Oh," Jennifer said, confused and trying to remember when she last talked with Matt. She believed it was yesterday, but she couldn't remember for sure. "I'll answer his text when we get in the lunchroom."

"Alright," Belinda answered.

Jennifer held the door, allowing more of the delicious aroma of cooking meat to ooze around her as Belinda headed toward the food lines first.

After paying, Jennifer set up at their usual table and reviewed the cellphone messages. There on the screen was a conversation she didn't remember. Matt planned to drop by her apartment on the last day of exams. She swallowed and opened up her calendar, setting her alarm with a quick reminder of Matt's visit.

Glancing around the room, she didn't recall the tile floor having a marble pattern. She remembered it being dark gray with specks of color. Checking her phone tracking app, it said she ate here yesterday. Why did it seem like twenty years ago? Like she was visiting a place she hadn't seen in years? Did her personality change from one day to the next? She felt like she'd lived hundreds of years in a few weeks.

Soon, several other friends sat at their table. Laughter, stories, and debates blossomed around her, allowing her to focus on the important thing—the succulent meal in front of her.

One person discussed a prank on a reality show—a bucket of water over a door. Everyone at the table giggled when they reached the punch line, yet there was nothing funny about it, so Jennifer just stared.

Another person discussed the stress they were under because she and a friend wanted to date the same person. A blond girl nearby gave her advice; none of that was important.

Were these things she enjoyed yesterday?

She placed her elbows on the table and used both hands to shove the hamburger in her face, finishing first despite having the most oversized plate.

"Hey, I'm going to the bathroom. Be right back," Jennifer whispered to Belinda, taking her tray to the trashcan.

An odd realization occurred as she shoved her waste into

the trashcan. She felt sexy, desirable, and wanted. As she headed to the bathroom, she wondered if she'd always be THIS confident. She didn't think so.

Most people didn't know about the cleanest bathrooms in the student center. The closed door near the kitchen hid a long, narrow hall. The corridor, blocked off on both ends by doors, became an extremely excluded area not really meant for foot traffic and had such a small width that she could touch either wall if she stood in the middle. When she and Belinda accidentally found it, they kept it a secret among their group, though others were aware. She'd seen other people walk in and out of the door, not many, but a few, probably going to the student center.

Cracking the door, she noticed the lights were out in the hall before she had a prickling sensation of being watched. She continued to head toward the bathroom while glancing over her shoulder at the cafeteria. She recognized Johan's hungry eyes sizing her up. Then bumped into something solid, bounced awkwardly off, losing her hold on the door as it closed. As she watched the ground coming closer, she stumbled forward, and powerful arms grabbed her.

The second he touched her, her skin became alive. First, the passion only existed as small points where they made contact, but the anticipation branched until the sensation revived the intense desire from this morning. Her traitorous heart beat in expectation. Her breath became shallow.

She knew who held her elbows. Even if she couldn't smell the cashmere, sandalwood, and slight mold, she'd still know. He was her own personal Gancanagh, her Irish fairy of seduction—wanting her to succumb to the urges of Niall's sin.

A weird, peaceful lust shifted in her being as she grabbed onto his arms to stabilize herself. Strange completeness settled with the strong desire to become one with him—to be his and him to be hers.

Staring up from the ground, she lost herself in Petr's eyes, daring him to do more than just hold her arms.

You can kiss me if you want.

The surrounding air sizzled and popped, the noise reminiscent of water hitting an electrical powerline during a rainstorm. Neither of them glanced away to investigate the sound as an awkward pause swept over the moment.

Eventually, as in whispered surprise, he spoke her name and let his arms drop. "Jennifer."

"Dr. Smith," she panted.

Does he need me as I need him?

Raw urgency to take him as hers so strongly overcame her body that she clenched her hands into fists to keep from leaning in and kissing him. She didn't miss the fact that he stayed in her personal space. A slight movement of her head, or his, and she couldn't stop herself. Her skin burned for him to smother the flames of desire.

"Are you okay?" he whispered.

No. No, I'm not. I need you, my Gancanagh.

"I'm fine. I'm sorry, I," she stammered, glancing back at the door to the cafeteria. She was alone with Dr. Smith. No one would know if she tried to kiss him.

I could take you into one of these rooms. Would you let me?

She swallowed, taking time to clear the images pounding through her mind of her shoving him against the wall, her kissing him as she pressed her body against him. She said, "I thought I saw someone. Never mind."

Dr. Smith laughed awkwardly. A musk filled the room, and she wanted to make him purr like a cat under her continuous petting—to ride him while he fondled her breasts.

He asked, "You are okay, then?"

No. I need you, my Gancanagh.

There weren't many rooms off this narrow hall. Maybe one went to a coat closet. No one would know. No one had to know. In her dreams, it didn't even have to last long. It could be her secret...well, their secret.

"Why are you here?" Jennifer asked. She'd never seen a college professor in the student cafeteria.

At first, he didn't answer, like a deer stuck in the headlights. Instead, he stared at her mouth. She realized she nibbled on her lower lip.

Gancanagh, my Gancanagh.

As he searched her face, he said, "I turned in some final grades to the office to be put into the computer, and this is the fastest path. Otherwise, I have to walk around the building."

There was another pause; he continued to focus on her mouth, and she thought he might kiss her. He whispered in a rough sultry, bass, "Why are you here?"

Chills traveled up her spine, and she leaned a hair's breadth closer.

The bathroom, I can take him in the bathroom.

"I ate lunch with my roommate." She turned to point toward the cafeteria. "Do you—"

"Is Matt here?" he asked.

She was going to ask him if he wanted to go back to her dorm, or maybe his office, if he had one to himself. But at the mention of Matt, she paused and tasted the words.

Under normal circumstances, faithful, sensible Jennifer would realize her predicament and step away from the sin. But last night, she was Niall, and he partook of the flesh of another man's wife. The excitement of the forbidden fruit, Dr. Smith, not her boyfriend and a teacher on top of that, made her hungry for his carnal pleasures, and she moaned. She couldn't stand it anymore. Her eyes left him and searched for a private area, perhaps even the bathroom. She was desperate. *My Gancanagh!* She reached up to touch him—

The double door to the cafeteria opened. The rose perfume told her who walked into the hall, and she didn't turn to glance at her roommate. Right then, her prey stood before her, but Jennifer had regained control, her hand dropping. She breathed a sigh of relief.

"Jennifer? Is Matt here?" Dr. Smith asked again and took a giant step away from her.

"Sorry, I don't think so. We don't have time to see each other. Too busy with school." Ignoring the girl moving beside her, she said, "I have your class in the spring, your anthropology class."

She remembered that, registering for classes. Though it, like everything else, was vague.

Dr. Smith paused for a second. "Will you be going with us on the class trip in March?" he asked.

"What class trip?" Jennifer asked.

Belinda shifted her weight, almost touching Jennifer's shoulder in a motion meant to encourage Jennifer to introduce her.

But Jennifer didn't want Belinda anywhere near this man, *her Gancanagh,* so she kept quiet.

"I take a few students to a dig site in Elmo, Utah. It's open to anyone in my lectures," he responded, glancing nervously toward Belinda.

Acknowledging Belinda with a nod, she turned back to Dr. Smith and said, "I think I would like that. I guess I better get going. See you next semester, and sorry I ran you over."

Grabbing Belinda's hand, she opened the double door.

Once inside the cafeteria, the door flapped shut. Belinda pulled her arm free. "What was that?"

"What was what?"

"Was that a professor?" Belinda asked.

"Yes."

"You like him," Belinda accused.

"What?" More than like, he was her Gancanagh.

"Jennifer, your cheeks are bright red. It makes you look like a blond apple. To be honest, I'm surprised you didn't dream of him instead of Ava." She snickered.

Ignoring the Ava jab, she said, "Yes. He's attractive."

Conspiratorially, she said, "Yes, he is. Better not let Matt know. He texted me while we were eating and said to get lost on Thursday. He said he's coming by our apartment right after his final exam. I didn't tell him I was done Tuesday and wouldn't be there. Actually, I asked for twenty to leave. So, are you going to sip the milk? I mean, as crazy as you've been acting, you should taste something."

"Ha-ha," Jennifer answered sarcastically and changed the subject to Dick. While Belinda rattled on about the virtues of a carefree love life, Jennifer wondered, would she have tried to have her way with Dr. Smith if Belinda hadn't come into the room? She thought she would.

CHAPTER 29

PETR

THE DOOR CLOSED, AND PETR STOOD ALONE, FROZEN IN THE empty, dark hall. Thank God he'd already turned in the grades, or they would be forgotten, scattered on the floor when she bumped into him.

The shortcut by the student cafeteria was the most direct path to the office. The university required the original documentation as evidence; he might as well make use of the fastest way possible to deliver them.

When he entered the hall and saw how many bulbs this room had out, he promised himself to stop and count. As a good steward, he planned to report the issue to the maintenance department when he returned to his desk.

He faced the ceiling and didn't know who bumped into him—though as exciting vibrations coated his skin, he thought of Jennifer. After he straightened her upright, he lost himself in her face. Her cheeks flushed before she made eye contact, the room's air becoming saturated with lavender. Even now, parts of him radiated from the experience.

What happened? How did I lose control so quickly?

He stood there, watching her lips, wanting desperately to taste them, to taste her.

Neither of them moved. How long did he stand so close to Jennifer that he witnessed his breath move her blond hair?

Even now, he couldn't maneuver away, like she glued his feet to the ground. Lust so thick it permeated the air—his limbs heavy under pressure.

A student he didn't recognize walked into the hall, stirring the ether like walking through smoke. The person passed him without glancing at him and entered the bathroom, even though Petr stood awkwardly in the center. Light flooded the area and slowly darkened as the door closed.

"Come on, Petr," he encouraged himself. He needed to leave before the person returned.

Turning away from the cafeteria, he strolled to the other end to the second door. Once through, the sunshine poured into the university's student center. Music floated from the basement. A live band played downstairs as part of the celebration for the finish of the school semester.

The amps carried the loud bass; the boom bounced to a decent rhythm, and his mind made up words to the song. *Alone, there you are, alone, and she comes into the room. What do you do, Petr?*

Her perfume alone undid him as the lavender swirled in a fury of desire. He could drown in the scent.

Should I have said more to her? Could I have said more to her?

For a short time, while gazing into her eyes, he thought of himself as a fly stuck in a web. As if her presence alone controlled him to happily do whatever she wanted. Thinking he would break the spell, he mentioned Matt. Instead of calming her, it ignited something, like adding water to the coals in a steam room.

Next semester, when she takes my class, what will I do if we find ourselves alone? That was, if he maintained control.

Leaving the community center and stepping into the cold, the noise behind him diffused. A winter breeze washed over him, and he regretted forgetting his jacket in his office.

However, the spell she weaved seemed to dissipate. While he moved faster to get warmer, he decided he needed a plan, something he could fall back on when passion piloted his actions.

Passion? More like she spelled him with magic…or poison.

His hunger for Jennifer bordered on obsession—like being thirsty after working outside for hours on a hot day and getting that glass of cold water. It was like having an itch on your back and finding a back scratcher—calming, peaceful, calamity, chaos, overpowerful, consuming...too many conflicting words.

"Words are great, Petr, but what do you plan to do?" he asked himself.

A student nearby stared at him, then at his pants. Because of Petr's excellent hearing, he heard the man whisper to his buddy, "He calls his junk Petr."

That was definitely the part of his body controlling his mind right now.

Sure, he believed in fate and destiny but trusted in preparation to avoid pitfalls. Typically, he didn't need to discuss his life with anyone. He knew what to do. But today, he wished he had someone in the same time zone. The only person he would've confided in had she still lived was his sister Roz, his twin. Roz, his sister who fed him crushed dragon heart without him knowing—he would have asked her.

He imagined the conversation with her...

Him: Roz, I'm attracted to Matt's girlfriend. Matt, your son's descendant.

Roz: Petr, you're old and hesitant to be attracted to anybody. Find pleasure where you can. Matt is young. He'll find someone else.

Him: You don't know what it's like to love someone and watch them die.

Roz: Hogwash! Petr, I watched my mate die. If you like her, risk it. Risk trying.

Him: It's just lust. Why commit something against my beliefs for one night of pleasure? Plus, if I love her, she will age and die.

Roz: Please, brother, you're too cautious and should live a little. There are other ways to live forever than eating a dragon's heart. If you like her and then love her, you will find a way.

Right then, the ache of not having his sister felt raw...Also, he would never have told her about this. She would give terrible advice.

Shaking his head, he opened the door to his office building and headed upstairs.

At the door to his office, he stopped. Petr had heard of dragons claiming their mate. Could it be a claiming? Could she be the dragon, and she was claiming him?

No. There was no way. Jennifer had a brother. She couldn't be the dragon shifter. He'd never get that lucky.

At one point, he thought she was going to kiss him. Maybe even tear his clothing off—he would have let her.

If she approached him while still dating Matt, he couldn't have a relationship with her. Being in a relationship with one person and dating another screamed a lack of commitment. Any woman he wooed had to be faithful. Lust or not, he couldn't be involved, even for just a night of carnal pleasure.

Another possibility was that Jennifer Wright was no longer in a relationship with Matt. In that case, he could date her and hunt for traits he liked. Sure, she would age, and he wouldn't, but he was willing to try for the right person. Besides, he knew a few ways to live forever; some didn't involve a dragon's heart.

Then, he had to tackle the improbable possibility. "Consider she is the one, Petr," he said to himself, thinking of the dragon shifter. Grabbing the picture from the folder in his briefcase, he leaned back in his chair, holding the image and rubbing his temple with the other. In the corner, the symbols marked reaching a dead end with potential dragon lines—all except for her father's father. He'd have to go out of town for that part of the hunt.

Well, at least in that scenario, he didn't have to find a way to keep her alive. Dragons lived forever. All it took was one physical encounter to lock two souls together. A long time ago, he decided that while not out of the question, mating a dragon should require a lengthy, non-physical courtship lasting longer than ten years. The risk of mating someone over lust, then discovering that you didn't really like them, was a possibility he didn't want.

From his understanding, the bonding occurred from the act of sex itself. For a dragon shifter, he wasn't sure if it happened before or after they became a dragon. He assumed after. If it happened before turning into a dragon shifter, he wasn't clear what would happen to people with several partners. Perhaps the dragon shifter would have a harem?

He placed the picture back into his bag and grabbed his coat.

As he locked the door in the hall, Thjasse stood outside waiting.

Glancing at him, key in the knob, Petr asked, "Thjasse, to what do I owe the pleasure?"

"Remember our conversation the other day, Dr. Smith?" he asked.

"I searched the video feed for who at this campus you've been stalking, and it's me. I can assure you I am not a dragon shifter," Petr said. He'd spent hours watching different cameras.

"We have other operatives following the dragon shifter, Dr. Smith. I've been hired to take you out of the equation."

Operatives—such an interesting word to use.

The term implied several people were involved. Ending this human now became an obligation for the safety of the dragon shifter. Overall, Petr didn't like killing, but sometimes bloodshed became a necessary evil.

Breathing out and accepting the challenge, Petr said, "I suggest we don't do this here in public. Eliminating a person can get...messy, and there is the issue of hiding the body."

"You have a point, Dr. Smith. Where do you suggest we go?" Thjasse kept pace, matching him as they marched through the hall and down the stairs.

Petr shrugged. "The mountains. You can follow...or I can give you an address...or schedule this for tomorrow if you insist it needs to be done."

"Not tomorrow. I have to be in California tomorrow."

Petr nodded. If things went as they usually went, Thjasse wouldn't make it to California. If the man had a family, and Petr killed him, Petr would feel guilty. Therefore, Petr didn't ask for any details.

Instead, Petr changed the subject. "Well, if you plan to kill me, care to give me a hint as to who the dragon shifter is? I'm not a Nose."

"Above my pay grade. I'm not a Nose, either. If it makes you feel better, they don't plan to kill the dragon shifter, only gather them to the flock, you might say."

Immortals killed dragons to harvest their body parts for the gifts they bestowed. To not kill a dragon was the exact opposite of normal Immortal behavior. Maybe there was a group other than the Immortals—something to consider later.

Thjasse tapped him on the shoulder and said, "Stop frowning, Dr. Smith. Look on the bright side, tomorrow morning, it won't be a worry. Let me ask you a question."

Petr stopped, curious, and turned toward him.

As they stood facing each other outside, in the dark under a pole light, Thjasse asked, "How old are you?"

"Haven't you ever heard it's rude to ask someone's age? Besides, what does it matter if I'm going to be dead tomorrow? I'll keep my age to myself until my death if you don't mind."

"Fair enough. You sure are taking this better than any of the other people I've killed. Because I like you, do you have a wife or anyone I should contact about your death?"

"If I have a family, it doesn't matter. Let my loved ones wonder. Do you want to follow me, or should I give you the address?" Petr asked, and they started walking toward Petr's car.

"Why don't we ride together—that way, neither of us will pull out any tricks? During my last fight, three men showed up out of the blue. My target hit a panic button. Jerk couldn't handle a straight fight," Thjasse said.

It occurred to Petr that if they drove separately on the way to the mountains, Thjasse would call the 'operatives.' Not that Petr minded if they showed up. He could fight more than one person at a time. Petr needed to stay off everyone's radar to protect his friends more than anything.

Anticipation rose in Petr's chest. How many years had it been since he used his body as a weapon? These days most people used guns. "You want an old-fashioned brawl to the death? Using fists? No guns or weapons?" Petr asked, a little excited at the prospect of testing his cunning, strength, and stamina in a fight to the death.

Thjasse put his arm around Petr, as if they were long-lost friends. "I like the way you think, Dr. Smith. This is turning out to be a fine night."

Petr reached the door to his car, unlocked it, and allowed Thjasse to sit in the passenger seat. Hopping into the driver's side and placing the vehicle into reverse, Petr reflected on his last fistfight. Like Thjasse, the man he killed stood taller, with broader shoulders. No one anticipated Petr's speed or the years he trained to fight dragons.

Thjasse wouldn't understand until it was too late.

CHAPTER 30
JENNIFER

OUTSIDE JENNIFER'S DORM, MATT STUDIED THE FOUNTAIN AS HE waited. She snuck behind him, tiptoeing, then standing like a ballerina en pointe, she covered Matt's eyes. "Guess who?"

I'm not Fiona. I'm Jennifer Wright. Don't say Fiona.

Instead of answering with words, he grabbed her wrists and forced them around his waist. Gently, he tugged her close to his chest. His body wash of mint, rosemary, and cedar-wood blended into a sexy, fresh, clean smell.

When she backed away to see his face, Matt's lips found hers in a possessive, demanding, powerful kiss. When he finished, he took a step back. "I had to kiss you."

Glancing around the area, she searched to see if anyone had witnessed the display of emotion. A girl down the hill came up toward them, but she had a stack of books in her hands, struggling, unaware of anything else. A guy was to her right, but he walked away, not facing them.

Matt followed her gaze, apparently also searching for onlookers. Then he turned his full attention to Jennifer. "I should have started with, how are you?"

Grabbing her hands, he stretched them out. Then, in a non-sexual way, like when a stylist prepared a model for a runway show, he checked out her clothing. She knew he saw jeans, a green ultra-soft hoody with a pocket in front, and her regular jogging shoes. Once complete, he let her hands drop.

At least his weird inspection allowed her to consider his question. How was she? Well, classes were officially done, despite spending most of the day as a carefree wind sprite named Fiona...Fiona was human but believed bizarre things, such being fairy of the forest.

"I'm fine," she answered. Then, seconds later, added, "How are you?"

He exhaled like he had been holding his breath for a long time. "I'm fine." Frantically, he searched around the area. Apparently finding what he wanted, he locked his hand around her wrist. "Come on." He led her to the unoccupied ornate iron bench.

Lucky for both of them, the wood seat did not hold the cold, which kept the day's chill from settling into their bones like something made of stone would have. Even after a few minutes of standing in the chilly air, Jennifer could see white puffs when she breathed.

He sat beside her, a foot between them, and she stuck her hands inside her pullover.

"This won't do," he announced. Scooting closer to her, he placed his arm around her shoulder. He leaned over to her ear. "I'm sorry, Jennifer."

Should she comfort him? Lean into him? Not sure what to do, she hyper-focused on a car leaving the parking lot by the dorm as the vehicle turned away from them toward the main road.

Still near her ear, he whispered, "I should have never gone to the beach without you."

That was what he was upset about? Mentally, she shrugged because she didn't remember or care about him going to a beach. Her demeanor, though, stayed calm, and she observed the busy street.

When he said nothing else, she knew she needed to respond.

What would Jennifer do?

Despite the cold, she placed her hand on his leg and squeezed. Turning at her hip, she faced him. His hair had grown, no longer cut short, and part of it landed in a jet-black curl in front of his right eye. She laced a finger through that loop.

She didn't remember Matt, not well, but the few memories there that seemed like centuries ago told him she cared for him, that he was a good guy.

Locking eyes with him so he saw her sincerity, she said, "You're forgiven."

Easy to forgive something you couldn't recollect.

As he sighed, his shoulders relaxed, and he pulled her head deeper onto his chest. To do this, she repositioned and moved so her neck rested on his lap, feet on the wood planks, staring at Matt's chin and the overcast sky.

That one strand of hair bothered her, so she tugged on it again. It wasn't the right color. The face in front of her was very handsome, indeed. But earlier, when she saw the message that her boyfriend Matt was visiting, she imagined a different face; one with auburn curls and a blond patch almost in the center.

"What's wrong?" Matt asked, and she realized she had scrunched up her face.

She didn't have an answer, so she did what Fiona would do. Locking her hand behind his head, she pressed him down and her up.

Dreaming almost every night about different couples since Thanksgiving had honed her talents in certain areas. Using the newly obtained knowledge, she kissed Matt in a way that made lovers drop to their knees.

It mainly involved the tongue and lips, but other parts, equally important and often ignored, joined in the seduction. With her hands, she caressed his neck. Without breaking contact, she maneuvered her body so that she straddled him.

This knowledge must be natural because he coordinated with the seduction dance. His breathing changed, and his heart raced as he rubbed and tugged.

While she forced her effort, she closed her eyes and thought of the other face. She wouldn't tell Matt about the other person—if she remembered a name or why the phantom man seemed important.

Eventually, he forgot the question, and she moved back to stare at Matt's face. He panted, his eyes half-masked, and a new musky scent of desire tinged the area.

"Wow," he whispered. Then he said, "I missed you."

Okay, time for her to lie. "I missed you, too."

She should miss him.

This time, he started the kiss by placing his arms around her and dragging her closer. She allowed him to reel her in and returned his energy level. As she sat up straight, she bit his bottom lip.

"Listen," he said, glancing around them and placing his hands on her calves. "Is Belinda still here?"

Gosh, another name that sounded familiar, but she couldn't recall. He must be referring to the person in the dorm room who wore rose perfume. It was empty when she woke.

"She's not upstairs," she answered honestly.

Now, the odor of lust was so strong it saturated the area like a fog.

Glancing at her face, he ran his hands up her back and into her hair. He sucked in with his teeth clenched. His words were barely audible and more like a grunt. "Why don't you sign me in, and we go upstairs to your room?"

It didn't sound like a bad idea, but it didn't sound good either. While she debated which emotion harmonized with

Jennifer Wright and which belonged to Fiona, the side of Matt's jeans vibrated.

As cheesy as it sounded, that slight movement caused unbearable desire, and she hopped off his lap and offered him a hand to help him stand. "Come on. Let's go upstairs."

As he stood, he said, "Before we go upstairs. I have to make sure you understand my commitment."

Tilting her head, she was slightly confused.

Had they never had sex before?

Honestly, she had countless memories of several people in multiple poses.

Sensing this was important, she stopped and faced him. Glancing up, she searched his eyes as he seemed to do the same with hers.

"I didn't mean to leave you here while I went to the ocean. I'm serious about our relationship." On top of the musk, a subtle floral scent crept into the mix. She couldn't distinguish the soft aroma from gardenia or rose.

"It's okay, Matt. I'm not angry about you having fun with your friends. You know I'm okay by myself."

"It's not okay, Jen. Listen, over winter break, I want you to think about something. I won't ask you until the end of the spring, but anyway." He dropped his hands, and she watched as he kicked a rock on the ground. "Doug and Lauren graduate soon. Doug told me he plans to propose on Christmas, and well, he plans to move out sometime this summer."

Taking her hands back, he made puppy dog eyes, pleading eyes with her as he said, "I know we haven't been dating long, but would you be my roommate? And I'm asking you to be my sexual partner as well as my girlfriend. I'm asking for a lot of firsts here."

He confirmed it! They had never had sex! A lot of firsts, indeed!

The idea of living with Matt didn't sound bad, but Jennifer had a problem. What would Matt do when he woke up beside Fiona or Niall? What happened if, one night, Jennifer disappeared? It seemed to her that Jennifer's memories came slower, like she slipped away more every day. Sure, she put on a good show, but even now, parts of Jennifer's personality seemed lost.

Sometimes, the emotions from the moment that ended her dream heated her day. How would he handle it if she talked to him in Gaelic for the first five hours of the day? Or used the trashcan as a toilet?

"I'll have to think about it, Matt, so thank you for the warning." Later, she would add this as a note. If they lived together, she would have to remind him of the dreams and let the full knowledge of how the dreams impacted her life be known. That part about having a partner sounded reassuring, though, someone to help find Jennifer Wright. So, she leaned over, and he met her halfway. When they kissed, to Jennifer, it felt less like lust and more like commitment, and she liked this better than the over-the-top, rip-off all her clothes sex.

When they finished, she nudged her head toward her building and said, "Come on. Let's go upstairs."

"Well, next time I chase the sun, I will have to take you with me," Matt said.

Standing in front of the door, hand-in-hand, she faced him. He had that giant, bright, white-toothy smile. "Please tell me it's soon," she pleaded.

The phone in his pants pocket vibrated again. Frowning, Matt pulled it out. "Oh, hold on." He let go of her hand and walked back to the fountain while she stood at the building's entrance.

"Mom," he whispered.

"When are you coming home?" Maria, Matt's mom, said.

When had Jennifer's hearing become so sharp that she could hear someone at least twenty feet away over a phone?

"Mom, I'm in the middle of something. I'll come home tomorrow morning. Okay? Probably in the afternoon."

"Not enough time, Matt. Our plane takes off tomorrow at noon. You need to come home now. I packed your things, but you need to go through it and ensure I got everything."

He sighed. He faced the English building, away from Jennifer, and placed his free hand in his jeans pocket. "Why can't I bring a friend?"

"This is a family trip. I only want family to go."

"Can I not just stay home, like Gung-Gung?" Matt asked.

"No."

"Well, let me tell Jennifer goodbye, and then I'm on my way."

"Tell her I said hello. I'm so excited. We haven't had a vacation like this since you were a kid," Maria said.

As he placed the phone in his pocket, he frowned and walked back to her.

"I'm sorry, Jennifer. I lied." Standing close to her, he longingly gawked up at her window.

"What?" Jennifer asked.

"My parents surprised me with a Christmas vacation to the Bahamas last night. That was my mom. She wants me to come home right now." He sighed and stared at her window again. When he glanced at her, he said, "I want your first time to be special, and I don't want to leave the next morning. I want to hold you in my arms when we finish. May I have a rain check for next semester?"

A little disappointed because there wasn't such a thing as 'bad sex' when it was consensual, she searched for an answer. Sure, she could wait, but would there be a Jennifer next semester, or would she vanish into a different person? She didn't know.

Using diversion, she asked, "When are you leaving?"

"Now." He frowned.

"Oh. When are you coming home?"

He sighed. "I won't be back until right before school starts. I'm sorry."

"What are you sorry for this time?" Jennifer asked.

Quickly, he peeked up, a sad expression on his face. "Well, I'll be gone for about three weeks. I just want more time with you," Matt answered.

"Matt, I'll be here when you get back. I'm not going anywhere. I'll see you when you return." She lied, but what else could she do? Tell him she was going crazy seconds before he left for a holiday?

"I can't kiss you bye, or I'll lose my resolve." Slowly, he checked out Jennifer, and she scented desire. Then he stared at her window. "I'll see you when I get back, okay?"

"Sure," she answered, and as he walked off, Jennifer hoped she spoke the truth.

CHAPTER 31

MATT

INFINITE POOLS, MILES OF WHITE SAND BEACHES, AND BRIGHT blues that landed on shades of aquas were arguably most people's version of paradise. Yet Matt's parents sold him on the trip by advocating for a family vacation.

Groaning, Matt placed the room card key and his parent's plastic credit card in his wallet and sat at a reclining chaise lounge beside the cobalt lake the hotel called a pool. Around him, steel drums played a festive island tune from hidden speakers.

In the distance, his mother weaved around patio furniture and vacationers toward a group of partiers. She stopped and turned. Always having to be perfect, she coordinated the reds in her one-piece bathing suit, lipstick, and glasses, all under a broad-brimmed sombrero and a white blouse that whipped about in the salt-flavored breeze.

She waved, and he wished he had something he could throw at her.

"I guess this is a working vacation," Matt yelled, sarcasm dripping from his lips. He smiled as he held his arm up and gave a similar gesture, but it was part of the show she required, and he didn't mean it.

Satisfied, she returned to her path, Matt forgotten. She bounced with the beat as she moved and pumped her right fist into the air. Under the white tent, someone gave her a drink with an umbrella. His dad came up behind her, swinging her around, and they disappeared into the sea of his father's colleagues from around the world.

On the table beside him, Matt had his own liquor since he met the drinking age on the island. Waving his arm at a waiter, he downed the rum punch, the liquid burning. As the man dressed in a white button-up shirt, black pants, and a red bowtie around his neck approached, Matt said, "Here. I want another one, please."

"Yes, sir. What room should I charge the drink to?" he asked as he grabbed the glass and placed it on a server tray.

"Room 415, please."

The poor waiter kept his shoulders straight, but that outfit, in this heat! Sweat beaded his forehead, and he appeared uncomfortable—Matt would hate wearing that outfit. "Oh, and give yourself and the bartender a twenty-five percent tip, please," Matt added.

"Very well, sir," the man said chipperly before leaving.

While Matt waited, he searched for his parents. When he saw the red of his mom's suit, Matt screamed, "See, Mom, we're having a great time bonding now!"

An older couple blocked his view of the white tent and turned to stare at him, mouths agape. But he didn't care. No one knew him here. The worst holiday in the world was being alone in a super fancy hotel in paradise.

Well, at least he could drink himself unconscious.

The waiter returned with a napkin and another glass. Beautiful scenery, and he was alone. He sighed, took another chug of the rum, and lay back in the chair. Twisting his feet to the music, he relaxed and thought of nothing.

"Matt?" an unfamiliar voice said. Matt was a common

name, so it probably wasn't him, but he opened his eyes anyway.

Standing at the foot of his recliner, between him, the pool, and the sun, was the form of a woman. Squinting, the short, redheaded girl seemed familiar.

"Um, yes." Matt tried to think if he had met her, possibly on the plane. He scooted up in the lounger.

She laughed, placing a large tan beach bag between them as she sat in the seat beside him. "I thought so. I haven't met you, but I've seen you around campus. I'm a South Holt freshman." She stuck a pale hand in his face for him to shake.

He threw his legs over the side and faced her.

Now, without the blinding light, he sort of recognized her. Not very tall, he guessed her height to be around five-four, maybe shorter. She wore dark sunglasses, so he couldn't glimpse her eyes. A splatter of freckles lined her cheeks. Her red hair was cut to chin length and styled despite the humidity.

When he took her hand and shook it, it laid lifeless in his fingers and lacked the professional four ups and downs of most people.

"I'm Amy," she said. Taking her hand back, she dug in the giant beach bag. "To be honest, I'm glad to find you. My parents abandoned me to go to some work thing."

"Are your parents at the bar, too?" Matt asked, pointing toward the tent.

"Oh, no," she said, then her pouty mouth pinched together in displeasure. "My parents canceled their plans to join me so they could go off to the Alps, I believe. Yes, I believe it was the Alps."

"I'm sorry," Matt sympathized. "But they could be here ignoring you." He pointed toward the bar area, where there was laughter, music, and dancing. "It's a work function. I don't think I'll see my parents except at night."

"Well, where's Jennifer?" Amy asked, glancing around the area, then returned to her bag.

She found what she was hunting for. Pulling out a tube of lotion, which he assumed was sunscreen, she lathered up her arms with a thick layer. Now that she mentioned Jennifer, he recognized Amy. A few times, he'd seen her and her red curls running around in front of the English building.

Before answering, he leaned over, grabbed his drink, and took a long sip. She stopped applying the lotion and followed the glass with hungry eyes. The ice cube clanked as the empty cup hung limply in his hand, and he searched for the waiter. Not finding him, he returned his attention to Amy.

He said, "I remember now. You live in Jennifer's dorm. Well, this fine trip was sprung on me. I wish I had time to invite her, but with only one day's knowledge..." He let his thoughts die off as he glanced at the white tent.

He recalled Jennifer standing on the steps of the dorm seconds before he left to drive to his parents for this vacation. Like a scene from a movie, the wind twisted her hair about her face. He'd known that moment was the time, the right time, to take her to bed and make her his in more than just name. When he returned, he'd have to prepare again, like a plane that had to overcome gravity; only at the right speed could he pull up and claim her body.

He wished she was here, or him there, in her bed. His virginity was his parents' fault.

As Amy squeezed the tube, it made a loud bloop noise while her hand filled with white cream. She rubbed her elbows and upper arms and said, "I'm sorry, sort of. I'm sorry about Jennifer, at least. But hey, at least there's a silver lining, at least for me. I was afraid I would be all alone at this hotel. When my parents said they weren't joining me, I decided I would go despite them canceling the plans, like in an act of rebellion. But I'm here alone, and as much as I really want to see the city, I wouldn't feel safe going out by myself. Maybe we could hang out? I mean, I know your girlfriend, so I'm not going to hit on you." She put the lotion container beside her on the seat and reached back into her purse. She retrieved a stack of brochures and handed them to him.

The first one had a boat and a guy reeling in a swordfish, a bright smile on his face, and water all around.

Surprised, he glanced up at Amy. He liked to fish, but that didn't seem like a normal girl thing.

Amy took off her sunglasses and laid them on the seat. Bending closer to his face, the corners of her mouth turned down, and she gave him a puppy dog stare with bright blue eyes. "I've always wanted to go deep sea fishing."

Scanning the next one, he stared at an ATV island tour. Lined up across the front, at least five men and no women or children sat on top of different cherry red four-wheel vehicles. Each held a drink. He raised his eyebrows and peeked at her. "This too?"

"Oh, yes, I would love to drive an ATV around the island and finish by getting plastered."

Amy was a strange girl, indeed!

He strummed through the rest of them. The next one featured a dive trip. There was one for swimming with the dolphins. Included in the list were parasailing and wine tasting. Even one called Dinner with the Sharks.

They all appeared to be fun, but he wasn't sure they would be able to do everything. As he stretched the documents toward her to return them, the one on top caught his attention, and he pulled them back.

The brochure had tropical trees that surrounded a stone structure. Underneath, it said, *Queen's Staircase.* That brought a memory of Jennifer reading the fashion book and their conversation about black sugar-rotted teeth minutes before leaving for one of their best dates, and he laughed as he handed them back.

"I know. It's a lot of money, but I would unquestionably

like someone to go with me and can't do them alone. Would you be my buddy and go with me?" she pleaded.

In his pocket sat the credit card. Surely, if his parents didn't want to experience the islands with him, they wouldn't mind if he did it without them. His dad did say go have some fun.

Drinking the water from the melted ice at the bottom of his rum punch, he thought, *What harm could there be in a few adventures with a new friend?*

"Do you want to do all of those?" he asked, surprised. He couldn't fathom Jennifer doing the dangerous ones.

"Yes, all of them."

"I don't think we have time for everything here. Which one do you want to do first?" he asked.

Would Jennifer consider his spending time with Amy cheating? He didn't think so. She had told him she didn't want to be *one of those couples*, the ones that cling to each other. Plus, Amy knew of his commitment to Jennifer.

"Parasailing. I want to go parasailing first. I've never been, and my parents have promised me every year." Her eyes became the size of saucers, and she placed her hand on top of his wrist, leaning forward, inches from his face. She asked, "You're not afraid of heights, are you?"

He wasn't, but he stared at the spot she touched. When she noticed where he focused, she moved it back over to grab the sunscreen, glancing away.

Patting the wallet containing the credit card in his short's pocket, he said, "Amy, I think we should."

"Good," she said and glanced up at the sky. "First, to recover from my plane flight. I plan to lie in the sun and get drunk." She waved over a cabana boy.

The same person in the red bowtie dashed over to them. "Yes, ma'am, what can I get you?"

"Sir, I would like whatever my friend just finished and keep them coming."

The man reached down, and Matt handed him his empty glass. "Would you like another?" he asked.

"Yes, please," Matt responded.

"Room 415, sir?" the server asked.

"Yes, and another twenty-five percent. Keep them coming for me as well," Matt said.

"And your room?" he asked Amy.

She laughed. "The irony of it. I'm just down the hall from you, Matt, in room 411. The same twenty-five percent tip, please."

When the man walked off, Amy stood and dropped her robe. Wearing a two-piece bathing suit, the freckles continued down her body. She had an hourglass figure rivaling the stars of the fifties, yet underneath were firm, hard muscles.

He stared too long, and he knew it, but she ignored him.

Turning around, she bent over, her tight apple bottom close to his face, and grabbed the cream again.

He gulped. If he didn't know better, he would think she intentionally tempted him with her luscious backside.

When she turned back toward him, she said, "Friend Matt, please be so kind as to apply the lotion to my back. Believe it or not, I wouldn't be comfortable letting you do this if you didn't have a girlfriend."

Huh, for a second, he forgot about Jennifer. What would Jennifer say? She didn't seem to care that he went to the beach without her. She didn't call him for days. Based on that, he doubted she would have a problem. Jennifer trusted him, and she should. After all, Amy was just an acquaintance. But just in case, he said, "Amy, I have a girlfriend, and I have this thing about commitment."

She faced him and pouted. "I don't want to get between you and Jennifer. Just relax, and let's have some fun."

What harm could there be in applying sunscreen and getting drunk? Would he do the same thing if Jennifer was here? He could imagine Jennifer sitting in the chair with him.

If she was here, Jennifer would probably rub the cream into Amy's shoulders.

"Just on my back, please," she said.

"Once again, just as friends. Jennifer, being faithful, it's all very important to me." With his hands covered in something that smelled like coconuts, he twirled his finger for her to turn around in the chair. Once she faced away from him, he carefully focused on only applying it in places she could burn.

While he buffed her back, the waiter returned with their drinks and placed them on the table beside his seat. Amy flagged the cabana man before he left and said, "Please bring another. I'll have this one finished when you return."

The white lotion clung to his hands, but Amy's back and shoulders had a glossy finish.

She leaned back in her lounger and handed him a towel. "For you to wipe your hands off."

With clean hands, he passed the small towel back to her. "Thank you, Matt. Would you please hand me my drink?"

Grabbing both glasses, he held out hers. Her fingers brushed against his when she took it from his hands. Did she do it on purpose?

She said, "I'm trusting you, Matt, to help me get back to my room. The number is 411. Do you think you can remember that? If you can, I'm going to get so toasty. I'll be crusty like twice-burned toast. There will be nothing left of me but ash."

"I'll remember," he said. With Amy's petite frame, he doubted it would take much.

She downed it in five seconds. "Well, that burned. So here's to catching fire before this vacation is over."

Taking a sip, Matt smiled. "I'll remember, 411," he said.

"Tomorrow, let's go parasailing and deep-sea fishing. I've always wanted to fish for sharks. And I'm not leaving until the day before school starts. When do you head out?"

"After Christmas, right before school starts."

"Well, then..." She leaned back in the chair and placed her sunglasses over her eyes. "We better get started. There's a lot to do before next we leave." She smiled.

Quickly, he glanced at the redhead, amazed at his luck—another strange bird like Jennifer—Jennifer, his bright, beautiful girlfriend, and Amy his crazy wild friend. Weeks of spending his parents' money and doing fun things around the island sounded perfect. Perhaps this family vacation wouldn't be so bad after all.

CHAPTER 32
JENNIFER

On Christmas Eve, Jennifer sat on the carpet in her bedroom at her parents' house amongst scattered books. The lack of distinguishing designs— such as unmarked tan walls, a champagne-colored bedspread, and generic print artwork— gave this area a guest room feel. Since she'd been home, she moved her personal photos to a drawer beside the bed so that in the morning, she could access them. Other than a few knickknacks on the vanity and the recent addition of stacked dirty clothes in a corner, the space was relatively empty. It lacked Jennifer's individual touches.

Technically, that was how she liked her things: neat, organized, and ordered. She moved her personal items into different locations. She added notes in her notebook on how to find them, using them like a treasure hunt to unlock Jennfier Wright each morning. It worked. The puzzle helped her adjust quicker and guided her mind, keeping her brain on track and working through sluggish synapses.

This dawn, like every day recently, she attempted to process her words in the English language. Even now, her thoughts chatted away in the Gaelic tongue.

Spread out in front of her, she had her grandfather's

genealogical research. Stewart Wright, her grandfather, loved history and spent more time studying the Wright family tree than anyone should. As she flipped through the pages, she hunted for a crazy person—someone who seemed normal until around puberty or a little older, a soul like her.

Glancing around the room, she searched for a clock, then recalled her smartwatch on her wrist—close to three in the afternoon. Sometime today, her brother would pound on her door, requesting her presence downstairs to decorate.

He'd knocked yesterday for the annual trip to the country to pick out a tree. Half out of her mind, she stumbled around the tree farm. The people in her dream didn't celebrate Christmas. Thus, purchasing something dead and flammable to make everyone merry seemed dangerous.

Luckily, last night, she dreamed of Alusdar. Instead of living his life, it was closer to a movie. She still saw through his eyes and witnessed his emotions, but the character of Alusdar, super strong and brave, reminded her too much of so many other stories that it was hard to believe he ever really existed.

His first memory started in the woods. Roaming around, searching for food, eventually found by a loving family. Only after he showed superhuman abilities did his adoptive parents reveal his origins. At this point, he was an adult. Good looks, super strength, an incredibly humble personality, and then, big shocker, he was a gift from the fairies. Of course, he grew up strong, triumphed over his adversaries in battles, and finished by marrying the most desirable, beautiful woman.

There was even a song that loosely translated to *Alusdar the Brave, Alusdar the Legend*. A catchy tune that rambled around in her head. She thought the dream would make a good cartoon movie.

After leaving campus, Jennifer settled into a routine. At

seven a.m., the alarm went off. For two hours, she did her best to recall her life as Jennifer Wright.

Some days, it was easier to shake off the life she lived the night before at her childhood home, surrounded by memories from her youth. As far as she could tell, her dreams had progressed backward to the fifteen hundreds, and all the individuals spoke Gaelic.

As she turned the page and stared at a man standing in front of a log cabin, she thought about how the dreams bothered her in two ways.

First, would she keep going back in time until there was no more time? What happened when there was nothing? Would she sit around all day as a vegetable? Or would her psyche invent aliens? Maybe she'd stomp around as a dinosaur or fish?

Second, she thought in words other than English most of the time. She found this trend more disturbing than getting up two hours early just to grab hold of Jennifer Wright. Did her mind create languages? She believed the dialogue to be Gaelic, but what if it wasn't? What if the complexity of her subconscious developed its own world? She could check the internet, but both outcomes, actual language and made up, scared her.

Was that the definition of insanity?

Staring back at the pictures of the obviously sane families, she wondered about the true meaning. Was she the first crazy person, or was there a trend? Say, every seventh generation, a deranged one popped out.

Earlier on the internet, she found a story about three daughters; two had inherited schizophrenia, which manifested after they hit puberty. There were even books written about other families with schizophrenia. *Hidden Valley Road* was one; she'd already ordered a copy online.

She guessed she could have schizophrenia since, according to the internet, delusions and creating alternate realities could be symptoms, and the first symptoms appeared between the ages of sixteen and thirty.

What if she had an extremely rare mental schizophrenia brought on by whatever happened in the woods—whether beer, bear, or hormones?

If that was what caused her to dream in other languages, then at least there was medicine to treat the symptoms.

Time to seek professional help. Frowning, she pulled out her phone and added a note to call the doctor on the calendar app. She would make an appointment and admit she might be sick.

Happy winter noises migrated to her room—joyous Christmas music about Santa, laughter from her parents, and all the cheerful festival sounds. She could tell her household later. Today, she'd let her family enjoy their holiday and keep all her psychotic episodes to herself.

Before Randy stood outside her door, she heard him pounding on the stairs and on the carpet in the hall. The way he moved with intent, a little faster than when he went to bed, taking a single step at a time, she anticipated his direction and knock. "Come on, Jennifer," Randy pleaded. "Dad and I put up the tree without you. This is about tradition."

When she opened the door, the scent of cinnamon from her mother's apple pie and spruce from the new tree overwhelmed her sense of smell. In a few minutes, her subconscious would dull the odors as they had this morning when her mother started cooking.

Her brother bounced from foot to foot with untapped youthful energy. In the month since Thanksgiving, Randy had grown an inch, and the top of her head came up to his nose. She wasn't sure how he convinced their mother to allow him not to have a military haircut. After a few months without shears, wisps of blond pulled free from the ponytail and poked his eyes, and he swatted at it. Like most teenage boys, he didn't like pants, so even though the temperature was freezing outside, he wore jogging shorts made of thin material and a hoody. She didn't venture far from insensible clothing herself, wearing jeans and a white T-shirt hanging loose around her calves that once belonged to her father.

"Listen, Jen," Randy whispered. "Whatever you do, don't tell Dad the tree is not straight."

"Why?"

"He made me reposition it a hundred times this morning! Tomorrow, we try to talk him into a plastic tree, a pre-lit fiber. Before he let me get you, he made me test all the old strings we had in the box. You should be helping with this."

At the bottom of the stairs, her father, wearing a gray sweater and jeans, poured water into the tree basin. "Stop trying to gather troops to argue your point. An artificial tree won't have the same feel," her dad replied. "Think of it this way, how blessed you are. When I was a boy, we had to get a tree out of the forest."

With a groan, Randy grabbed a string of lights and waited at the edge of the spruce needles. "Yeah. We know the story. Snow, walking, cutting down the tree. The year the squirrel got into the house, which I believe is in a movie, Dad."

Jennifer laughed.

Until she went to college, she thought every family had the same tradition of decorating the tree the night before Christmas. When she saw trees in movies or positioned in windows, she considered that part of the pre-Christmas decorations. It never occurred to her that those embellishments were the final products. After all, the Wright household blinged their house out the first weekend in December. Her dad went as far as putting a sleigh with six reindeer statues on the roof. "Dad, why do we put the tree up on Christmas Eve?"

"Well," he said, assuming his position on the other side. Randy handed him the roll of lights. "Your mother and I wanted to have traditions you and Randy would remember.

We knew one day you and Randy would leave, and we thought, if we had a tree ceremony, maybe the tradition could carry on to our grandchildren."

Jennifer took the string from her dad and passed the blinking bulbs to Randy. As he placed them on a tree limb, he said, "So, you're trying to bribe us to come home every Christmas?"

"Of course, son. That's what Christmas is for. Spending time with your family."

The double door to the kitchen opened, and Jennifer's mom, wearing an elf apron, glided into the room, holding a small present in her hand.

"Jennifer," she said, approaching her. "We have a change of our tradition, but only for tonight." She held out the gift, wrapped in blue paper with a bow as large as the top.

The lightweight box fit easily in her palm. "Will it break if I shake it?"

Now that Randy had placed the last row of lights on the tree, her father moved to stand beside her mother. He rested his arm over her mother's shoulder. "No," he said.

As she shook it, something rattled. Her first guess was a necklace, but the way her parents stood close to each other, smiling brightly, whatever was hidden inside cost a lot of money.

She tilted her head. "Me trying to figure out what is in my packages is nothing different from any other Christmas Eve. What's going on?"

"We're going to put the rest of the presents under the tree tonight like we normally do, and you and Randy can shake most of them when we bring them out. But we thought this one time, we would like you to open one present tonight."

As she ripped off the paper, Randy snuck beside her, glancing around her shoulder. Not so delicately, she opened the box and revealed a key on a key chain.

"Now, sky angel, you won't have to walk to class on rainy days," her father said.

Holding up the fob in the light, her hand shook. "No, this isn't?" She glanced between her parents, hunting for confirmation.

The grins on their faces and the glow in their cheeks told her what she wanted to know, but she asked anyway. "Is there a car here for me?"

Her mom nodded yes, and her dad pointed toward the door. "It's outside. I asked the dealer to drop it off. Your mom wrapped the keys while we put up the tree."

"There's a car outside for me?" Surprised, she glanced behind her, like she might see it through the walls.

"Let's go see it," Randy said, running to the door before Jennifer. He blocked his sister from leaving the house. "You don't want it. I'm fifteen; I'll take it off your—"

"Move, Randy!" Jennifer demanded, shoving her rock of a brother.

"Kids," their mom said.

Once through the door, cold smacked her arms, and the frozen porch blistered her bare feet. But she ignored it all—for parked against the curb, a four-door blue sedan waited with a giant red bow.

"The dealer had the car wrapped. She said it was part of the Christmas package." Her father cuddled her mom. Meanwhile, her mom rubbed her hands together to warm up.

Jennifer pointed and tested the fob. The lights blinked, and the car beeped. Jennifer giggled.

Aware that the noises coming out of her mouth were incomprehensible laughter, she drew in a deep breath and ran to each parent, hugging them and dancing, trying not to land on their toes.

"Why don't you take us for a drive?" her dad asked, pointing toward the steering wheel.

"I don't have any shoes," she said. She wiggled her toes.

"That's okay. We'll just go for a quick spin around the neighborhood."

Rather than walking to the car, she ran. At first, the bright red bow didn't want to budge, and she pulled and tugged. Finally yanking the ribbon off, she flung it to the grass and opened the driver-side door.

The gray cloth interior had that new car smell, and she drank it in. Instead of car mats, cardboard protected the carpet. She picked up the stiff brown paper and tossed it in the yard as well, almost hitting her dad.

He opened the passenger door. Patting the seat, he said, "This car gets great gas mileage. I thought it would be practical for when you graduate. It should last at least ten years if you take care of it."

"Oh my gosh!" she squealed, moving behind the wheel. "Hurry, get in!" she demanded.

Her dad sat beside her, reminding her of when she learned to drive. Meanwhile, her mom bumped the back of Jennifer's seat with her knees. Randy grabbed her dad's headrest. Leaning forward, he said, "Neat, the dash lights up blue. I want one, Mom and Dad."

Because of the time of day and since they'd only be cruising the neighborhood, they left the house's front door unlocked.

Turning on the lights, she started the car and maneuvered onto the street.

❧

The excitement continued the rest of the night as they finished placing ornaments on the tree. Then they ate home-baked cookies while watching Christmas movies in their pajamas, spending another Christmas Eve at the Wright household.

At the end of the night, her mother pulled out a brown

package from the decorations box. Instantly, Jennifer recognized the tree topper from past Christmases. As her mom and dad placed the faded angel on the top, she remembered all the holidays from her dreams. The first recollection was when her grandmother, Josephine, bought that ornament for her first Christmas with her husband.

Thinking back to her conversation with her dad, she realized having tradition did more than build a legacy. The consistency gave her a sense of stability, something she desperately wanted. The peace she'd been missing overcame her, and she slept.

CHAPTER 33

JENNIFER

THERE WAS NO COLOR OTHER THAN SHADES OF GRAY, BROWN, and yellow. A dog as big as a two-story house sniffed her, forcing her to the cold ground. Jennifer concluded either everything in this dream was giant-sized or she was miniature.

A voice whispered to her, "The name is Barry. These are my memories."

The first thing that drew his scrutiny was his three-fingered, clawed hands. But that didn't last because the aroma of fried eggs, pure protein, and something edible, caught his attention and he drowned himself in consuming the flaky brown remains on the ground. Every scrumptious bite held an extra crunch similar to salt-rich potato chips. When he had finished, still hungry, he sniffed to find more.

The nest dug deep into the dirt made for a perfect hatching bed. Nearby, an unhatched egg rested sideways on a mud bank. The creature, Barry, crawled on all fours to the yummy smell. Driven by instinct, he licked the outside, discovering a flavorful, tasty salt. Using his beak-like nose, he hammered until a loud crack announced a yellow-brown cream as it oozed down the side. With the fresh, meaty scent emanating from the liquid, he devoured all of it despite the squirmy brown part in the middle.

Hunger temporarily sated, he thought about the familiar creature that slurped down his throat. He acknowledged and didn't care that he ate one of his brothers or sisters. If survival involved cannibalism, then so be it; serve up the next sibling. Lifting his head, he noticed a third egg.

On his way to the next scrumptious meal, a lizard with rows of sharp teeth, the same height and shape as him, slammed into him, knocking him from his feet. Momentum caused him to roll and tumble until, with a thud, he smashed into a rock. He didn't have time to contemplate the sting from that impact, because a relative targeted his chest for dinner. He shoved at the body to escape. There was no bitterness as his family tasted his flesh.

An acute stab transmitted through the dream. The wound was pure torture around Jennifer's tummy, right under her ribs.

The effort to flee drained his attention, and he missed the robust outdoorsy scent of sweat and the shadow that overcame the sun. A chunky toddler's hand the size of a small plane scooped him and his sibling up. She caged the two dragons in the palm of her hands. As she walked, she sloshed them around in the man-made earthquake.

"No, no," the female child chided as she opened her hand and lifted the other lizard creature. Gently, she placed that dragon on the ground. The tail of his kin disappeared behind a tree as his family evaded capture.

Then, none too gently, the girl dumped him into a basket. "I will take care of you."

Ripe blueberries and blackberries made an aromatic bed. As the container moved like a bed of balls, Barry sunk lower into the luscious fruit. His stomach growled, and he tasted his surroundings.

Hunger and pain became one sensation as he devoured all

in sight. Only on some level did he recognize the gash on his side no longer ached. Nothing demanded his attention anymore as his wound healed, and he curled up, lulled to sleep by the swinging.

Maud, a small raven-haired girl with freckles on her nose, couldn't have been much over six when she found the baby wyvern. She hid the creature where no one would see it in a small bed of hay in the corner of her parents' farmhouse.

The first word he understood was what she named him: Barry. She explained that he blended in with the dark blue of the berries, and he loved to eat them. Therefore, he should be named after the tasty little morsels. Personally, if a color decided a name, grass worked just fine because everything in his world existed in shades of grays, yellows, and browns.

The second tangible item he associated with sounds, as well as the third, fourth, and fifth, belonged to food groups. Initially, he survived on goat's milk and small crumbs left over from her meals, but he grew quickly, and so did his appetite.

Months went by, and Barry grew to the size of a small, miniature dog. One night, as Maud's father relaxed after a day of work, he said, "Maud, why is your bed moving?"

Under the thin covering, the round apple became a ball. Barry had just retrieved it from the table. Her father watched him as he climbed on the surface, grabbed the meal, and scurried back to the covers. This puzzled Barry. Father knew that Barry was there. Why did he ask?

Ignoring the toy, Barry stuck his head out and searched for his Maud. She reclined on the ground. In her lap, thread spilled around her, and she made eye contact with Barry. Her large, oval eyes and mouth opened.

That second, Barry realized not everyone knew and

accepted his presence. All this time, he thought they belonged to him, like a family. Maybe his species saying of *'hate humans or love them as dinner'* was just propaganda, a way to preserve the purity of the wyvern lineage.

Then again, perhaps not.

Maud stood abruptly, scattering the threads on the planked floor. As Barry grabbed her leg, she said, "It's just a lizard I found in the woods. I want to keep him, Fadres. He's fun and, and he really doesn't eat that much."

Sensing his time for introduction, Barry stepped forward and wrapped his arms around Maud's legs. Glancing upward, the broad-shouldered, dark-haired man had his thick eyebrows pressed together, and he inspected him. The scrutiny became uncomfortable, and Barry moved behind Maud, peeking over between her father and mother.

The fair-haired woman, Maud's mother, wrapped up in cooking something in a pot over a fire, didn't glance up—until Maud's father cleared his throat. The ladle dropped from her hand, but after she spotted Barry, her eyes never wavered...or blinked.

Patting his head, Maud said, "His name is Barry. I named him after the berries. See the resemblance? He is all purple and blue. When he could fit in my hand, I could hide him in a basket full of fruit, but usually, he ate most of the ones I picked. He loves to eat them."

"Is it…?" Her mother stood, her hand covering her mouth. Without glancing away and fingers blocking her lips, she walked sideways toward her husband, standing behind him, like Barry was positioned behind Maud.

"It's a wyvern," he confirmed, looking at his daughter.

By now, Barry understood their words. Of course, he was a wyvern. What else would he be?

"Maud, you have to kill it," her father continued.

So, the wyvern memory, *'hate humans or love eating them,'* was a truth. He glanced up at Maud and saw how her lower lip trembled. He didn't hate Maud, and he couldn't eat her.

With saucer-sized eyes that gleamed with tears, Maud picked him up like a doll and hugged him close to her chest. Barry scented the outdoorsy sweat, like how the grass smelled after a rainy day, and he embraced her back. His tiny wings flapped loosely to his sides. "No, Fadres. Barry is my friend."

"Maud, it's a baby wyvern. They are huge meat-eaters. When he gets larger, he will eat our goat, the town sheep, and probably people. You need to kill the thing."

Barry could never hurt Maud! Because of her, her family was safe. The goat in the front yard, though...he licked his lips.

"But, Fadres." The waterworks began, showering Barry in a salty solution.

"Maud," her mother said with finality in her voice, "Your fadres is right. Put Barry back in your bed. But tomorrow, take him into the woods and put him to sleep forever."

They started off early the next morning. Barry rested on Maud's shoulders and thought about survival. The plan consisted of running when she sat him down. He could hunt for himself and find smaller things to eat until he grew into his wings.

He expected her to find a rock close to her home. Yet she surprised him and walked well past the entrance to her family's farm and away from other humans. Eventually, she turned onto a stone road with weeds and young trees growing through rock cracks and other debris from lack of use. She stopped in front of a forgotten straw-and-mortar home.

Despite his well-thought-out course of action, curiosity

locked his feet in place. He moved out of her reach but waited to see what she would do.

"Barry, according to my parents and other people in my village, this place is abandoned. Several people lived here once, but they got sick and died. Legend says the forest is haunted by the creatures that gave those that stay here the disease. But I don't think it is. I've been here before and found some pretty things. I think the people that lived here just died.

"Anyway, I thought this would make a good home for a wyvern. The nearby villages are afraid the ground is cursed. They believe anyone who visits will awaken the vengeful fairy who will take their souls to the fairy court. No one will bother you. You can hunt around the area, and if you like, I'll bring you food from time to time. Maybe we can eat together like we do now. There is a stream nearby with little fish. I can teach you to swim. We can play and talk. Nothing will change."

Reaching into a satchel, she pulled out a cloth. "I've been saving this for you. For your birthday." She laid it on the ground. "Now you can have a blanket with my scent." Then she retrieved a loaf of bread and some berries. "And now you have something to eat."

She glanced over toward the forgotten home. The thatched roof collapsed some time ago. A small tree sprouted from inside. Scattered in the area were iron pots, broken furniture, and metal gadgets.

"It might be a few days before I return, but I will, and we can play. I'll come when I finish my chores so I can stay longer. I won't do it, Barry. I can't kill you. Even if one day you grow large enough to eat a hundred people. You and I are friends, and we belong together." With that, she stared away, refusing to make eye contact or say goodbye—tears freely fell.

He moved to the forgotten road, watching her leave, her quick steps making swishing noises. He heard her cry, but he didn't follow. At this time, he understood all her words. She was his best friend, and he loved her.

At night, he missed the girl's warmth, but during the day, Barry hunted. He grew. And when she came around, he played, soaking up the sunshine that was Maud.

Maud came back day after day, week after week, month after month. She even found ways of visiting him for short periods every day in the winter. Their friendship blossomed. He learned about her mother and father. She shared the birth of her siblings and how she hated them crying at night or changing their diapers. Her least favorite chore was cooking and cleaning, preferring to work in the garden or gather wild berries, but she gladly finished if it meant she could run to visit him.

While there, she taught him her tricks. She didn't realize it, but without words, she learned his language. Eventually, after years, they understood each other. If he tilted his head to the right while she talked, she knew he needed more details. If he patted the ground, he expected more food. A swish of his tail in the summer meant let's go fishing. That comprised of Barry diving into the water and bringing back a scrumptious meal. A quick run in one direction, followed by a turn-around, he interpreted as let's play hide-and-seek.

When Maud didn't show up, Barry hunted away from the village, typically wild bunny rabbits or boars. Until he required more food to sustain himself, then his diet consisted of cows and sheep in neighboring towns. He made sure he stayed away from anyone who might know Maud.

The day Barry learned to fly, everything changed.

Lately, Maud visited only once a week. The morning he expected her to drop by, he practiced taking into the air, balancing on the wind, until he felt confident. He intended to surprise her. One of her wild, crazy, repetitive dreams was of flying through a puffy cloud. Today, as a gift, he planned to fulfill that desire.

When he heard the crunch of her familiar gait on the stone steps, his heart sped in his chest, and he thought about how he should pose when she walked into the clearing. Should he sit in the sun or off in the shade? Should he lie casually on the blanket beside the flowers he gathered for her?

When she came into the clearing, the look on her face caused all his thoughts to disappear. Instead of a bright smile and flushed cheeks, she stared at the ground, a frown on her beautiful face. He thought about running to her, but he stayed back. Flowers, similar to the ones on the blanket, were laced into her hair, and he smelled a strange oil that reminded him of what she called roses. The basket in her hand dangled as if she didn't care about what was in it.

Then, the copper scent of blood and bitterness of disappointment hit him, and he froze.

He'd kill whoever hurt her.

But the more he hunted for wounds, the more she came across more sad than injured. This puzzled him, so he tilted his head to the side, asking her, with his movements, what was wrong.

When she glanced at his posture, she nodded. "Nothing is wrong, my friend Barry. It is a joyous day," she said, but the tone of her voice did not sound happy at all. Her shoulders slumped as she flopped the basket on the blanket. "Thank you for the flowers, Barry." She hugged him, the copper scent even stronger. Tense, he shifted on his legs.

Sighing, she perched on the ground beside him. Even though she was now an adult woman, when she stood, Barry towered over her by a few inches. Now that she sat, he lowered close to the ground and placed his head in her lap. Absentmindedly, her fingers rubbed the top of his head. "If only you were a human, Barry."

He took a claw and gently tapped her leg. "You want me to go on? Okay, I will. I am now a woman." He glanced up. She blankly stared at the woods across the old, forgotten road. "Fadres says it is time for me to marry. He has announced it to our town and the neighboring villages. Barry, I don't want to get married. When I do, that will mean even less time I will have to spend with you. The only good news is Fadres is allowing me to choose. I'll come as often as I can, but when I marry, I will have to leave for good."

CHAPTER 34

THE DREAM OF BARRY—JENNIFER

LATER, HE CURLED UP ON THE BLANKET SHE HAD GIVEN HIM IN his broken-down home, very much looking like a dragon protecting his precious treasure. His thoughts were drifting back to Maud and marriage.

When he blinked, he could see her married to a man, pregnant with his child, and Barry nowhere near either of them.

You're foolish, Barry thought to himself in Maud's tongue. *You're a wyvern. Your kind is meant to eat humans, not protect them.*

Barry turned in a circle like a cat chasing its tail, trying to get comfortable. When the spot felt right, he closed his eyes, and instantly, the picture of Maud married to someone else was in front of him. The thought hurt, and he cried out in pain.

Human-eating wyvern or not, he had to do something. He could not lose his Maud. If she married someone else, he would eat them.

He imagined her crying, the feet of her spouse dangling from his jaw.

Who was he kidding? He couldn't kill him because it would hurt her if he killed someone she loved.

What would she do if he turned himself into a human? She mentioned in passing that she wished he was a man.

Dragons remembered, not just their lives but all the ancestors before them. Sure, he had to search and tug to reclaim something buried in his DNA, but Maud was worth the pain. There, he found the ability to shape-shift. A great-grandmother or something turned into a woman so she could lure lonely men to her stomach. Great-grandmum had the idea after meeting a male dragon married to a human female. If other dragons used the skill to blend, she could use the talent to feast.

He'd use the experience to lock Maud to him if she'd have him. Closing his eyes, he pictured becoming human. Nothing happened.

Trying again, he experienced a tingling sensation like the start of frostbite. This time, he kept his talons and his lizard feet but had hair.

On the third attempt, he thought human—a warmth and tickles spread along his skin, then he noticed human hands. But his feet were lizard paws.

Again, he tried, the image solidifying in his mind. The heat spread over his face and into his limbs. When he opened his eyes this time, things around him seemed different. He was still color blind, but his vision changed. All the surrounding objects appeared closer, like using a looking glass. The sensation of blinking up and down instead of sideways unnerved him not only because of the vertical action but the absolute darkness that came with closed eyes. Wyverns could see even when they slept.

Touching his soft face, all his nerve endings registered texture. As a wyvern, most things, regardless of the bumps and dents, seemed similar. Closing his eyes, he ran his fingers over the wall of the old home, greeted with the even, cool material. Excited, he skipped through the area, placing his hands on everything: grass, bark, and rocks. He even stepped on a stick and felt pain.

Next, he tested his vocal cords. "Goo- good morning." Barry's masculine voice startled him, causing laughter. The human mouth could say human words. "Well, isn't this a wonder," he said.

The sun wasn't up yet. With the first step of his plan in place, he surveyed his surroundings. What did Maud require to call this her home? The dilapidated structure needed repairs.

The wind blew, and he felt a chill. The unfamiliar sensation of goosebumps brought a smile to his lips. Glancing at his fair skin, he required clothing. He could do this; he would find a way to keep from losing Maud.

Naked, Barry began that night on the thatched roof. Over time, he switched to wyvern, finding human hands provided finer details, and wyvern muscle worked best on strenuous tasks.

While he busied himself, he listened for Maud's approach, but after she became a woman, she seldom visited. If Barry hurried, he could surprise her without having to scare off any potential suitors. To keep his secret, he slept on the path, barring the way. When he heard her, he ran. Before she reached the abandoned house, he found a reason to go another direction, such as for a swim, to collect berries, or to see something rare. So far, he successfully kept her away.

The day after a visit, he snuck into various towns and studied how to make furniture. He flew miles away to get the items he needed. These secret missions he sometimes did as a wyvern and others as a human, stealing clothes when necessary.

He wasn't sure how he had done it, but in a few months, he had learned the human way of hunting, tanning skins, making furniture, and thatching roofs. To his surprise, he enjoyed crafting things out of wood. As a wyvern, he would knock down the tree he wanted and use his massive claws to whittle the hard wood into something unique and beautiful. He thought it ironic —his favorite human trade was something he did as a wyvern.

Discovering the complexity of the markets astonished him. He relished haggling. If other wyverns ever took the time to study buying and selling, they would all turn human. He started taking furniture he made to the city squares. What fun there was in seeing what all he could earn!

As demand increased, he needed help getting the merchandise to the store. As a wyvern, he could easily carry the items to the market, but he couldn't lift them as a human. His wheelbarrow seemed awkward, unbalanced, and often fell. After clothing, he purchased a wagon and a horse.

Picking out the right horse was also an issue. Even if Barry appeared human, he smelled like a wyvern. It took time, but he acquired a mare who either had no sense of smell or just didn't care. A beautiful girl with a white and black nose and blond mane, he named her Buttercup, mainly because she was peaceful, like a flower. He then had to build a barn. He found another horse that didn't shake in fear of him and two barn cats. All the restoration occurred as Barry detoured Maud away from seeing the cabin.

In their talks, when Maud visited, she kept Barry informed of her courting. She didn't have a suitor, and so far, no one had asked for her hand in marriage. Barry hoped his luck held until he finished making her a home.

In the winter, Barry, as a human, made his way to Maud's house. He brought two of his more decorative tables and some coins he'd earned. Nervously, he knocked on the door.

Her father answered. Silver replaced his black hair. His clothes were messy and covered in dirt. Strong body odor followed him like he hadn't bathed in a while. Barry didn't blame him, staring at the layer of snow. Who wanted to get wet on a day like today?

"Sir, I would like to marry your daughter," Barry declared without even a greeting.

"Who are you?" Maud's father replied, squinting as if blinded by the outside light.

"I'm Barry, the furniture maker. I have brought you two of my pieces and some money for her hand. I have a small cottage nearby and can provide for her needs."

Her father rubbed his stubbly chin and studied Barry. He glanced over to the tables stacked tall. "Do you even know my daughter?"

Yes. She is my best friend, he thought, but he answered, "I know of her."

"I have heard of you," her father said, still surveying the furniture in the cart. "Let me call Maud out here and see what she says."

Maud's father disappeared through the door.

A few minutes later, both Maud and her father exited the home. The unique fragrance that surrounded her wafted over to him. He could dance on the scent of rose oil and the outdoors, like right after a spring rain shower. Her dark hair was on top of her head, except for a strand. She blew to move it out of her eyes as she dried her hand on the cloth wrapped around her waist.

"Excuse me," she said to Barry, wiping the sweat off her forehead. "The fire is hot," she continued, unaffected by how the world seemed to focus solely on her.

Standing beside Maud, her father said, "This man asks for your hand in marriage."

"Does he?" she said and inspected the human Barry. "I don't think I have ever seen him in town." Her voice lacked the tenderness she used when talking with him as a dragon. To his delight, she didn't recognize him yet.

"I have seen you," Barry announced, aware he wore a mischievous grin, though he tried not to.

"And why do you want to marry me?" she asked.

"Why wouldn't I?" Barry responded.

"Come back tomorrow, and I will give you my answer." She stormed back into the house and disappeared.

Rubbing his chin, her father stared at the furniture. "Well, that is better than a no. So far, all I've heard her say is no. Maybe you will be the yes."

Her father moved over to the wagon. "Leave your wares here. You can get them tomorrow if she says no."

"Has she said no often?" Barry asked.

"Aye, every opportunity she has," Maud's father answered. Barry clearly remembered that Maud had told him she hadn't had any offers.

"I'll just leave the wagon here. I can collect it tomorrow if she doesn't accept my gift," Barry said, unhooking Buttercup and turning to go.

Before he asked for her hand, he expected today to go differently. He thought for sure that she would recognize his soul no matter what outside shell he presented. After all, it wasn't her appearance that he liked enough to become human. It was Maud herself. If only she had asked his name, the name she gave him, she'd have realized it was him; he was sure.

Distracted by the disappointment, when he returned home, he took off his clothes and sat them on the bed he made for them. Then went outside to work on furniture as a wyvern.

So, in tune with his project, he didn't hear the footsteps behind him or smell the rain shower of roses.

"Barry?" Maud whispered.

He forgot the work in front of him, a simple wood chest, and turned toward her. With a puzzled expression, she surveyed her surroundings. Then, as if she understood, her facial features relaxed. She suspected the truth, he figured.

She passed him, not saying any other words, and touched the small dragon he'd added as a detail in the furniture's design. Slowly, her eyes drank in the cabin, no longer in pieces, and the barn, where Buttercup neighed in delight. Finally, her attention focused on him.

"I don't know who that guy was, and I'm not sure how he had your eyes, but you and he are in this proposal business together. Did he make you a deal? He would marry me so we can be together?" she asked.

He shrugged, and his wings bounced nervously, so he pulled them in tight.

He stepped closer, unaware of how shifting from a dragon to a human appeared, but she needed to know the truth. How else would Maud realize it was him? He concentrated on his human form.

Within minutes, Barry, the human, stood before a very pale Maud, her mouth open.

"Barry?" she asked and touched his hair. "Barry, it was you? So, there is no other man. You?"

Dragon's memories didn't do the extra nerve endings humans had justice. When she touched his hair, his soul felt on fire. The experience couldn't be equated in all the generations of genetic recollections. Running his fingers across her chin and up the sides of her face, he drank in his Maud. "It's me, Maud," he whispered.

"Barry?" She brushed her fingertips over his nose, across his lips, over his eyebrows.

"Yes, Maud."

"How?" she asked.

"All dragons can become human."

"Why now?"

"I..." Barry glanced at the ground. "I couldn't lose you. If you got married, I would never see you again."

"You proposed marriage?"

"I am a dragon, a wyvern, to be specific. All dragons can take on a human form. Some dragons spend their lives as humans. However, wyverns pride themselves on hunting and eating humans. So, I've broken my poor parents' hearts by deciding to spend my life with you."

"Wyverns see humans as food, aye," she said, chuckling. "Is that what you thought of when I found you wrestling with the other wyvern?"

He stood up straighter. "Maybe. I'm continuously hungry."

"Yes, you are always hungry. Are you ravenous now?"

His stomach growled, and they both laughed. "Not until you mentioned food."

"I don't understand why you waited until now to become human. Why didn't you become human earlier? We could have played in the creek, or you could have helped me gather wood."

"I had no desire to be human then."

"No desire?"

"You were with me. Why would I want to be human if you are with me?" Barry asked.

"The only reason you want to marry me is so you won't lose me? Barry, that seems foolish. Marriage is about love, children, and a home."

"Marriage is a human term. I want you as a mate. And not just a mate, a true mate."

"Marriage, mate, what's the difference?"

"A mate is for life, and it will be a long life. With a true mate, there's a bonding that happens. Your love will be for me, and my love will be for you."

Leaning close to her ear, he nibbled on her lobe and listened to her breath change. From the aroma in the air, she desired him as well. How he loved her and wanted her as more than his best friend. But not without the whole truth. He needed her to understand the consequences.

He whispered his warning near her neck. "If you have sex with me, it will bond us. If you die, I die. If I die, you die. Wyverns, my line of dragon, we rarely bond for life, not in true mating. We have two ways of reproducing. One way would be laying eggs. That is what I am: a hatchling. But our children will be born as human."

Standing straight but keeping her hips close to his, she pulled a lock of his hair. "The blond in your hair has a red tint. If I were going to choose a color for your hair, it wouldn't have been blond, and it would never have had a touch of red."

"It wouldn't, would it?" Barry asked, placing his hand on her back and pulling her lips into his. She tasted of fall apples, of summer blueberries, of, well, everything he loved.

When he finished, rather proud of himself that she let him kiss her, he grabbed her hand. "Let me show you our home, the dragon cabin."

Before they walked in, she paused and demanded his full attention. "You were the first of six suitors to whom I said maybe. But there was something about you. I couldn't say no. I wonder if I just knew it was you? Like our souls are cut from the same stone."

The next day, Maud agreed to marry Barry. A week later, they went to a church and signed their names in a book.

Their life was peaceful.

On a beautiful spring morning, Barry rose early. In wyvern form, he stood on his back legs, extending his wings, pulling them taut.

"There you are," Maud said as she exited the barn. When

he didn't lower his wings, she asked, "What are you doing, Barry?"

In response, he fell with a thud and walked over to her, nudging her limbs. She understood his language, no matter what form, and placed the basket on the ground. "It better be warm up there, husband. If I get cold, you are in trouble."

After hopping on his back, Maud straightened her dress as much as possible, and with dragon panoramic vision, he saw her knees showing and watched as she reached around his neck. As soon as he knew she was secure, he took to the air. It was exhilarating to fly, and he loved hearing Maud's breath catch, followed by giggles of pure joy. He drifted between clouds and down into a spiral, all the while aware of her positioning.

While he glided and soared, he desperately searched, and finally, he found the perfect field. Off in the corner of the woods, far away from their home, he found a peaceful meadow covered by Maud's favorite flowers.

White puffy pollen dropped around them, like snow from a cloud. Maud dismounted.

"This is lovely."

Human, Barry thought.

Even after years of marriage to Maud, his heart accelerated in anticipation. "Do you regret our true mating?" he asked. He knew the answer. He just enjoyed hearing her say it.

"Never," she responded, melding her body into his.

For his response, he removed her dress.

She tugged on his wavy hair. For some reason, she enjoyed straightening it just to watch it bounce back. "Rose blond, the blond still surprises me."

He wasn't sure if it was her or him that pulled them onto the ground; he only knew he was on his back, and she was on top of him, embraced in a kiss. A soft layer of moss grew under the dark cover of trees, making a natural bed for them.

When Maud sat back, Barry froze, entranced by the look of his wife above him. He promised himself, no matter how long he lived, this moment would burn in his mind. Maud's black hair, straight and thick with a hint of some color he assumed was purple, fell across her face and over her hips. Dark brown eyes peered into his soul with an overpowering purpose. Her cheeks were flushed, her lips puffy and darker from their kissing. Round firm, breasts and her stomach covered in a layer of fat. Even her breathing was erratic and erotic.

Barry would never forget this.

CHAPTER 35

JENNIFER

THE DRAGON AGE PROPHECY

SOMEONE TRIED TO OPEN JENNIFER'S EYELIDS. SHE SWATTED AT the person, but her hand met no resistance, slicing through the air.

"Come on, Jennifer," Barry, the wyvern from her dream, said. "It's Christmas Day. We didn't celebrate Christmas in the fourteen hundreds, so this should be fun." She recognized the voice, the accent, and even the musky scent of fall leaves and campfire smoke. Without a doubt, the odor belonged to Barry, Maud's dragon.

Heart racing, she sat straight up and surveyed the room. Daylight coated the walls from the closed blinds, and her furniture remained empty, except for the pile of Grandaddy Wright's genealogy studies.

Also missing from her living space was the intruder she expected to find. She exhaled. Finally, she'd broken; for now, she hallucinated odors.

"No, you're not crazy," Barry said from behind her left shoulder.

She glanced toward the voice. Barry stood at the edge of her bed. She estimated his height at 6′1″. Neither skinny nor muscular, he reminded her of an average person. Cut in a mullet, his wavy blond hair had slight strawberry highlights. His nicest feature, by far, was his blue-green eyes that bore into her, his sole focus. For an outfit, he wore blue jeans, cowboy boots, and a band shirt from the seventies.

If she saw him outside her room, she'd quickly dismiss him as a pacifist or strange and not a dangerous predator.

Why would a fifteenth-century dragon want to wear concert shirts?

The figment shrugged. "I like the clothing of this era better, and the music is amazing," Barry responded to Jennifer's thoughts.

"How?" she asked, trembling.

"Well, you remember a few nights ago. As I told you, you're not human." He moved to sit beside her and hugged her.

She experienced the pressure!

Leaning away but leaving his arm over her shoulder, he said, "You made it! I'm glad to say you made it through your last dream without me. From now on, it's you and me, dragon girl! I will help you understand the ways of dragons." He paused. "Though you could have chosen better."

"The ways of dragons? This isn't real. This can't be real."

"Oh, Jennifer, that's not how you talk to your grandpappy, is it?" He kissed her cheek and stood up to stand in front of her. With the back of her hand, she wiped where he touched.

"Trust me; you've made it to perfection. Humans are so…" He paused. "What is the word? Dull. Unfortunately for you, you're not pure wyvern."

A white presentation board on a tripod appeared beside him, as well as dark-rimmed reading glasses over his eyes. He cleared his throat. "You're a combination of different dragons. It makes you not very perfect. I'll forgive you for not being pure and all…Oh, you have a word for it, *mutt*."

A laser pointer in his right hand magicked into existence. Waving his arm, a photograph of her sat in the top middle of the poster. Under it was the word *mutt*. He ran the pole down the paper, and a list of names appeared, ending with an image of him as a wyvern. "These are the dreams you just had. They led to me, your dragon ancestor, and your dragon guide. But dreams of your ancestors are far from over."

He sighed, then the red dot started at her pic and ran down the right. More surnames flashed onto the screen until it ended in an emerald green and electric blue dragon. This picture reminded her of the dragons on Chinese calendars, complete with whiskers and lacked wings.

"From looking into your mind, you've got two more dragons you are related to, so you have quite a few dreams to go. You are descended from an ancient or prime dragon named River." When he said *River*, he jabbed the pointer over the green-blue dragon.

"The other dragon," he said, bitterness in his voice. The wand ran from mutt down the left. A new list of names bled into the page. The screeching of women, which reminded her of Halloween tracks of people in hell, reverberated. "Sorry for the dramatics," he said. "I'm not looking forward to these dreams."

On the presentation board, a video image of a light sky-blue serpent swimming in a dark blue ocean appeared. "Jormungant. He is an ancient dragon and a nasty fellow, and also the third dragon you are descended from."

He patted the display twice, and it vanished.

"Wyverns, your thoughts that we are overgrown salamanders with large heads, sharp teeth, and wings, that is us in a nutshell. So, what are you, if you aren't crazy? And that is a great question."

The room shifted into the forest from the weekend before Thanksgiving. She recognized the scenery, the trees, and the bear. Standing behind the bear, she watched her likeness slowly rise from the ground and dust off the leaves while the bear lunged at her. A loud, high-pitched gong clanged.

Watching, she missed when the clothes she wore ripped apart. The other Jennifer's limbs expanded, her neck exploded outward, and wings grew. When it finished, the claw of dragon-Jennifer held back to push the beast away, and the movie stopped.

Standing beside the dragon-Jennifer, Barry said, "You, Jennifer, are a dragon. More appropriately, a dragon shifter. Some dragons never shift, but all dragons can shift to human form. If a human descends from a dragon, some of those children will have the ability to turn into a dragon."

Walking over, she noticed the leaves on the ground didn't make a sound. "I take it this is a memory?" she asked.

"Yes."

"Am I still sitting on my bed?" she asked.

"Yes. This is what I call dragon vision or second sight. I can focus on memories to help you."

This allowed her to study what had happened. The tiny scales coating the body resembled blood-red gems, glistening in the moonlight. Even the underbelly of the elephant-sized Jennifer held the same color. She reached out and placed a finger on the scale, and the heat forced her to pull it away. "Why am I hot if this is my imagination?"

"Well, this isn't your imagination. This is a fact you recorded. Human brains collect a lot of facts. Typically, unless there is a reason to remember something, your brain will remove it. Becoming a dragon changes your human chemistry. It's like going from a 32-byte computer system to a 128-byte system. You have more cells to store data. Thus, you remember the exact location of the trees, the sounds of the creek in the distance, even that your dragon skin burns." He tilted his head, studying the dragon-Jennifer. "Notice your canines are longer than an average wyvern's. Your nostrils are more flared, and your face more swollen than mine."

He was right. The dragon's face had strong similarities to

a wyvern, but the neck of this dragon was beefier and shorter. The face was larger and more filled out.

"I believe the shape difference is from River. Your wings appear heavier, bones thicker, but you do seem similar to a wyvern. Enough that most people would call you one."

Something bothered her, so she asked, "How is a person from medieval times able to tell me about computer information?"

He sighed. The forest disappeared. "I have instant access to all your memories. Things you learned at one time or another are at my fingertips. Which reminds me, before you ask, I have no idea why you are red.

"I live in your head as your dragon guide. My thoughts and emotions are independent of yours. You can't see them or feel them unless I want you to. I know yours at all times. I'm glad you have programs because, in a way, that is what I am. I'm the representation of your dragon ancestor at the moment you were conceived. I'm not real. Based on your dream of my son being raised by someone who thought he was a gift from the fairies, I'm dead. I'm not sure how I feel about that. I'm still processing.

"Dragons that are born dragons do not have dragon guides. Only those that are born human. You had an option to choose one of us, and you picked me. I don't know why or how your subconscious made that choice."

Yes, I'm crazy, utterly insane. Blinking several times did not cause Barry to disappear. Nothing changed.

"You're not crazy. You are a dragon shifter. Come, show me Christmas."

"And what will my family say when they see you?" Jennifer asked, grabbing her phone off the charger.

"Unfortunately, I am a product of your imagination. Dragons live forever. In my case, only in their descendants' minds. They won't be able to see me or hear me. I'm here more as a guide."

Barry's odor wafted past her, fall leaves and an outdoor fire, as she opened the bedroom door.

They headed down the hall, pots and pans clattered, her father and mother talked about the best way to cook creamy spinach, and anime played from the living room. She wondered if others could detect so many distinct sounds.

"It's not normal for a human to hear those sounds through all the walls," Barry whispered in her right ear, sending a chill up her back. "But you're not human anymore."

Turning, she searched for him, but he wasn't visible anywhere around her.

"And the eyesight? Is that why I have the weird everything is bright at night unless I'm inside?"

He laughed a disembodied sound. "Yes. Your vision changed as well. So did your appetite. You need more calories."

"Oh." Everything made sense. The Barney challenge, eating raw meat—she burned more energy than others.

"Well, I still could be going crazy," she said.

"Those days are over. From now on, your dreams will be like movies, and I will be beside you, helping you daily," Barry said.

"Thanks, Barry," she answered.

Around the corner, her brother held a strip of turkey. "Who's Barry?" he asked, then shoved the meat in his mouth.

"Nothing, just thinking," Jennifer answered. Barry laughed.

Randy passed her and headed toward his room.

"Don't answer me out loud when you are in a group. I can hear your thoughts," Barry warned.

As her sibling went down the hall, he sniffed, then called out to her. "Do you smell it?" he asked.

She stopped on the stairs, one hand on the rail. "Smell what?"

"I don't know. It smells like a campfire, and in a way, it

smells like the woods in the fall, kind of musky. You know, the rotting leaf smell."

"Um, maybe Mom burned some food," Jennifer answered, surprised.

"Oh well. Hey, that movie you watch every year is about to come on."

"It's A Wonderful Life?" Jennifer asked.

"Yeah, the *lasso the Moon* movie. Anyway, thought you'd like to know."

"Thanks," she said.

He went into his room, shutting his door.

"If I have all these above-average human senses, how did my brother sneak up on me?" Jennifer asked.

"You need to learn to stay aware of your surroundings." Barry materialized in front of Jennifer, starting as a faint outline and slowly filling in. "I saw the fading-in thing in a memory of a movie you watched on a sci-fi channel. And the outfit in a spy movie." He straightened the brown polo shirt he wore over a pair of slacks. "It looks more festive." He paused for a second. "Your brother could smell me. That's very interesting, indeed." He sniffed the air. "And I don't smell like rotting leaves."

"Why didn't you tell me they could smell you?" Jennifer asked.

"I didn't know they could. I'm in all new territory on what can and can't be done. While Jormungant knew human-born dragons, he didn't have memories talking about the dragon guides. I probably should mention, and I'm just stating the obvious, but your brother also has the potential to go dragon."

Nodding, she headed right instead of left. She needed to see if her parents really gave her a car or if it was a dream. She opened the front door and stared at the new dark blue vehicle parked on the curb. "Well, at least that was real."

Barry said, "Tomorrow, we should head to the mountains.

You need to practice turning into a dragon. Even before my big reveal as your dragon guide, you would have noticed a dragon. They smell—"

"Like that Johan guy? He smells of danger," she thought.

"No. Not like Johan. You'll recognize it if you ever come near it. You could be the last dragon alive."

Her phone rang, and she grabbed it out of her pocket. Matt's number flashed across the screen. She slid her finger across the surface to answer. "Hello."

"Hey," Matt said, but static and background noise made his voice choppy.

"Hey, Matt. How is your vacation?"

"Good. I can't talk long. I just wanted to say Merry Christmas, and I miss you."

"Miss you too, and Merry Christmas," she said.

"Maybe next year you can join us?"

"That's a nice thought. Please be careful. I guess I won't get to talk to you until school starts," she said.

"I'll call you as soon as we get back to Charlotte, okay? And the weekend after, we can get something to eat and catch a movie."

"Sounds good."

"Bye, my sweet Jennifer."

"Bye, my sweet Matt," she replied. When she stared down at the screen, she had a text message from a number she didn't recognize. She opened it.

> OTHERS KNOW OF YOUR EXISTENCE, DRAGON SHIFTER, AND YOU ARE NOT SAFE. DON'T MESSAGE ME ON THIS NUMBER. IT'S A BURNER PHONE. TRUST NO ONE, NOT EVEN PEOPLE YOU REMEMBER FROM YOUR DREAMS. BE CAREFUL, JENNIFER. YOU DO HAVE FRIENDS. – THE WHITE JAGUAR.

As her hands shook, she slid the phone back into her pocket. To her left, she noticed a person sitting inside a fancy red car parked in front of her neighbor's house. Across the street, Fred Harris pruned for the fifth time this week. Behind her, Barry materialized, and she jumped.

She thought, *"Tomorrow, Barry, we go to the forest, and I learn to shift into a dragon."*

The End of Book 1,
The Dragon Age of Prophecy

ACKNOWLEDGMENTS

I have this amazing support group, that starts around my family. Thank you, husband, daughter,oldest, and youngest son for putting up with my continuous devotion to writing. I am blessed to have you in my life. I love you, all.

Mom and Dad, thank you for being a good role model and encouraging me to pursue my dreams.

Thank you, Vickie F. for reading each page of the first version. For saying you loved it and giving me your thoughts. Even though hardly a single word is left from that revision, the story is the same and you helped shape it.

I've been blessed to find several groups of like-minded individuals:

HEA Editor Jessica Snyder.

The *Six A.M. Group* for listening to my success and my woes (Ali, Amy, Shanna, Zee, Erica, Karla, Katharine).

The *2020 Finish Strong Group* put together by Dale L. Roberts (for advice on publishing, please visit: https://selfpublishingwithdale.com). Thank you, Andy and Guen.

YouTuber, artist, and writer H.K. Darkwood (https://hkdarkwood.com) and Melissa Eick, for being there. For seeming excited every time, I mention what I'm working on. You're both incredible, and I'm so glad I got to know you.

I am blown away by the artwork from Neal at Elerfine - Etsy. Thank you for bringing Jennifer to life.

My first editor Vicki, thank you for your patience and for helping me learn along the way. Because of you, I improved so much I had to scrape the first version and update it. www.vickiedits.com.

If each time your ears tingle when you return a round of edits to me, Jennia, it's because I'm saying, "Wow. That's incredible. I love it." She went above and beyond to point out loops and mistakes, questioning the motivation of my characters. I appreciate every challenge she gave me to make the story stronger. Thank. You.

Roxana added the final touches to the work. Reading through it in record time and surprising me at how many mistakes were left. Her attention to detail is much appreciated. https://proofreadebooks.com

My editors are amazing. Each did their best to lead me to a powerful story. All the mistakes in this book are mine.

ABOUT THE AUTHOR

Let me share with you a secret. Well, it's not a secret to those that know me. I love math—believe it is God's language, perfect like he is—I adore math! My devotion is so strong that I've threatened to ground my three kids if they brought home anything less than A's in math. Math, to me, is natural, like breathing. Unlike grammar, where letters like to flip around and change positions, math stays faithful.

I thought grammar, like math, was something you understood from birth. And in college, I gave up my dream of sharing worlds with other people to go into engineering, because I had no clue what a passive sentence structure was or how to correct it. I wasn't one of those gifted with grammar.

Don't get me wrong, I love my day job. I love looking at data from machines and interpreting their language—Do they need maintenance? Is it failing? Is it behaving normally?

But I missed English and stories.

Then, one day, while cleaning my house, I listened to something I thought was an autobiography. It turned out to be a self-help book. In it, Scott Adams explained what a passive sentence structure was, and that grammar was learned.

What?!

Not only that, but the first time you write a story, it can be a draft that you change, manipulate, and update.

Oh my!

Finally, I could do things I never knew were possible. I could write a book. I love to make up stories and worlds.

Thank you for reading my story. I hope you enjoyed it, because I loved writing it.

-N. A. Hydes

Find me at https://nahydes.com or on discord at https://discord.gg/tdnwDVu2R4

www.ingramcontent.com/pod-product-compliance
Lightning Source LLC
La Vergne TN
LVHW010641110826
845149LV00014B/2916
* 9 7 8 1 9 6 3 6 4 3 0 1 5 *